James Noble is a Yorkshire author, who previously wrote a non-fiction book concerning the travels of the Buffalo Bill Wild West (Show) in Yorkshire and Lincolnshire. Apart from writing in several genres, his interests are many, including Napoleonic History, restoring elderly model steam engines, model soldiers and computer modelling and animation. He also paints in oils, mainly wildlife and local pastoral scenes, and has a healthy sales record locally.

James Noble

THE MAN WHO STOLE MIDNIGHT

AUSTIN MACAULEY PUBLISHERS™

LONDON * CAMBRIDGE * NEW YORK * SHARJAH

A CIP catalogue record for this title is available from the British Library.

ISBN 9781035847723 (Paperback)
ISBN 9781035847730 (ePub e-book)

www.austinmacauley.co.uk

First Published 2024
Austin Macauley Publishers Ltd®
1 Canada Square
Canary Wharf
London
E14 5AA

Chapter One
Eighty Dollars and the Man
Who Stole Midnight

Town of Dogwood, Wyoming Territory, 1867

He waited on the raised sidewalk outside Mr Bridey's store, sitting back on the old rocking chair and letting it roll to his weight as he nervously changed his position. This was not the first bank he had robbed, but then he had been younger, and lucky that the war had come along and covered his tracks and the misdemeanour. But this one was different. These people had been his neighbours for a year, and up until five days back, he had no intention such as the one he now considered and had decided upon.

Through the glass of the store window, he could see the big hand of the clock on the wall edging towards nine-thirty. Soon, the bank would be open. It was Saturday morning, and most of the town were down by Seawell's blacksmith shop and livery, waiting for the race to start, three hundred yards down the single street. It happened every month, another way for Bellfield to take money from anyone crazy enough to fall for a one-way gamble.

The race's course was three times around the town, and open to any cow pusher that fancied his mount against a dead certainty, a half Arabian, half Mustang that had the speed and endurance of most of the others put together. The dash would finish back at the blacksmith's, and then would come a noisy parade back to the 'Longhorn' bar where Bellfield would buy a drink for those who had nothing left to pay for one themselves.

He had ridden all night and told no one of his intent. By now, they would all be awake and wondering where he was, but they would soon know. He had reached the town at dawn and tied the horse out of sight, then waited behind the livery to avoid any suspicion, especially from the Marshal and any nosy deputy.

When the onset of race time drew out the people, he had eased into the street, and found the rocker outside of Bridey's.

Two minutes and he would go. He looked up, beyond the wooden canopy that covered the side walk, at another bright sky that had traded blue for the early clouds. His right hand slipped down to the handle of the Colt's Walker pistol that hooked into his broad leather belt and felt the smoothness of the walnut grip. A brown left hand pulled down the brim of his faded black hat and settled it firmly over his eyes. There was little point in trying to hide his face with a bandana as he would be easily recognised, and it would be almost an insult to think they might not. He had nothing against these folks, far from it, as they had accepted him for what he was, even though they had little knowledge of his past. All that was about to change.

He rolled forward on the rocker, took a deep breath, checked both ways down the street and found them empty. He had planned it that way. Rising, he adjusted the Colt as the rocker headrest thumped against the wall.

The bank was a few yards to his left, and as he walked slowly in that direction, he heard the soft metallic noises that told him it was opening time. He paused and went through the routine in his mind, as he had done so many times in the last hour.

Outside of the double doors, he halted as casually as he could, and again checked up and down the street to make sure that the race had pulled most of the population away. Still clear, apart from the occasional dog that sniffed around the spaces beneath the sidewalk, hoping for something to kill.

In he went, the green blinds trembling on their rollers as they closed behind him. At first, there seemed no one between the brass screen that separated the teller from the customers and the big iron safe, green with the gold lettering that curved above the brass combination lock. But then a bald head rose to a full height of five feet five. Beneath the space where his hair had once been, a friendly face beamed through the cross hatching of the security brass.

"Mr Standing. Good morning." It was a stern voice, not intimidating but authoritative and respectful.

"Morning," William Standing returned the greeting. "All on your own today?"

Weaver, the bank manager and main teller, spread his hands.

"Last Saturday of the month. Arthur's gone down to the race as usual," he explained. "How could I stop him; Lord knows it's hard to find employees who can add in this town, and he's the closest I can find."

Weaver smiled, and Standing had no idea whether he was joking or otherwise.

"Now, how can I help you?" He said. "If you want to negotiate a loan, I told your sister and her husband how matters fall. It's a matter of collateral, as I explained previously, we don't just give money away, you know. After all, it's not my money."

William Standing looked quizzical. "Collateral?"

Weaver nodded and smiled. "It's what we call a good enough reason to lend the money out—"

Standing pulled out the Colt and held it rigidly at arm's length, hoping Weaver would not detect the empty chambers.

"This a good enough reason?" Standing asked, raising an eyebrow.

The bank manager's arms jerked towards the roof and his expression changed.

"Don't shoot! Please don't shoot!" Weaver coughed, choking on the words.

Standing twisted the corner of his mouth as he moved closer to the counter.

"Hell, I'm not going to shoot you, I have to make a withdrawal, and cash, no cheques before you ask…" He felt humour might calm the situation. "…You can put your hands down if you promise not to go for a gun or such."

Weaver nodded and began to open the drawer that housed the cash. Standing kept the Colt braced, just in case, although what might happen should his empty weapon be challenged, he had no idea. A heap of untidy banknotes began to slide from a pile on the counter, tens, fives and a few hundred-dollar bills.

"What the hell are you doing?" Will Standing asked.

Weaver stopped and looked at him through the brass screen and shrugged his shoulders. He thrust his palms forward and out, in a questioning attitude.

"Getting the money," he said. "Getting you your money."

"Who asked for all that?" Standing asked. "Huh?"

"Well, I… You don't want it?"

Will Standing shook his head. "Seventy dollars. I want seventy dollars."

Weaver looked down at the heap of money waiting to be taken. He indicated the pile with both hands. "But…"

"Seventy, that's all."

As Weaver began to count out the amount in ten and single notes, Standing glanced out at the street, a little surprised at how easy it had been, so far. The manager finished and pushed the money through the semi-circular hand access.

"What do they charge for cartridges these days?" Standing asked, remembering his empty Colt. "Down at Bridey's?"

"Oh, a dollar five for fifty, I guess," Weaver said. "Or thereabouts, I never bought any."

Standing thought for a moment. "Better make it eighty."

Weaver added two more fives and Standing grabbed the money and pocketed it. He looked through the mesh of the brass screen.

"You know I gotta tie you up a bit, Mr Weaver," he told the manager. "If you promise to not shout for fifteen minutes, I won't knock you on the head. How about it?"

Weaver nodded enthusiastically. "Fifteen minutes," he said, "that sounds reasonable. But you know they'll come after you."

Standing slipped the Colt back into his belt where it belonged, and opening the hinged countertop, made his way around to where Weaver stood, wide-eyed. He pulled a cord from his other pocket and made to tie the other up, then noted the rest of the bills cascading across the polished oak. He jerked a thumb over.

"You better put that away safe," he advised, "never know who's around these days."

Weaver swallowed.

"You don't seem the regular bank robber, not that I've known…" he said, scooping the pile of green paper back into the drawer. "Not that I've known many."

Will Standing went back to tying up the man, fairly tightly behind his back, and easing him down onto the floor.

"Well," he said, "takes all kinds. Honest robbers and them that ain't. I hope you take me for the former. I never harmed you or nothing, nor took anything personal, your watch or the like."

Weaver pushed his back against the wall as Standing returned to the other side of the counter and looked up at the big white clock on the wall, with its black hands and polished surround.

"Can you see the time?" He asked of Weaver.

"Sure."

"So, fifteen minutes from now, agreed?"

Weaver nodded. It was thirty-six minutes past nine.

"Fifteen minutes, OK," he confirmed. "Good luck, and thank you for your forbearance."

The comment made Standing smile as he left and closed the door behind him. Down the street, he could see the main population excited and animated as the horse race was already in progress. He hurried along the sidewalk and entered Bridey's store.

Bridey was a small, middle-aged man with a soiled white apron that covered his ample appetite. A heavy crop of dark hair fell over his forehead and invaded the spectacles that he wore. He came from the execution of some tasks beyond the counter. Standing touched his hat.

"Morning Will!" Bridey smiled a greeting. "You not at the race?"

Standing shook his head and said that he was not, and feigned disinterest.

"How much does my sister owe on account?" He asked.

"Seven dollars, forty," Bridey confirmed.

Standing took out the money in his pocket and dragged off a ten-dollar bill and laid it on the counter.

"Is that enough to add a couple of boxes of forty-four ammunition?" He asked. "And maybe a can of that sweet milk that Molly likes."

"Sure, and ten cents change," Bridey told him, moving along the line of shelving to where each item was stacked.

The storekeeper found the cartridges and the can he asked for, and placed them on the counter, scooping up the ten-dollar bill and sidestepping to the old brass till. He pressed the levers and found a ten-cent piece and handed it over.

"You want a sack for those?" He asked, offering a small hessian pouch, and filling it with the purchases when Standing decided that he did.

Standing looked up at another clock. It showed forty-one minutes past nine.

"That right?"

"On the button!"

Standing touched his hat again. Time was running its own race and he had the most important thing yet to do. He grabbed the sack and made for the door.

"Thank you, Mr Bridey. Bye now."

He did not wait for further conversation and closed the door behind him. As fast as he could and trying to seem casual, Standing made for the throng of people jostling to see the winning horse come around the side of the livery stable, and nearing the crowd he looked for Bellfield. As usual, a knot of the latter's employees gathered around their boss, the usual grimy bunch, unshaven and bored, just waiting for the inevitable win and the blowout that followed. Standing wondered how people could be so stupid as to continually think that the Bellfield horse could lose. In the year that he had been back, it never had, but still some felt the need to try.

Will Standing pushed through and pulled the remaining bills from his pocket. A hand fell on his shoulder. He half turned and found the town Marshal holding him back. For a moment, in his mind, he could see himself with the shadows of bars over his face but fifteen minutes were not up yet, not quite.

Deerbolt had been the Marshal for several years. Standing knew the type, brawny and bought by whoever made the offer, and sustained in his position by votes purchased by the same hand. In short, he was Bellfield's man and seemed unashamed to show it. Standing flashed the money.

"Here to pay up, if Bellfield still wants it," Standing said.

For a second, Deerbolt held his gaze, then raised the carbine that he held and used it to clear a way through to where Bellfield stood, watching for the first sight of his winner.

"Somebody to see you, Mr Bellfield," Deerbolt called out.

Bellfield turned as if the words irritated him. He ignored Standing and turned back to the race. Standing clutched the money and glanced back towards the bank. Still no sign of Weaver. It would not be long now, and he wished he had said twenty minutes instead of fifteen.

"What do you want, Will?" Bellfield asked without turning to face him, more intent on the race.

Standing pressed a little closer. He grabbed the hessian sack and held it tighter, wishing he had taken the time to reload the Colt.

"Molly sent me with the water money, seventy dollars."

Bellfield turned his head slowly and held out a hand. In fact, Molly had no idea of what he had decided to do to and would by now have woken that morning and wondered where he was. He could visualise her and Henry scratching their heads and shrugging their shoulders, looking around the place to see if they could find him.

"Always surprising, the Hendersons and their brood." Bellfield twisted a lip.

"I need a receipt. Molly was insisting on that," Standing said, pulling back his hand a little.

"You don't trust Mr Bellfield?" Deerbolt asked for his employer.

Will Standing shrugged. "Oh, it ain't that." He grimaced. "I just wouldn't want to go back without one. Not if you know my sister, Molly."

"Maybe she needs it to put against expenses…" Bellfield laughed mockingly.

He continued laughing to himself and twirled a finger at the nearest man to him, in order to offer his back as a desk. He pulled out a notepad from the inside of his expensive jacket pocket and fumbled for a pencil, beginning to write. He then stopped.

"Just for the year, tell Molly," he growled. "Then another seventy, or I hold back the water."

He continued writing until a loud cheer made him look up to see what he had never doubted, a coal black stallion with no other horse in sight, rounding the corner of Blaine's livery and making easy progress towards the finish line. On its back, a colourful rider in simulated English fashion tapped the animal's flanks with a whip and urged it on. Reaching the open space where Bellfield's entourage stood, the horse was pulled up in an explosion of dust and small stones, still filled with the excitement of the run, wide-eyed and chewing the bit between its teeth.

Standing looked nervously back down the street. Maybe he had tied Weaver up too tight, maybe he had fallen asleep, maybe he had a heart attack, and they would take him for murder. He turned back to Bellfield, whose attention was still on the horse.

"Mr Bellfield…?" He asked, reaching for the receipt.

Bellfield pushed his big grey moustache further up towards his nose in frustration. Quickly, he scribbled a signature on the paper and thrust it forward for Standing to take, dropping it before the other could grasp it. Bellfield ignored it and strode quickly towards the dismounting rider as the rest of the runners came around the side of the livery. As the jockey turned, Bellfield knocked him to the ground and held back another blow, instead grabbing the whip and beating the man furiously about the head and shoulders.

"You lay another finger on that horse, and I…"

Will Standing scrambled in the dust and the milling legs to retrieve the receipt that he had at last won. Somewhere in the distance, he heard the sound of smashing glass and a disturbed voice that sounded like Weaver's, a plaintive call for assistance. Few had yet heard the call as they were still eager to see who might have come a close second to the big black horse.

Weaver's voice claimed a larger response as Standing managed to secure the receipt and rise from the dust. He thrust the paper into his pocket and looked across to where he had tied off his horse, now well covered by the increasing number of townsfolk who were responding to the wailing Weaver, still with hands tied behind his back and stood upon the sidewalk outside of the bank.

Standing decided that Weaver had given him an extra minute and mentally thanked him for it, but knew he could never reach his animal before the bank manager spotted him and exposed him for the thief that he was.

Even Bellfield had heard the commotion and left the knot of horses to investigate, with Marshal Deerbolt already increasing his strides up the street. Only the berated jockey seemed thankful for the distraction and began to stand, brushing off the dirt and the admonishment.

Standing stood for a moment as the crowd slipped by him, then turned his attention to the jockey who was bending to retrieve the whip that Bellfield had thrown at him. Taking the loose rein, Standing threw a well-aimed boot at the jockey's rear and sent him falling back towards the ground. In an instant he was up in the saddle, his legs dangling and feet unable to reach the high mounted stirrups.

The horse reared a little as Will Standing pulled its head around and towards the open ground outside of the town. He kicked the flanks and gave the horse its head, allowing it to find a pace that would take him away from the trouble behind him. The other contestants in the race had dismounted and milled around, gathering their breath and looking forward to Bellfield's celebrations. As the black horse gained speed and leapt among them, mounts were pushed aside, and pulled and dragged their riders, many losing grips on their animals as they reared and bucked in the melee and the rising dust.

So fast had he made an escape that Standing was almost out of pistol range, just the odd shot that chased him and was well wide of hitting its target. Within minutes, he was into the timber and circling back towards home, where he would have to say goodbye and then stay ahead of the posse, and hope he could avoid it. At least he felt that he had successfully done what he had intended to do, pay back his sister's kindness with the receipt in his pocket that would secure their water supply for a year, and give her and her family a chance in this open country.

There were always people like Bellfield, with money to buy up the valleys and the river heads, and manage the run off to make homesteaders pay for what should be free for all. In Will Standing's mind, the fight against them would always need to be a little creative.

If it were just one man, Standing thought, *it was worth a confrontation, but it was never just one man, especially one with the law in his pocket.*

Back in Dogwood, Bellfield watched Standing riding off into the trees. His anger turned his face redder than the colours of the jockey who was sprawled in the dirt. People hurried in both directions, many running into those running in the opposite direction, their priorities on crime depending upon their predilection for horse theft or bank robbery.

Bellfield pushed through the confusion, finding one of the two wranglers he had brought with him. He grabbed the man by the shirt and pulled him close.

"Back to the house," he told him. "Get a half dozen good riders and extra horses, food for a chase and meet me at the Henderson place. And don't waste any time."

The man hurried off to find his horse in the disorder, but commandeered a loose one and ignored the pleading of the owner, who was also looking for his mount and saw it go. Bellfield became aware of the other issue that Saturday morning, a knot of townsfolk already gathering around the manager of the bank and attempting to remove his binding. Avoiding a loose horse, Bellfield walked quickly over to where the Marshal was dealing with the situation. Deerbolt saw him coming and met him in the centre of the street.

"William Standing," he told Bellfield. "Robbed eighty dollars from the bank."

Bellfield looked at the Marshal in amazement. "Eighty dollars?"

Deerbolt threw up his shoulders. "Just eighty dollars."

Bellfield suddenly realised how it was all unfolding.

"Which I gave him a receipt for…" he admitted. "Bastard stole my horse, stole my Midnight, best damn horse this side of St Louis." He turned and looked back in the direction that Standing and the horse had taken. "He's a dead man, only he doesn't know it yet."

Bellfield looked back at the Marshal.

"Get some people mounted and follow me to the Henderson place," he said. "And bring a rope."

***

Will Standing found the racing saddle hard to sit, his legs dangling down by the horse's sides and gripping its flanks. Once into the timber, the ground rose up to a high ridge and the big black hose hardly slowed its pace, even more astounding as it had just run a race and won. Standing was impressed, although he knew that his actions meant more trouble than he knew how to handle. Maybe he should have thought it out better, or not at all, and hoped that he could avoid bringing the whole damn situation down on Molly and the family. Whatever happened now, he was on his own and had no future anymore at his sister's place. He knew that they would soon be on his tail and what the outcome would be if they caught him, and he also knew that they would by now have figured out what his first stop would be. There would only be time to hand over the receipt for the water, then keep moving until they overtook him, or he lost them.

Standing wondered about the receipt and hoped the crimes would not cross over, and it would at least be worth it, but he could not be sure and damned himself for making such a mess of it.

Once at the crest of the ridge, he hauled back on the rein and then gave the horse his head for a moment. Midnight was breathing heavily and panting at the exertion, but he had not given in and maintained the pace until halted. Standing looked back over the trees to where the town was just visible. He wondered if they were already mounted and coming on, and how many they were.

He knew the horse deserved time to recover and any normal horse would have been blown for the rest of the day. However, he gave it a minute or two, then remounted that imperfect saddle. He slapped the animal on the neck with his left hand.

"I know it's not right, but I gotta ask you to run a little further."

He touched the horse's flanks with his boots and Midnight threw back his head and snorted away the weariness, lunging into the timber that led down into the next valley.

Chapter Two
Dog Soldiers

Henry Henderson rolled out of bed, his back still aching from the day before, when he and Tom had finally hauled the stump out of the ground and filled in the hole. He looked through the small window at the sunrise, then back at Molly who was still sleeping. At the end of the bed, Sam, a big brown and white mongrel dog raised one eye to see if he might be called from his restful night, his chin slumped across one paw.

Slipping his braces over his shoulder, Henry winced at the pain where the sun had burned and wished he had left his shirt on yesterday. Across the room, a rough crib held the latest member of the family, a three-month-old infant that they had named William after his uncle, and who like his mother was sleeping late. Henderson smiled down at the round, pink face, twitching in some distant dream.

Pushing back the blanket that divided the room, he walked over and opened the door, letting in the morning light. He glanced back into the room, to where his eldest son and his daughter were stirring from their small, handmade beds near the stone fireplace.

Outside, chickens were squabbling over the remains of yesterday's corn and waiting for replenishment. A cow 'hawed' in the lean-to barn. Henry went outside as he always did, and watched the early mist drifting across the valley towards the treeline. He loved this place, and no amount of work to make the place right was too much.

Somewhere near the distant treeline, a chevron of Canadian geese announced the morning and cackled their way skyward. Redwings hovered around the cleared space that surrounded the building, and waited their chance to steal the chicken's breakfast. Henry cranked his neck back and looked for the buzzards that were always there, gliding effortlessly and aimlessly in a weightless world of their own.

Back in the cabin, he heard the sound of the children rising and glanced back to see if Molly was too, his tall frame silhouetted in the doorway.

"Better git fire goin', Tom," he said, stretching off the last of the sleep stiffness.

"OK, Pa," came the reply. "What we doin' with that old stump?"

Henderson smiled at his son's concern. "Oh," he answered, looking back again to see if Molly was rising yet, "cut it up for winter, I guess. Make a few blisters, but we'll be glad of it."

Henry stepped out into the light of the rising sun, still half hidden by pink morning mist that would be gone in an hour. He walked around to the side of the cabin, to where their only cow waited for attention and release onto the sweet grass. Beside the cow, two mules also waited and shuffled restlessly across the dirt floor.

Henderson turned as he heard movement behind him and he swivelled his hips to see Sam loping around the edge of the building, interested to see what breakfast might bring. The man grinned down at the dog as it fell onto its haunches at his feet. The dog grinned back, a long pink tongue lolling to one side and a wet nose aimed skyward.

Something was missing and Henderson noticed immediately when he reached the enclosed animals. He checked the rough fastenings and found them intact, so he walked around to the lean-to behind the cabin and heaved open the rough timber that made up for a door. It was empty.

Sam followed as Henderson made his way back into the cabin, where the children were already dressed and young Tom was building the fire, while Alice spread a worn blue and white cloth over the wooden table. Henry pushed aside the curtain and looked down at his wife, who looked up with drowsy eyes.

"Will's not here!" He told her.

Molly opened her eyes wider, raising her brows to show her lack of knowledge, or apparent concern.

"You know what he's like," she answered. "Always up early and around. Maybe he went to shoot a bird for breakfast, who knows? You know what he's like."

Henry shrugged off the idea.

"His horse is gone; you think he went into Dogwood?" He asked. "Never said anything, never said he was going."

Molly turned over.

"Ooh, you know what he's like, he'll turn up when he's ready," she mumbled. "What time is it?"

Henderson had no watch, just a natural instinct for the time of day.

"After four, I guess."

Henry left his wife to rise in her own good time. He knew she would be up soon and call everyone to breakfast as a matter of routine, just as she always did. His mind drifted to their main issue and wondered how they might deal with it. Once more at breakfast it would be the topic of conversation, how to pay for water rights when Bellfield dammed the river, which he surely would in the weeks to follow.

Henderson knew the score and why the man was so unreasonable, he knew it was a way to force off the settlers who dotted the valley. But with Bellfield's resources in men and money, there was little option but to pay or leave, and they had put so much work into the place. It was an ongoing stream of taunts and threats whenever the two sides met, with accusations of all kinds. Sure, Will might have come across a stray steer sometimes, and brought it back to see them through, but he always butchered it well away from the homestead and nothing had ever been proved. Maybe that's where he had gone that morning.

Attempts to dig a well and avoid Bellfield's powers of control had been unsuccessful, the water table being too low to find. Henry had cursed the time that he, Tom and Will had spent sharing their single shovel, sweating for days to gain nothing.

The fire was spreading through the logs in the stone hearth and Henderson nodded affirmation of a job well done to his son when Sam began to bark outside. Alice stood on the rough wooden bench and looked out of the small window to see what had unsettled him, but could see only the distant hazy trees.

"God-damn that dog!" Henry growled as he went out into the morning.

He walked over to where Sam was posturing into the mist and knelt, rubbing the animal's chest to calm him down.

"What the hell's got you all fired up?" He asked, as if expecting a reply.

The dog still kept its attention in the same direction. Henderson followed its line of sight and saw nothing at first. But then, just a shadow or a drifting of light through the dissipating mist.

"Will?" He called.

Almost as soon as he had said the name, he knew that it was not his brother-in-law. The single shadow was now five, emerging slowly, deliberately, each becoming clearer, more defined, into something he had dreaded. He had heard the stories, suffered the warnings, but they had never been optimised and such dangers always appeared so far to be a world away. Henry backed slowly towards the cabin door while Sam continued to bark. He knew that if he ran, it was all over, but in fact whatever action he might take, the outcome would be the same.

Five riders now advanced, their horses painted with bright symbols of hostility, buffalo leather bridles strung with feather embellishments and beads. They halted, in a line abreast, some six feet apart and twenty feet from the cabin door, showing no signs of fear or caution. Magnificent specimens of the wild life they were, bodies toned and faces painted, their heads decorated with differing feathered head adornments, symbols of their clan. One had halted a few feet ahead of the others, his horse's breast muscles highlighted where a painted hand had left its marks in red. The horse danced in response to the rider's gentle nudges with his heels, keeping the animal in motion and attention upon the man on its back, its dark brown and white patched hide rippling with the movements.

Henry halted and it seemed a lifetime that he stood there. He knew that the rifle was where Will had put it, up on the rafter out of the way of the children, and tested the odds as to whether he could reach it in time. Somewhere just behind him, he could hear the children busying themselves with the morning chores, unaware of what was taking place outside. Still, Sam barked his defiance at the intrusion of the horsemen.

Then, breaking the moment, Tom's voice cut in from just inside the door.

"Pa, what's Sam…" His question was made short by what he now saw. "Pa!"

The paint horse reared a little as the rider raised the feather-decorated lance that he carried and let out a shrill cry that penetrated the morning silence. Immediately, three arrows appeared in Henderson's chest and sent him crashing backward onto the porch, one arm struggling to find support from the timbers that held the roof overhang, the other clutching at his chest and the arrows that had appeared there, their points emerging ragged red from his back.

"Pa!"

Tom clutched the door jamb as first one, then two arrows appeared in his father's lower abdomen. Henderson fought to rise and leant to one side as more arrows hit his left upper leg and side. The lead horseman was already urging his mount into the narrow doorway, leaning forward over his horse's neck, brushing Tom aside and onto the floor. Screams from Alice aroused her mother who was already on her feet and responding to the commotion, still unsure as to what was causing it. Tom rose and rushed to his sister.

The hooves of the paint horse thumped on the earth floor as it twisted and danced in the enclosed space and sent the table and benches and all that was set for breakfast clattering across the room. The rider hunched over to avoid hitting his head on the rafters and the metal oil lamp, and swung his lance around him to clear any enemy that might be there. Molly pushed aside the blanket that gave privacy to their space, still in her night dress, her face contorted in fear and disbelief at what was occurring. She leapt towards her baby as it began to cry in response to the unnatural cacophony of sound that awakened it.

Outside, more arrows found their mark, loosed into the prone man by dismounted attackers, who kept up the action until no movement could be seen. A yelp announced the demise of Sam as the animal denounced the intrusion of strangers. Two more warriors entered through the single door, and one made for the two children who hunched in the far corner, while the other avoided the lurching paint horse and threw back the curtain that had temporarily hidden Molly and the baby.

The cabin was filled with whoops and cries of the confident warriors, the crash of broken ceramics and pewter mugs and cutlery, to which was added the cries of Molly as the baby was ripped from her and thrown without care into its wooden cradle. Across the room, the children screamed as the other invader grabbed them roughly and dragged them, kicking, towards the door, avoiding the mounted warrior as he urged his horse back through the entrance and into the sunlight.

The warriors who had not entered the cabin pressed their attention on the livestock, chasing a chicken that came too close and opening the rude door to where the mules and the single cow were housed. A flash of bright iron ended the cow, while the mules were driven into the yard and plaited rope fitted around their necks. One mule bucked at the harsh treatment and was checked by a fist to the side of the head which did little to settle it down until the warrior managed to grab an ear and bite hard. The animal backed away, dragging the attached human but seeing the error of its ways and giving in to the rough handling.

The mounted rider swirled his horse in the dust of the yard, allowing the animal to rear in high spirits and fix the moment with an aggressive yell of victory. He dismounted and left the horse untied, then made his way back inside the cabin, where his companion still struggled with the two elder children who had managed to escape their captor and were avoiding him by slipping through the debris of the room and the upturned table.

Molly's screams and the tearing of cheap fabric determined her fate, to the increasing screams of the baby. Once inside, the dismounted warrior grimaced at the sound of the child crying and he made his way quickly across the room and thrust a hand inside the crib. He grabbed the small legs and hauled the baby out, swinging it around until the small body smashed against the stone hearth.

Seeing the fate of their sibling, the children fought harder to avoid capture, but it was in vain, and at last hard brown hands secured them and thrust them towards the door, a camouflaged blessing that they avoided what else was happening inside.

While one of the warriors inside the cabin was occupied, the other tore through the few belongings that the family owned, casting aside anything that he found useless. A tin half full of cinnamon gained his attention and he scooped up a heap with his finger, spitting it out shamelessly when he found it not to his liking. Casually, the two inside the cabin traded places and were joined by a third who had chastised the mule.

Tom and Alice were still in shock at what they had seen, heard and experienced. They winced at the sound of shrill yells from inside the cabin, sounds that were to become familiar in the days to come. Roughly, the children were each thrust onto the back of a mule. A cord was tied around their waists and secured around their mount's neck and each mule was guided by another cord, fixed to a bridle that had been fashioned from the same material. They remained there in shock, until the business of the cabin interior was over.

"Tom!" Alice had called, locating her brother, terrified at what they were experiencing.

Tom turned quickly to his younger sister and shook his head, finding the presence of mind to understand what might not be tolerated by their captors. A chicken found itself outrun and was quickly despatched by one of the warriors outside and its neck hung loosely as he pushed it roughly into a bag that was carried around his horse's neck.

Alice saw the brown and white shape of Sam on the ground where four arrows had put an end to his warnings. Her face contorted into what might have become loud sobbing had not Tom once more signed her to be resilient.

Another loud yell came from inside the cabin, shriller than before and more intimidating. One of the Indians lumbered through the open door, carrying an armful of stolen property, fabric, pots and a knife. He found a skin bag to contain them, and fastened it to Alice's mule, briefly looking up at the tormented face of the young girl, then returning unmoved to scour the place for anything else worth stealing.

Molly's last, desperate scream cut through the morning air and both of her surviving children knew it for what it was. Alice's face screwed up again with the torture of the cruel reality that was happening all around her. Tom's demeanour was frozen, a stone acceptance of their fate and what was to come.

Soon, all of the warriors had taken what they wanted from the Henderson place and were mounted once more, turning their horses to the north. A few embers from the fire had been kicked by the horse and set one of the children's simple beds alight, the flames moving steadily up the wall and spreading to the animal enclosure on the other side. The surviving chickens hastened away from the smoke and out onto the sweet grass that surrounded the homestead, soon to be given attention by the coyotes and the buzzards as their luck ran out.

***

Will Standing kept the black horse moving at a steady pace. He knew they would soon be organised and determined, and wondered how many might be in pursuit. For certain, he had no time to lose, would drop off the receipt, say his farewells and maybe head west for the high plains where he might throw them off his trail on the rocky ground.

He knew that Bellfield would not give up easily. Midnight was his prize possession, after the big house that money from poor homesteaders had bought, and if they did catch up with him, a noose and a tall tree was his ultimate destination. Standing's mind wandered to the steady beat of the horse's hooves, wondering if they might not have had the will to follow if he had stolen another horse, or managed to secure his own. Hell, it had only been eighty dollars he had robbed, would they have chased him up for a few bucks?

He reached down and rubbed Midnight's neck, finding flecks of foam, so pulling back easily on the rein, he slowed to a steady walk. If the horse gave up and he was afoot, then Heaven help him, because no one else would. Turning on the racing saddle, he looked back at the low hills he had left behind but could see no sign of immediate pursuit, no dust, and no flash of sunlight on their rifles. Guessing that it would take time for Bellfield to send for more men and supplies, he tried to calculate his lead in hours and came to no more than three at the most. It was ten or twelve miles back to Molly's place, through the timber, across the river and another half mile to the cabin. Once there, he reckoned on no more than twenty minutes rest for the horse before he must move west, keeping close to the other farmsteads and hoping to gain more time, as he knew Bellfield could not pass them by without searching for him.

Standing shuffled on the uncomfortable saddle, unused to such a useless piece of leather. He knew that Henry had another saddle, old and beaten up from the horse that had died in the previous winter, so once back he could swap it for something not so harsh on his sitting parts. Of the horse beneath him he had no doubts at all, and thanked his lucky stars that he had stolen one so finely honed for the benefit of a thief. Half Mustang, half Arabian, this animal had all of the advantages of both, stamina and strength, speed and endurance, and Lord knows he would need them all.

The rider gently tapped the horse's flanks with his heels and urged a little more speed. Midnight responded and slipped into a canter, kicking up a little more dust that Standing hoped might not be seen by those that followed who might have a long glass. Ahead, the terrain opened into large areas of prairie grass, dappled green and ochre where the bleached older growth gave way to younger replacement. The big black horse took each stride with confidence, a rhythmic movement that covered the ground with ease.

Miles passed, and up ahead, Will could see the timber that led to the river. Soon he would feel the trees around him and the comfort of their safety, blanking him from the open spaces where he felt more exposed to anyone with a long-sighted rifle. He was sure that they were still too far back for that, but it paid not to be too confident in his situation.

Reaching the tree line, standing hauled back on the rein and let the horse rest again, allowing it to graze for a minute or two while he checked for any pursuit. He climbed up onto a low branch and looked hard but could only make out the lazy movement of the grass as far as he could see, until it merged into a mirage of pastel shades in the distance.

His back ached with that damn saddle and he looked forward to the comfort of a style that he knew better. Mounting again, he tightened his grip on the rein and guided the black horse back into a slow canter as they negotiated the timber.

Once moving he let the animal find its own way, just occasionally keeping it heading in the right direction with a gentle tug. Will's legs still hung down, loose and free of the highly fixed stirrups that he had no time to adjust.

Twenty minutes later, the sound of moving water told him that they were close to the river. Soon, the reflected sun on its surface cast dazzling, flickering shafts of light through the trees and following the downward slope of the terrain, they found the river's edge. He slipped down from the discomfort of the saddle and let the horse drink, cupping water for himself from one hand while keeping the rein in the other.

Crossing the water was easy at this time of the year, barely touching the horse's belly and soon they were on the other side and climbing the gentle slope through the aspen that came right down to the water's edge. From there it was a short distance to Molly's place and a better saddle.

Pushing aside the last of the aspen branches as they found the top of the slope, Standing looked across at where the homestead was. He saw smoke as he expected but not in the way he should. Instead of the lazy grey drift from the stone chimney, it was dark and threatening in volume and told him that something was wrong. He kicked the horse's flanks with his heels and urged it on with some speed, covering the ground in minutes.

When almost there, Standing saw the cabin clearly, still burning on the side of the animal byre and the body of the cow slumped before it. Two horses were tied off some distance away and around the corner of the animal enclosure, two figures appeared carrying water pails. Something was slumped over in front of the door and when a little closer, he saw it for what it was. Henry's body was still where it had been left, the arrows protruding in varying angles from his torso to his legs.

Will recognised the figures as they flung water from the buckets over the remaining flames. One was their neighbour down the valley, Albert Dawson, and with him was his youngest son Charlie, a boy of sixteen. They paused as they saw the rider coming closer, putting the pails down just in case danger might be returning.

The black horse skidded to a halt and Will dismounted untidily, leaving the rein loose to fall to the ground. Albert ran forward and grabbed Will, in an attempt to stop him going further. Standing struggled, but paused to look down at the body of his brother-in-law. His face was grim and set.

"You don't want to go in there…!" Albert told him.

Standing looked him in the eye. "The hell I don't!" He shook himself free. "The hell I don't, Albert!"

Dawson stood back and grabbed a handful of his long beard, watching as Will walked over to Henderson's body and knelt for a while. Then, he stood and looked through the open door, surveying the upheaval inside. He turned his head to the side of the building where Charlie was. He nodded.

"Charlie," he said in a kind of greeting to the boy.

Charlie shuffled, uneasy at what he knew was beyond the door.

"Mr Standing…" he replied, trying for a half-smile that was useless.

As Will walked slowly through the doorway, his neighbours continued to put out the last of the flames. Inside, it was horrific. He walked over to where the big curtain had been torn down and now covered the big, handmade bed, pulled it aside and looked down at the torn and twisted shape that had once been his sister. A red strip ran across her throat, below the tortured features that had once been a pretty face.

The tears would hold no longer and as they lined his dusty cheeks, Will Standing gently placed the curtain back over her body. He turned to the foot of the bed and began to lift the crib back into place when he saw the baby. He froze into anger and sorrow, swallowed hard and somehow found the strength to lift the infant from where it had been left. He pulled back the curtain again and placed him beside his mother, carefully moving Molly's arm around the small body. He moved back into the centre of the room and looked around, taking in the broken cabin and what few possessions had been left behind in pieces that were of little use to anyone. Slowly, he righted the table and looked beyond at the charred wall.

A shadow in the doorway made him turn. It was Albert. Standing took a deep breath and wiped away the wet from his face. He headed for the door and Dawson stepped aside for him to pass. Once in the yard, Will looked around and cupped his hands to his mouth.

"Tommy! Alice!" he shouted, letting the call drift across the open ground.

Dawson put a hand on his arm.

"They ain't here, Will," he told him. "We looked. They ain't here."

It was a long hard look in return. Will's frown held for a moment. Albert told what he knew.

"Cheyenne, looks like," he said. "I think they took them kids, took the mules too, took whatever they wanted, looks like."

The worse just got worse.

Words just would not come. Will Standing stood rigid with the shock of what he was seeing, his hands on his hips and his eyes on the ground, his mind working in a muddle that refused to clear. Anger began to take over his whole body and he began to shake with the need to hold someone responsible. Gradually, it subsided into knowing what he must do, putting things into a perspective of some kind of order, some kind of decency, some kind of responsibility.

"I'm really sorry, Will," Albert said, reminding him that he was still there behind him. "They was good folks, real good kids."

Will nodded, the tears finding a way through again.

"Thank you, Albert," he answered, realising the good that his neighbours had done. "You too, Charlie."

Albert screwed up his lips.

"We saw the smoke from up on the hills a-ways," he explained. "It was like this when we got here. Nuthin' we could do for your kin, they was already gone. We're real sorry, we couldn't do much." He paused, holding back his words for a moment. "We can hold on for a while if you need help with the graves…"

Will turned to look at Sam's body, a short distance from the cabin, then back to Dawson.

"I ain't got no time for graves, Albert," he said, walking back over to where his brother-in-law lay.

Standing bent over and slipped his arms beneath the man, lifting him, arrows and all and took him inside the building to lay him beside his wife and child. Going out again, he did the same for Sam and placed him with the others, the whole family together again, aside from those who had been taken. Albert appeared in the doorway again.

"We better get off, Will," he said. "In case them heathens circle back to my place."

Standing walked out into the yard after his neighbour. He knew that Dawson had three more older sons back at his homestead. Albert threw a hand over the open ground in a gesture that added to the facts.

"Four or five of 'em, looks like, heading north," he explained. "I heard they hit Fort Wallace a few days back, big band of Cheyenne under Roman Nose. I guess they'd break into smaller bands to avoid the army and make their way back up north, maybe join with the Sioux over in the Black Hills or further north into Montana, where they can skip over into Canada if it gets too hot for 'em."

Will Standing was releasing the racing saddle from the black horse. Albert looked quizzically at the animal. He pointed. "Hey, ain't that…"

"Sure is," Will answered. "And I'll need him where I'm going."

"You ain't damn crazy enough to chase on after them Cheyenne, Will?" Dawson asked, finding the thought incredible. "Ain't no sense in it, just a dead man's ride…"

Standing threw the racing saddle on the ground and rested his forearms on the back of the black horse, looking out towards where the Cheyenne had ridden off.

"Got a damn fine horse that can catch 'em," he answered. "If I can catch 'em, I can kill 'em. If I can kill 'em, I can get those kids back. If I can get them kids back, I can live with myself."

Albert said nothing. He just twisted his lips and understood.

Standing had found the old saddle, just a little charred, and was slumping it over a blanket on the back of the black horse. He tightened the girths and made his way back to the cabin while Albert continued to protest gently with sad eyes. Once inside, Will reached up onto one of the rafters, finding the long-barrelled Sharps rifle that he kept out of reach of the kids and pulled it down together with the small box of cartridges and percussion caps. He was surprised that the Cheyenne had missed it, but glad they had. If he got the chance, he would make them sorry that they had.

Picking up an oil lamp from the floor, Standing shook it and found it still had fuel inside the reservoir. He opened the cap and began to throw the thick whale oil around the interior of the room, especially the bed where the bodies were. Standing still for a moment, he looked around the room, remembering the laughter, the joy when young William was born, and the conversations of what the place might be like ten years from now. He took a match from where it lay with others on the floor, struck it and threw it near the bed, waiting for the flames to rise. As the fire increased, Standing reached into his pocket, found the receipt for the water rights that he had taken from Bellfield, crumpled it in his hand and threw it into the flames. One last look, and he returned to the yard, pulling an arrow from the doorjamb and sticking it into his belt.

Albert and his son were already mounted. They watched the cabin begin to burn while Will walked back to the black horse.

"You got supplies?" Albert asked.

Will mounted and shook his head. Dawson rode across to him and reached behind his saddle, found a hessian bag and handed it over.

"All I got is some corn sticks, fresh cooked yesterday, but you're welcome to 'em," he said.

Will grasped the bag and tried to smile in response to his neighbour's kindness. He added it to the bag that he had got from Bridey's shop. Also inside was the box of cartridges for the rifle and the percussion caps. The Sharps he had tied with a cord to the saddle horn by the grip.

"Appreciate it, Albert," he said. "And all you done here." He reached over and shook the other man's hand. "If you see the army, maybe you can tell what happened. Tell them the Cheyenne took the kids, and I'm up along after 'em. Maybe they'll send soldiers on after us, even the odds a might."

Albert shrugged off the idea. The cabin flames rose higher.

"Wouldn't bank on it, guess they have their hands full all along the Kansas border, following up into Wyoming after them Cheyenne." He frowned. "Maybe you should think twice on what you're doin', Will."

Will Standing pulled the black horse's head around to the north and jerked his head towards Albert and his son.

"I already thought twice on it, Albert."

Chapter Three
Chasers

It took Marshal Deerbolt an hour and more to calm down what had been an eventful morning, despite Joshua Bellfield's insistence that they set out right away after the horse thief and bank stealer, William Standing. On the one hand, he knew his authority was needed to investigate the situation, not least in case Standing had committed more crimes during his morning spree, and as it turned out, fraud could be added to the list when Bellfield confirmed the receipt issue.

On the other hand, Deerbolt was aware of the Fort Wallace incident a few days before, and to sally forth unprepared with the Cheyenne around was a game for good Samaritans and fools, and either one would be wishing themselves elsewhere by nightfall.

Deerbolt walked a fine line trying to please his patron while doing what he was paid for by the territorial purse, and wished no loss of revenue from either. Bellfield followed him around in protest at his lack of action to catch the man who stole his black horse, and made it clear that there was a tight timeline to be kept in the rendezvous, with his employees despatched to the Henderson place. And so, at last giving in to the passive threats of the more lucrative of his financial options, the Marshal gathered those who were willing, and armed them from Bridey's store, with a generous supply of ammunition and supplies. Mr Bridey on his part was not totally happy with the arrangement, complaining that once the weapons were returned, they would be in less than pristine condition and might have to be offered at second-hand prices. However, once Bellfield had assured him that he would cover the loss, at manufacturer's costs of course, Bridey saw the error of his objection and gave in. Joshua Bellfield was a persuasive man.

Around eleven that morning, seven men rode out of Dogwood, with two mules trailing and carrying supplies for an uncertain pursuit.

The ride to the Henderson place proved uneventful, the only incident to break the monotony being a short shower of rain, which despite passing quickly, caused a brief delay when they halted to don their oilskin dusters, which avoided the possibility of a chill or worse. Bellfield ground his teeth at the delay, but did likewise and without admitting it, was glad that he did.

Marshal Deerbolt continually cautioned Bellfield to take the ride steadily and not tire their mounts, as an exhausted animal is the last thing you need in the open. But cautions made, it amounted to a situation where Bellfield surged ahead and the others followed.

By the time they found the river, the horses were all but blown and breathing heavily, sweat heavy on their flanks and necks. Deerbolt was the first to see the smoke, heavy and grey against the blue and white of the sky. Once over the hump of the opposite bank and clear of the aspen, the situation was unmistakeable. Bellfield's men were already there and had been for some time, five of them with three spare horses and more supplies.

The cabin was still burning, reduced to just what was left of the walls to define its original purpose. Deerbolt dismounted and walked as close as he could, feeling the heat on his face.

"Lord love a duck!" He said slowly.

Deerbolt saw the dead cow and where arrows still held in the timbers, and found it hardly difficult to deduce what had happened. Taking off his hat, he nodded a greeting to Bellfield's foreman, who stood holding his grey horse some way from the fire.

"Gaskin," he acknowledged the man. "Anybody still alive from this?"

George Gaskin shook his head and said the obvious, "None that's still in there." He changed his weight from one foot to the other. "Ran across old man Dawson on the way down, he says them Cheyenne took the kids, the oldest kids, all the rest is in there, looks like."

"And Standing?" Bellfield asked.

Gaskin threw up his shoulders.

"Didn't say nuthin' about him."

Bellfield raised the corner of his mouth in what was meant to be a smile.

"I'll just bet he didn't."

Marshal Deerbolt turned back to the still mounted Bellfield and put on his hat.

"Mr Bellfield, maybe we'd better get back to Dogwood. Who knows how many Cheyenne are around, we got women and children all over this valley? I guess most will head into a town until the army catches up with those Cheyenne."

Gaskin cut into the conversation, "Dawson said 'they' was four or five of 'em hit this place, just a bunch split up from the Fort Wallace fight."

A rider, who was further out and searching the ground, came in. He pulled his mount close to Bellfield.

"Four or five unshod ponies," he told his employer. "Two mules, looks like, and a set of shod tracks over 'em, heading just east of north."

"William Standing, the horse thief," Bellfield said, "that's who those tracks are."

Deerbolt walked over to his horse and looked up at his patron.

"God-damn, he's got stone balls, I'll give him that!" he admitted. "Seems like he's gone after those kids. Lord help him if he catches up with 'them' Cheyenne, because nobody else will."

Bellfield crossed his arms over his saddle horn and bent over. He spoke directly to Deerbolt, "Well, either way, he's done for. I just want that horse back. The Cheyenne can have him, but just so long as we catch him before that."

Chapter Four
Captives

The Cheyenne and their two young prisoners left the burning cabin behind. From the backs of the mules that they were tied to, the children looked back at what had once been a home and family, and wondered what days might come. Still in shock, they clung to their mounts and feared falling off, with strong hide cord securing them to the animals that did little to make a secure deck.

Tom glanced ahead at what he assumed was the leader of the band, his headdress like a feather porcupine fluttering in the breeze, and the war shield strapped to his back with symbols of horses, buffalo and stick people. All of the Cheyenne wore loose deerskin shirts with short sleeves stretching as far as the elbow, decorated with feathers, beads and cord edgings. On their chests were bone strip breast plates, also decorated and supported by a strong plaited cord around the neck. The boy could see the weapons they carried, bows, hatchets and knives, and long lances with iron tips with more dancing feathers at the base of the blade. The leader and one other also had firearms, breech loaders strapped to their horse's flanks, but now without ammunition, what they had once had been expended at Fort Wallace.

For a mile the party moved a little east of north, then turned to true north, hoping to delay any followers who might try to anticipate their route and cut them off. And yet they moved without haste, knowing that the army might be in pursuit, but unafraid and even welcoming the confrontation should it come, for these were not just warriors, they were dog soldiers of the bear clan, the elite fighters of the northern Cheyenne.

Finding a minor tributary of the Laramie River, four of the small band crossed to the other side, leaving the mules and the children with a single warrior mid-stream. The four then backed their mounts into the water again, and joining the others turned against the mild current and followed the stream for a mile.

Finding thick undergrowth, the warriors pushed their animals through until they found open ground beyond, in the simplest way to disguise their passing.

It was mid-afternoon before they halted, dismounting in thick timber and dragging their captives roughly from the mules after releasing the cord around the animals' necks. Pushed onto the ground by one of the party, the children's neck constraints were transferred to a branch above them and tied off.

Tom reached out a hand to his sister, whose face was pale and filled with the terrors of the day. Her face began to contort with fright, and Tom saw it. He remembered the fate of his younger brother when he became an irritant to these men and feared what could happen if Alice made the same mistake. He gripped her hand.

"Alice," he whispered. "Don't cry. Just bite your tongue and don't cry."

His sister looked at him and bit her lip, holding back the tears. Tom tried to smile back but it was hard to do. He tried the noose around his neck, to see what resistance there was, but there was little if any, and it would take more than a tug to release it.

The five warriors had tied off the animals and sat in a small circle. Tom listened to the high-pitched sound of their language, the singing vowels and long climax to their sentences. He wondered what they were talking about and watched their faces, trying to try to interpret expressions to meaning. Occasionally, one laughed and pointed over to him and his sister. Another found something to eat and chewed while speaking, denying the manners that the children's parents had instilled in them.

It went on for a half hour, then the porcupine headdress rose and walked over to the captives. He looked down at them and spoke in Cheyenne, long complicated words that meant nothing to them. Tom looked up into the man's eyes with the hate that was impossible to forget. The warrior laughed aloud and, raising a moccasin clad foot, pinned Tom's neck to the tree. He held it there and Tom fought off the urge to grab it and thrust it away. His sister pushed herself back. The Cheyenne kept the boy restrained, pressing with his foot until Tom began to gag. Another moment, then he took his foot away and threw something down between the two children and walked back to the others.

Tom looked down and saw two pieces of grisly meat, half raw and mainly fat. He swallowed hard and reached for one of the pieces, offering the other to his sister. She shook her head in disgust and pushed it away. Tom thrust it at her again.

"Eat!" he said. "Eat it!"

To encourage her, he raised the meat to his mouth and bit off a piece. It tasted foul and nothing like his mother's cooking, but they must eat and survive. He knew that, and his sister must understand that too. Tom felt that he had aged many years since he woke that morning.

Alice took the greasy food and held back the tears as she swallowed without chewing. Her face was dirty with the dust and grime of the journey, unlike the pretty girl her mother kept so pristine and urged to be ladylike. Those days were gone. She took another bite and the fat oozed out and down her cheek, clearing a little of the dirt in a streak of pale skin.

Tom smiled as best he could to show his satisfaction that she comprehended his concern. He glanced over at the Cheyenne, who still sat in conversation. Opening a hand, concealed behind his leg, he drew Alice's attention to it with his eyes.

"Look," he whispered.

Alice dropped her eyes and saw the stone in Tom's palm, a sharp-edged, ragged stone that might just give them freedom. She held back any emotion or expression that would give it away.

"Tonight," Tom mouthed.

Within an hour, they were moving again. The captives were once more tied to the mules and from the position of the sun, Tom could see that they were heading north. He tried to put away the shock of the day and tried to think clearly. Perhaps their lives might depend upon it. Fort Laramie was somewhere behind them, and he wondered if there might be soldiers in pursuit, coming to find them. He hoped they were. If they could free themselves and lose their captors, he resolved to make sure he knew where south was, and kept an eye on the sun as it sank into the trees.

With nothing between their legs and the back of the mules, the children's thighs were sore, especially Alice who only had her torn dress. Tom was in a better way for at least he had his grey serge trousers beneath a jacket. Alice had also lost one shoe and the other was so damaged by the rough handling that it was of little use and hung loosely by the delicate strap that might give way at any moment.

For the rest of the afternoon journey, Tom mentally rehearsed what his intentions were, what he must do to protect Alice's feet and what their escape plan must be. He knew that against these people, their chances were not good, but the alternatives were worse. For a fourteen-year-old, Tom's presence of mind was astounding, born of the fear of the unknown and the experiences of the day. Alice had become almost silent and morose, as if in a dream that would soon break and return her to the normal life that she understood, and rarely responded to Tom's whispered encouragement when he risked the chance to speak to her. When discovered in this, a rawhide whip across his back was his reward from the closest Cheyenne.

Nightfall came as a blessing to dismount from the mules and ease the soreness from the constant rubbing from their hides. As before, the children were tied by the neck from a branch above that was out of reach, with just enough slack to avoid strangulation. Also, their hands were tied with the same cord and made movement almost impossible.

Both Tom and Alice were desperate for sleep, but the discomfort of their bindings made it difficult for any rest. It was becoming cold, and Tom saw his sister shivering with only her tattered dress for warmth. Despite this, he saw her eyes begin to droop and he slowly moved his leg to touch hers and keep her awake. He recalled what Uncle Will always said, 'any problem is best sleeping on and sorting in the morning', but tomorrow they would be weaker, less able to attempt escape.

The Cheyenne tethered the animals and began to settle down for the night. The warrior that Tom decided was the leader with the porcupine-style feather headdress eventually came across to them and threw over a worn blanket, which Tom was grateful for, not least to cover his work with the sharp stone that he hid in his pocket when the time came.

After some animated conversation, four of the warriors lay down and pulled over their blankets to sleep. The fifth sat with his back to a fallen log to keep watch. Tonight, there would be no food, an issue that both Tom and his sister would hardly complain about.

Tom shuffled his back to the tree and tried to make himself more comfortable. Immediately, the watchful Cheyenne turned towards them and barked a curse in his own language, the words lost on the children but the meaning obvious. Alice let out a sigh and Tom knew that this was having a serious effect upon her physical and mental health.

Somewhere above and behind the tree that held them, an eagle owl protested their presence. Seconds later, it was answered by another further away. Tom observed the watchman intently, hoping he would fade into sleep, for only then would they stand any chance of finding a way out of their predicament. After what seemed hours, the Cheyenne reached out a hand and woke another, who with bleary eyes still wanting sleep, took his place on watch.

Tom felt the night eluding them and knew that with the first light, their chance was gone. But, shortly after, he saw the first sign of freedom as the watchman's eyes drooped a little and his head began to fall lower onto his chest. The owl protested again and he jerked out of the torpor for a moment, then slowly began to give in to the drowsiness he obviously felt. When his chin touched his chest, Tom felt for the stone, with difficulty due to his tied hands. He managed to slip it from his pocket and work on his secured wrists under the camouflage of the blanket.

Looking to Alice, he saw her frozen stare and moved his leg once more to gain her attention. She turned slowly as Tom's wrists broke free. He reached across with his free hand and touched her on the arm, glancing back to ensure that the Cheyenne was still asleep. He was.

Reaching up with the stone, he sawed its edge to release his neck binding, feeling the relief from the tension. Still under the blanket, he eased across to his sister and with one more glance at their captor, cut Alice's neck cord, steadying her movement as she relaxed. She seemed to return to her old self as he began to cut the wrist cords.

"Tommy?"

Tom reached up and put his hand over her mouth, checking the Cheyenne watchman again. His head moved slightly, then gave way to sleep again. The boy looked hard at his sister and put a finger to his mouth and shook his head. Alice seemed to understand.

As quickly as he could, Tom cut away the bottom of each trouser leg, still under the blanket and working blindly, he fashioned coverings for the girl's feet which he secured with the cords that had once held them prisoner. He worked quickly, knowing that they might be discovered any moment and punished in whatever form the Cheyenne thought fit.

Alice smiled at her brother when she realised that they were free. Tom secured her silence again with a finger to his mouth, then used the same finger to beckon her after him, around the tree that they had been secured to. Finding Alice's hand, he pulled as silently as he could, bringing the blanket along with her until they were around the other side.

Within seconds, they were into the shadow of the timber and avoiding any underbrush that they could see that might be noisy to navigate. It was very dark, and doing so was not always successful and the scrubbing of sharp foliage did little to help their advance. Tom tried to take the worst as he pushed through, and made sure that the blanket was wrapped around his sister as best he could, while holding her by the hand and pulling her along. The owl hooted and flapped away somewhere above them, only just audible on silent wings.

Tom guessed the importance of making as much distance as possible between themselves and the Cheyenne, fully aware of their skills at tracking. He hoped that the night was their friend and only at first light could their trail be followed. Every flat rock he could see became a way to disguise their tracks and once on top he adjusted their path to leave by a different direction in order to delay pursuers that would be coming on behind.

The boy hoped that the Cheyenne would not bother to follow, but in his heart, he doubted that was the case. Maybe their luck would be in and they might come upon soldiers in pursuit, or other friendlies who might help them.

"Tommy!" Alice called to him.

The boy halted and turned to his sister and pressed his face close to hers. He took her arm firmly.

"Alice, we must be quiet," he told her. "We must be quite as a mouse…"

His sister looked at him.

"I need to pee…" She said in a low voice.

Tom almost smiled, but then he saw the torches in the trees behind them.

***

They were awake well before the dawn and it took only moments to see that the children were gone. Deciding against fire the previous night in case of pursuit, it took a little time to make flame enough for torches. Two Cheyenne remained behind to ready the horses for travel while the other three searched in the limited light of the fire sticks to find signs to follow.

It took little time to find the children's trail around the tree but more difficult to follow up in the dark of the twilight; had it been daylight, their quarry would be easier to find and secure. Added to the difficulty of the task was Tom's attempts to put the Cheyenne off their track and until more light filtered through the trees, it was working. But with three searching for signs, and the rising sun making an ally to the warriors, the end was inevitable and only delayed.

"Heneheno (Here)!" The leading Cheyenne found where Tom had slipped from a rock, apparently trying to keep Alice moving.

Immediately another warrior, his fur headdress swaying with his eagerness to be the first to find the children, stepped ahead and was halted with a hand to his chest. The lead warrior smiled and saw it for what it was, Tom's attempts to throw them off the trail. To a trained eye, the ruse was not hard to interpret, but the Cheyenne nodded his deference for such pluck in so small a boy, and a white boy at that.

"Ma'ehoohe hetaneka eskone (Fox boy)!" He smiled.

The third warrior yelped his delight at being close, for they could see that the trail was fresh. All three spread out and began to understand the rhythm of their quarry. Now that the light was improving it was a simple thing to avoid Tom's attempts at misdirection and follow through the trees.

As they advanced, the sound of moving water filtered through the forest, not too far ahead. Wild turkey skittered up from undergrowth between the trees and all three of the warriors paused to see if it were they or the children who had alerted them, but soon it was clear that they must go further to find the captives.

Still thrusting the torches out before them the three followed the signs of the children's passage through the woods, laughing quietly to one another as they overcame each tactical manoeuvre to offset their pursuit. Then, the trees became sparser as they neared the edge of a river, the bank of which fell abruptly down to the water but was covered in thick undergrowth. The warrior with the porcupine-like feathered head display held out his arms as a sign to halt and move forward in line. He could see where Tom had made a good effort to cover their footprints over the open ground, but not good enough.

Slowly, they edged forward as the first of the new day's sun filtered through the branches and clothed the forest in a pink light. It glistened on the moving water below and sparkled back at those who watched above.

The Cheyenne leant forward and looked over the edge.

***

Tom heard the water and glanced back. The torches were pin pricks of twitching brightness through the thick brush in between.

"We got no time, Alice," he told her, his sister still needing to halt for a moment for what comes naturally.

"But…"

Tom took her hand and pulled her roughly after him, ignoring her whimpers and wondering if the sound of moving water was to their advantage or otherwise. He knew that their captors could not track over water and hoped for the best. Soon, he was disappointed.

Their escape was blocked by a river too far below and too far to jump. Even if it was not deep, he feared for Alice, knowing she could not swim and even though he could, the dangers outweighed the reward. Tom thought for a moment. He sat Alice down near the edge and pulled the blanket around her, then went back to the trees and taking a fallen branch, brushed away their footfalls to the river's edge, backing away as he returned to her. He threw the branch into the water and watched as it floated downstream.

"Listen, Alice," he whispered. "We have to hide from those Indians, we can't go back and we can't go across the water. There are roots and branches down the bank. I'm going to let you down, so find something to hold and grip on tight, then I'll follow you down. If we can find cover down there, they might go away."

He held her hand and looked into her eyes and saw the fear in them. She looked down at the precipitous angle of the riverbank.

"Tommy, I'm scared," she sobbed.

"Me too," he confided.

Not waiting for protest, Tom eased her down and held one hand as she descended into the scrub that littered the way down. The blanket fell away a short distance as she searched for a handhold, finding a branch to steady her. Tom was almost flat to the ground above, his arm over the edge as far as he could reach. Suddenly, Alice slipped and thrust out a hand, finding only the loose blanket that came away and fell with her. Her brother felt the weight of his sister and would not let go and he slipped over and followed her down, head first.

Tom felt the edge with his toes as he slid over, but his hand found a root and still holding Alice's hand, he swung around, making a human chain that kept them from a cold, wet destination. He felt the root give a little, then hold firm.

"Hold on," he said in a low voice to his sister. "Just hold on, and quiet as a church mouse."

It felt like they hung like that for an age. Alice sobbed a little but quietly when Tom shook his head at her. Then pink and amber rays invaded the last of the twilight and awarded the morning for its patience in the dark.

Tom tried not to breathe. He heard a noise, hardly a sound, like a feather on the cheek. He looked up into the face of the Cheyenne and his heart dropped into his boots. A hand reached down, almost benign, almost helpful with no anger on the face behind it. There was nothing for it, it was over, they had failed to escape. The fingers of the hand flexed, beckoning Tom to take it.

"Heestan, heestan (come, come)," the Cheyenne said.

Tom had no idea what the man said, but dug in his heels and tried to do what he was indicating. If he let go of the root, then both he and Alice would pitch into the river below. He thought about it for a moment and came to the same conclusion that he had done before. Then, without warning, he felt his wrist grabbed and a strong arm hauled both himself and his sister onto the edge of the bank.

The children sat there, exhausted, demoralised and afraid. The warrior looked down at them without any emotion in his face. Alice began to sob again and Tom dried her eyes with his sleeve. He turned and looked at the Cheyenne, eye to eye. The Cheyenne maintained the gaze with just the hint of a smile beneath the war paint.

"Ma'ehoohe hetaneka eskone (Fox boy)!" He said, again.

***

The children were unceremoniously dragged back to where the horses and mules were waiting. There they were met with harsh expressions from the waiting warriors. Alice limped with the help of her brother, still with his makeshift coverings on her feet and sparing her the worst on the walk back. They were flung back up onto the backs of the mules and the party continued in a northerly direction. This time, they were not tied to their mounts and Tom wondered why, especially after their recent failed attempt to escape.

That morning and part of the afternoon, they rode in single file through the trees, the children in the centre of the column, winding along and making a trail through the standing timber. Since the previous morning, the children had not had anything to drink, and ate only the unpalatable meat that they had been given.

Tom's stomach rumbled and complained, empty where there was normally his mother's home-made biscuits, beans, and eggs if she could find some freshly laid.

In mid-afternoon, they halted and let the horses graze in an open space between the trees. The children were pushed down beside another large tree as before, but again were not secured by rawhide. Four of the Cheyenne hunkered down in a circle a little way off and as the previous day, began to eat. The feather headdress who found them by the river walked over to where Tom and his sister sat, and offered food, this time a dry meat of some description, hard and fibrous and with little taste, but acceptable for one who was hungry.

The man also carried a skin flask, clearly a water container with a wooden plug at the short end. He spoke in Cheyenne, words that were lost on the children, so he cupped his hands as an indication for Tom to do the same, which he did. The plug was pulled and the man poured a stream of water into Tom's palms and the boy drank it down eagerly. He turned to Alice, but she was engrossed in chewing the hard meat that she had been given, so the Cheyenne cupped his own hands and filled them from the large flask wedged into his knees, and thrust the water to her mouth. She dropped the meat and drank, until the man grew tired and took it away, throwing the remainder to the floor.

The Cheyenne walked back to the others, and Tom watched as his spiky feathered headdress danced at each step. He sat and began to eat, with apparent little concern that there might be another escape, confident that he had proved the futility of such endeavours. As the warriors conversed, Tom saw how they used hand signs as additions to the spoken word. Often the same sign was made as a reference to themselves with a directional shake of a head, apparently to reinforce what was meant. It looked to the boy that there was a difference of opinion as to their fate, with odds of three to two against, but the leader confirmed his wishes with a slap on his chest, and another on the back of his hand as it was pushed towards the dissenting warriors.

Tom wondered if their escape might have changed the Cheyenne's attitude towards them and decided that captivity might be the better of two evils.

A half hour later, Tom and his sister had drifted into a fitful drowsy sleep, having had little the night before when escape seemed worth the loss. A painful kick in the leg woke the boy, and opening his eyes found Alice being dragged roughly across the stony ground towards the mules by one of the painted warriors. Immediately, Tom responded to his sister's screams by leaping forward to pull her away from the man, cursing with words that his father would have paddled him for.

Another warrior joined in and put a second constraint on Alice, while kicking Tom away with a well-aimed foot that sent him back against the bole of the tree in a cloud of dusty debris. He scrambled up again and tried again to aid Alice but was met with the back of a hard fist that floored him once more. Before he could make a third attempt, a short buffalo tail whip appeared and flashed across his face, striping it red from cheek to chin. He raised an arm to defend against another strike that never came.

"Nehetaa'e (Enough)!"

As Tom dropped his guard a little, he saw the Cheyenne leader reaching forward to grasp the whip arm that was poised to strike again. His face was stern to reinforce his authority and there was no dissent, the other warriors fading back to where the horses were being readied. The man looked at Tom's face and then pressed his own close to the boy.

"Nehetaa'e (Enough)!"

Chapter Five
Horse Soldiers

William Standing soon picked up the trail of the unshod ponies of the Cheyenne. They were strung out abreast with the mules behind and a single rider coming up in the rear, the overlay of tracks made it clear, at least for the moment. They were moving slowly, as if unafraid of pursuit or desiring it. He could see from the pace of the mules that they carried the children.

Over sections where the long grass gave way to open ground he moved quickly, but even after a few hours, where the grass was long, it had already sprung back into place and helped cover the riders he followed. Standing found that it was better to look far ahead to get the faintest difference of the lay of the grass, rather than pick up a sign on the ground. It proved easier knowing how the Cheyenne were spread out. Once that trick was discovered, he could encourage the black horse on much faster.

At mid-day, he paused to rest his mount and eat a couple of the corn sticks that Albert had given him. His mind wandered over the preceding hours that had completely upturned his life. Of course, he knew that nothing would be the same again when he levelled his Colt across the bank counter, but that had been his choice, and he had been completely willing to accept the consequences, if they caught him. Now here he was, wanted not just for the theft of eighty dollars, but as a horse thief, maybe a fraudster and who knows what else Bellfield would throw at him. His family gone, he had no choice but to do his best for his kin that survived the attack on Molly's place, but who would ever imagine the pursuer pursued? Those children's lives depended upon him staying ahead of those that hunted him, just as the Cheyenne would do well to stay ahead of him.

He watched Midnight for a while, calmly grazing and completely oblivious to the dramas that were surrounding him. For perhaps the first time he realised his luck in stealing the animal, almost by default. Any other horse, including his own, would have been outmatched by the circumstances, and it might even be all over by now. The thought made Standing take a look back to see if he could observe any signs of those that were after him, but it was still clear. He wondered how many there might be coming up behind, and guessed at maybe eight or ten.

The black horse stopped grazing and looked over to him. It pawed the ground in impatience, the sun reflecting blue from his dark hide. Will Standing smiled for the first time that day.

"Lord, you're a damn fine animal," he said aloud. "You got more insides in you than I have for this work."

Before he remounted, Will checked his bag of ammunition for the long rifle. Ten caps and five cartridges. He wished he had more. The rifle was taken from a Confederate prisoner at the end of the war, traded for a generous bag of supplies to see the man back to Kentucky, when Mr Lincoln and General Grant allowed them their freedom. It was a good piece, 1863 model with the octagonal barrel that Sharps sold as a sporting gun, but Standing guessed it for a sniper's weapon in the hands of 'Johnny Reb' and he wondered how many federal soldiers had seen their last day at the crack of the thing. Of course, he still had two boxes of ammunition for his Colt and was glad that he did. He pulled it from his waist band, took cartridges from one of the boxes and slipped them into place, leaving the hammer on an empty chamber.

He thought for a moment at the predicament that he was in. Ahead and behind were people he would avoid on any normal day, but maybe, just maybe, he could set off one against the other. If he could stay ahead of those that hunted him long enough, until that perfect moment when he might catch up with the Cheyenne, perhaps he would find the reinforcements that he would need to turn the odds in his favour.

He wondered about the children, how they were faring, and if it came to trading more than insults, how they would be entangled in the middle of such a situation. It was something that could not be avoided, either he was intending to get them back or he was not, and whatever lay in between must be suffered.

***

Mid-afternoon came hot and gave little encouragement to someone in a hurry. Cresting a low ridge, Standing was drawn to a wagon cutting obliquely across his path. It was still some way off so he turned in its direction, and approached carefully lest they mistook him for a Cheyenne. Nearing the wagon, he recognised the driver and called out, waving a hand in greeting as the mules that hauled the thing were pulled up. On the board seat was a man in his forties but looking older, his clothing worn and needing repair, a dark broad brimmed hat with the front turned up on his head. His face was grizzled with an unkept beard. Beside him sat a woman, better dressed with her hands in her lap.

"Mr Prescott." Standing half smiled. "You're a-ways from home, ain't you?"

Prescott returned the acknowledgement, leaning forward and easing the long leathers that controlled the mules.

"Will." He nodded. "Could say the same about you."

Standing stretched his legs and stood in the stirrups for a moment, then returned to his original position.

"Guess you know the Cheyenne are around?" He warned. "Not safe to be caught in the open if a bunch turns up unannounced."

The man jerked his head upward as the woman spoke up.

"We heard about your kin, Will," she spoke. "Darn shame. All gone under?"

Standing nodded.

"All but the two eldest, Mrs Prescott. Them Cheyenne took 'em for a purpose, I guess," he told her. "That's where I'm heading now, see if I can catch 'em, kill 'em and get them kids back."

The woman pushed back the linen bonnet that she wore and looked concerned.

"You're on your own after them Indians?"

Will Standing turned in his saddle to look back.

"Well, I might have some help coming on up behind," he explained, smiling, but avoiding the explanation "just don't yet know how many, or when."

Prescott shook his head. A young girl's face pushed through between her parent's heads from the back of the wagon.

"Elizabeth." Standing smiled at her.

"Mr Standing," she replied, an awkward expression on her face.

"Them Cheyenne catches you strung out on your ownsome, I wouldn't give a pig's ear for your chances, son," Prescott told him.

Standing shrugged.

"Where you heading for, Mr Prescott?"

"Fort Laramie, I guess. Least till the emergency is done, when them Cheyenne's clear. Seems like the safest place to be until they're well gone," he supposed. "I heard the army's coming up behind so maybe we'll see some if we keep on south east."

Standing agreed.

"Seems the sensible thing to do. They say Fort Wallace got hit a while back. Roman Nose's bunch. Some people got killed down there too. Appears like they split into parts and are making their way back into Montana, but there's nuthin' to say there ain't more where this bunch come from, on their way up."

"Maybe you should think this through, Will," Mrs Prescott told him. "Come with us to Fort Laramie and let the soldiers deal with them Cheyenne."

Standing shook his head.

"Can't do that Mrs Prescott," he replied. "Least I can do for Molly is chase up them kids and try the best I can to get 'em back afore they can't be found by anybody. They're all the kin I got now."

"Well, I wish you luck, Will," Mr Prescott said. "I think you'll need it."

"Will Standing took off his hat to the women."

"Take care, Mr Prescott, Ma'am…"

Prescott was about to hurrah his mules into motion when he paused. Will was turning the black horse away to the north.

"Hey, Will!" He called after the rider, recognising the horse. "Ain't that…"

Standing turned in the saddle and called back, waving his hat in a goodbye.

"Damn sure is!"

Midnight loped along at the steady pace that Standing urged, and the man grew accustomed to the rhythmic thump of the horse's hooves on the ground, while his eyes followed a regular path through the long grass. Here and there he had to stop, when time returned the country to its original state, and aided the Cheyenne in hiding their passage through. After dismounting and looking closer, he always managed to regain the trail and pushed on, coming to terms with the imaginary target on his back that he constantly felt was always there.

Close to the river, the ground became more open and he could make progress to the flowing water. Glancing ahead, it looked a perfect place for an ambush, trees lining the banks in just the right places, plenty of underbrush and undulating ground, plenty of cover to hide horses from the view of a victim.

Standing pulled up the black horse and unstrung the Sharps from his saddle horn. The sun was to his left and thankfully not in his eyes. He tied up the horse, pushed the linen cartridges and percussion caps for the rifle into his pocket and advanced on foot upon the river, taking advantage of every piece of cover he could find. Some way off he halted as a brace of wild turkey fluttered and squawked away to announce him. He listened for any sound that could give him an advantage, and hearing none, made his way forward. The water was just a few yards away, swishing and gurgling slowly eastwards, down towards the main tributary. He could see the clear tracks of the Cheyenne ponies, entering the water and also the marks where they had exited on the other side. A thought suddenly passed in his mind. Maybe they had crossed, then come around behind him, and were already about to put a bone-tipped spike through his back. He jerked around, wide-eyed at the trick his mind played upon him, but would not let him pass off as just paranoia. But these were Cheyenne he was chasing, and not to be taken lightly. If he was to stand any chance against them, his paranoia was a guide whose nervousness he would have to endure.

Standing waited for some time, deciding that if some possible bushwhacker was there to end his days, impatience would motivate them before he would make the same mistake. Instinct told him that he should take care but he moved to the water's edge anyway, mindful of falling behind too far to stand any chance of getting the children back.

Only the running water invaded the afternoon's silence, along with the chatter of small birds that reassured him of being alone. Just in case, he drew the Colt and put the Sharps on the ground before crossing over. If there were Cheyenne around, the side arm was the best option in an enclosed space such as this. Also, he would need to conserve the rifle ammunition. Once a linen cartridge was slipped into the breech and the lever pulled back into place, the block would slice off the rear of the round and leave a trickle of powder in the breech which would be ignited by the percussion cap when firing. If not fired, the powder might be blown away and the round wasted, a waste he could not afford.

Levelling the long barrel of the Colt ahead at arm's length and pulling back the hammer to rotate the cylinder onto a live round, he negotiated his way through the water and up onto the other side. Following the tracks of unshod horses, he made his way up the bank and onto the level ground that extended beyond the treeline. He glanced into the distance but could make out nothing, no dust, nothing but more open ground that stretched away to more woodland.

Will Standing followed the trail, until it stopped and disappeared into thin air. He examined the ground, looking on either side and wondering how horses could just vanish like that. Dropping the Colt to his side and releasing the hammer in case he shot off his foot, he pushed back the deep hat that he wore by the brim and scratched a dusty forehead with his thumb. He shook his head and looked back at where the animals had emerged from the water.

Walking back, he examined the tracks again and realised that they were thicker than they should be. Despite the horses bunching up onto dry land, it looked like there should be twice as many and he realised how the disappearing trick was done. The Cheyenne had made the opposite side of the river, then backed them out into the water and diverted downstream to throw off a pursuer or at least cost them time. Depth of the hoof marks in the wrong places confirmed it.

Something else he noticed. Only unshod horses had exited the water when he knew two shod mules were present, and he guessed that the animals carrying the children had been kept mid-stream for the sake of speed. Strange hostiles these, he thought, appearing to travel easily as if fearing nothing that might follow, and yet bothering to take the trouble to cover their tracks whenever possible. Perhaps it was just the way they had been raised; a different culture has its ways.

Standing waded back into the water to see if he could decide which way they went, upstream or downstream. If he were pulling the same trick, he decided that he would pick upstream as the flowing water would carry debris to quickly obliterate any sign of passing horses. He could be wrong. Keeping to his idea, he moved knee deep upstream and looked for something to give away the direction of the Cheyenne and the children.

Smiling to himself, he found it. A series of stones visible through the clear water that were clear of the algae that others carried, kicked over by the hooves of large animals, and many of them. He would follow upstream.

Before changing direction, he let Midnight drink and filled his canteen, then swung up into the worn saddle and headed upstream, still with one hand on the Colt. Some way along, he found where the party had exited the water, and congratulated himself for getting it right for a change. He urged the horse over to where the tracks were and took a long look to ensure that it was not another false trail. Satisfied, he advanced up the bank and took another look out towards the distant treeline. Somewhere out there, he told himself, the children were being taken, terrified and unaware of his attempt to recover them, wondering what their fate was to be. He wondered that too.

By now, the sun was descending quickly. Standing thought about continuing in the dark, but decided against it. He dared not use a torch to follow, wishing not to waste the element of surprise, and without light he might lose the trail completely and waste time finding it again. He hoped that those who chased him would feel the same way. A fire would also alert them to his position, so it was a cold sleep with just a corn stick to stop his belly rumbling in protest.

***

It was indeed a cold, fitful half sleep, with fearful, dreamed images always there whenever he managed to discount the world around him. Waking when it was still dark, he rose and shook away the stiffness and the realities that flooded back from the day before. Midnight was still where he was the night before, tethered on the long rope that gave him the freedom to graze.

Will Standing put the old saddle over the blanket on the horse's back and gave him a slap on the neck. Slipping home the bit, he attached it to the bridle and threw the reins across the withers, ready to move as soon as it got light. Having no time piece, he could only guess at how long it would be before the light would be breaking, but from the indigo in the east guessed at an hour or less before he could be back on the track of the Cheyenne.

Standing reached into the sack for the corn sticks and found only three. Once gone, it would be a hungry ride, for he had not the time to stop and hunt or forage for food that grew wild. He took one to arrest the hunger pangs and made it last, making water fill the gap where food did not.

He wondered again about his kin, somewhere ahead on the deck of a mule, and mulled over what night they might have had. A certain guilt overcame him, like a voice in his ear, asking why he had not been there to defend them, to stop whatever ills he imagined they were going through, to catch up and make things right all the quicker. And then there was Molly and Henry and little Will, all gone, with the responsibility beginning to find a seat on his shoulders, right or wrong.

As the sun rose, he warmed and eased into the ride. The trail had now all but gone, thanks to the long grass returning to its original upright position. Pressing Midnight on, he found occasional clear patches of ground that gave his quarry away, and Standing made a mental note of the place where they might be entering into the distant treeline, calculating a direct route across the open ground. If he was wrong, then he could at least ride along the edge of the trees until he found where they had entered.

Something took his attention to the east. He pulled the black horse up and squinted into the distance, just a hint of dust on the horizon, a halo of lighter value against the blue. Could it be the chasers? If so, they had covered a lot of ground to move around from south to east and cut him off. He doubted that was possible with such a horse as Midnight under him. But maybe they had travelled all night. He doubted that with Cheyenne around, unless they were crazy as hell and it was catching.

If it was those who wanted his neck in a noose, they were too close for comfort and his shaky plan to need them at the right time might be falling apart. He decided to wait and see. The dust increased to outline the encased riders, and he reached for the Sharps and checked the cartridges in his pocket, just in case. Now he could see the shape of wagons, but how many was unclear.

Midnight whinnied with impatience, and Standing reached down to calm him with a slap on the shoulder. He raised a hand to his eyes and narrowed them to find focus. A guidon fluttered above the dust now, twitching with the breeze and the movement of the rider that held it. It was red and white and carried symbols of the unit that followed. The Seventh.

When a half mile away, Standing's concerns were not only salvaged but bolstered into relief. He could see them clearly now, United States Cavalry with three wagons and pack mules, pretty as you like and coming his way. Standing turned the horse around to meet them head on, and gave a cheery wave as they closed the gap between them.

At the head of the troop was a young officer in dusty blue with a fatigue cap on his head. Beside him was a flamboyant character in buckskin shirt, held at the waist with a broad belt and large buckle, wide brimmed hat and deep leather boots. On his hands were beaded gloves of Indian style. The officer held up a hand and halted the column, then advanced his horse to meet the single rider, the buckskinned man a yard behind. He saluted.

"Lieutenant Miles, of the Seventh Cavalry, out of Fort Hays." He smiled good-naturedly. "Good morning, Sir. Are you alone?"

"Fort Hays?" Standing asked. "You're a long way from home, Lieutenant," Standing answered. "Yes, I am alone, but glad to see you, Sir. I surely am."

Will reached out a hand, and shook that offered by the officer.

"You know of the Indian emergency?" The soldier asked. "I understand they are raiding all along this valley and moving north. I would advise you to come with us for your own protection, they may be anywhere around the area for some time."

"Seen it first hand, Lieutenant," Will told him. "They hit my sister's place yesterday, killed her, her husband, and three-month-old child. Took two older kids for captives, and that's where I'm going, after those kids."

"I am sorry for your loss then," said the officer.

The buckskin man urged his horse nearer. He held a long-barrelled rifle by the barrel and rested the stock on his thigh. He nodded a quick greeting.

"Chasing up those Indians alone would not be the sensible thing to do…"

The lieutenant apologised.

"This is Mr Cody, our scout for the present." He turned back to Standing. "I did not catch your name, Sir?"

"Didn't give it. But it's Standing. William Standing. Late of the Henderson place, as was." He looked at the buckskinned rider. "Cody? Billy Cody?"

The other nodded courteously.

"The same, Sir."

Standing nodded back.

"Last I heard of you, you were killin' meat for the railroad…"

Cody smiled, and raised his brows.

"I was that. But the railroad is almost complete and a fellow needs employment so I signed up for scout during the present unpleasantness," he answered. "I am sorry to hear of your loss."

Standing curtly nodded his appreciation of the words.

"Well, I fixed on their trail, heading north up into Montana, seems like. Making slow but cautious way along." He pointed to the distant treeline. "Towards the timber. Guess they made it there already. When I set out, I was about six hours behind, but I think I might have closed the gap a little."

The officer looked across to where Standing was indicating, the distant treeline.

"Well," He explained. "My orders are to report to Fort Fetterman, where a joint effort to pursue the hostiles is being arranged. I would urge you to listen to Mr Cody's advice and come with us, for your own safety." He paused when he saw Standing's expression. "I'm sure an effort will be arranged with some despatch to pursue your missing children and that the outcome will be successful."

It was not the outcome that Standing wanted or expected.

"Lieutenant, those kids are not missing, they are taken," he said angrily. "And right now, they are just a ride away and farther by the minute. All I ask is four or five soldiers to help me track 'em, get those kids back where they belong. I kind of had the idea that you people are there to protect folks in times like this?"

"Mr Standing, I have my orders, which are very specific. I have forty mounted men and infantry in the wagons, and supplies for a field expedition destined for Fort Fetterman by tomorrow. At this time, I cannot release men for the purpose of an enterprise which has little chance of success. I am sorry, Sir."

Midnight shuffled in impatience, and Standing pulled him up. The man was exasperated by the refusal to help him. The lieutenant added what sounded like a consolation.

"What I can do Sir, is offer some provisions if you are determined to continue your pursuit of the hostiles. You look a little short on comestibles."

"On what?"

"Comestibles, Sir," he explained. "Food?"

Will Standing tried to calm his anger. He did need food to keep him going, and if that was the least he could get, he would be a fool to deny himself. The young officer had ordered a sergeant to return to a wagon and he soon returned with a hessian sack that Standing added to his well depleted one and hooked it onto his saddle horn.

"Well," Standing said. "I thank you for that at least."

"I do wish you luck, Mr Standing," the officer told him. "I hope you regain your family."

He saluted. Cody leant forward in the saddle and eyed the animal that Standing rode.

"That is a remarkable beast, Sir. If I may say so. He has Arabian in him, has he not?"

"And some Mustang I hear," Standing added.

"You are lucky to have such an animal," Cody said, in admiration of the black horse.

"Yeah. I get that all the time," Will agreed. "What about you, Mr Scout, I hear you have a reputation for chasing Indians when there's money in it. You feel like helping a fellow in need of some assistance? Don't have much to offer but you can have anything I got, including the horse, if we get those children back."

Cody allowed an expression of disappointment to flow across his features.

"Alas, Sir. I have a commitment to the army, and Mr Custer back at Fort Hays. I fear what reputation I have would be sorely dented if I failed to rise to it."

Midnight reared, wanting to go, and Standing touched his flanks to give him his head, but the man had time to call back.

"Then go back to shootin' poor dumb animals, and you can go to hell!"

Chapter Six
Trails

It was past mid-morning when Bellfield's party crossed the river. They had lost Standing's trail and drifted more to the west, but rose early and kept up a pace from early light, hoping to pick it up again on the more open ground on the other side. Making the far bank and halting at Bellfield's order, the latter drew a brass telescope from his saddle bag, extended it and put the small end to his eye. He slowly scanned the country ahead, moving left to right, and then back again.

Then, he froze and concentrated on one place in the middle distance. He handed the telescope to Deerbolt and pointed.

"Take a look," he ordered. "There. Where I'm directing, what do you see?"

Deerbolt took the instrument and looked closely at it, unfamiliar with such wonders, then realising Bellfield's impatience, put it to his own eye and screwed up the other. He moved the view around and finally saw what the other had seen.

"Dust?" Deerbolt asked, already fully knowing what it was. "But who's?"

Deerbolt dropped the telescope to his chest and looked again.

"Cheyenne?" He asked, aware of the concern of the others at the suggestion.

Bellfield took the telescope and looked again at the object of their concern.

"Maybe a pennant, or a guidon," he suggested.

"Or a war lance?" added the Marshal.

Bellfield kept the telescope steady for some moments, then confirmed his hope.

"No. Its cavalry, and wagons, and coming this way."

The party of horsemen immediately set off to intercept the distant troop, covering the distance at a steady pace. When some way off they observed the small cavalcade halt and look earnestly in their direction until certain that the newcomers were not Cheyenne. Bellfield took the lead and rode close to the commanding officer at the head of the column, who saluted and greeted them with his name and rank.

"Lieutenant Miles, Sir. B Company, Seventh Cavalry."

Bellfield touched his hat.

"Good day, Lieutenant," he grunted. "We are a deputised group from Dogwood, a small town south of here." He poked a finger at Deerbolt. "This is the town Marshal, Mr Deerbolt."

"Mr Deerbolt," returned the officer, wondering why a deputy appeared to be taking charge over the peace officer. "You are a-ways from home, considering the current emergency with regard to the Cheyenne. You know that Fort Wallace was attacked some days ago?"

"Roman Nose's bunch, I heard," Deerbolt confirmed his knowledge.

"The same," Miles agreed. "It appears they broke up after the attack and are heading back north in groups to avoid direct contact with the authorities."

Deerbolt nodded and pushed his hat back.

"We already had a taste of 'em," he explained. "They hit a homestead yesterday, south a-ways, people killed and children taken…"

"I am aware, Mr Deerbolt, of that sad event. I am sorry that I cannot be more involved in returning the children, but to abandon the whole area for a pursuit that is likely to end in failure is against my orders," Miles told him.

"I understand that, Sir," Deerbolt agreed, a sad note in his voice. "I only wish we could apply ourselves to a more agreeable chase."

Bellfield was becoming irritated. The Cheyenne were not his priority.

"We are in pursuit of a criminal," he said, "a bank robber, horse thief and fraudster, and perhaps more that we have yet to discover. Have you come across any individuals recently?"

Cody urged his horse forward and halted by Lieutenant Miles.

"Does this individual have a name?" He asked.

"Standing by name," Bellfield answered. "William Standing, of dubious character and ill disposition. A taker of what does not belong to him, nor ever would."

"And what will you do to this ill-defined character, if you come across him?" Cody asked.

Bellfield looked aghast at the query.

"Why, hang him, of course. From whatever tree or high place presents itself."

The sergeant, who sat the horse behind the officer spoke up without being asked.

"Sounds like the one we cut trail over this morning, Sir."

Miles, who was annoyed by the verbal intrusion, snapped back.

"I am aware of that, Sergeant."

Cody, who had leant over and crossed his arms over the saddle horn, turned and gave a long glance back at the non-commissioned officer. Who knows if Lieutenant Miles or Cody had intended to give Standing the benefit of the doubt? Whatever the truth, the path was now clear.

"We did come across an individual earlier," the lieutenant confirmed. "Following hostiles who had taken some children," he said, looking at Cody. "Can you recall the name?"

Before Cody could answer, the sergeant did it for him.

"Sure was Standing, Sir. I remember right clear."

The officer nodded, trying not to show irritation.

"I believe that was his name."

"Riding a black horse?" Bellfield needed no more confirmation, but asked anyway.

"Remarkable animal," Cody said.

Bellfield allowed his anger to show. He tugged the rein of his horse.

"You have no idea, Sir," he told the man, then looked back at the officer. "And you say you came across him back there? How long?"

"Oh, a few hours ago."

Alexander Bellfield glared across at Marshal Deerbolt.

"Let's go. We're wasting daylight."

With no further conversation, Bellfield spurred his mount away and along the line of the column. Deerbolt tipped his hat and thanked Miles, then galloped along after his patron and the rest followed. At the last of the wagons, Bellfield turned north east, hoping to cut Standing's tracks or find where he might enter into the distant trees, a blue line along the horizon, much as his quarry had done in trailing the hostiles.

Cody looked at the officer by his side.

"Interesting," he said.

***

Often, the Cheyenne halted to listen. The big trees grew close like buttresses in a cathedral and seemed to add the same echo to any reasonably loud noise. The calls of small birds that made their way through the lower canopies were amplified into a crescendo of white noise and distant woodpeckers appeared much nearer than they were.

Tom had not wasted the short time between discovery and continuing their journey. Keeping both eyes on their captors, he gently tore off small strips of Alice's dress where they would not be noticed, and applied similar attention to the pieces of his trousers that he had tried to use to bind his sister's feet. The results were pushed into both of his jacket pockets.

Four Cheyenne still rode abreast, a few yards ahead, and then the two mules carrying the children, and finally the last of the Indians, unfortunately the most aggressive and unforgiving that Tom had already had dealings with.

As the horses navigated between the boles of trees, Tom leant over the neck of the mule as if saddle sore, and this gave him the opportunity to look back. Whenever his mule turned one way or another, the angle gave one of Tom's hands the freedom to take a piece of fabric and drop it onto the ground, in a bush, or other places where he hoped it would not be observed by the rider behind. There were only so many pieces of cloth at his disposal, so he knew that the distance between each must not be too far, nor too short. He glanced over at Alice, who looked on without expression at what he was doing, and he hoped that she would not give him away by her attention.

For some miles Tom managed to seed the trail with cotton fragments, thankful that the Cheyenne following them rode close behind. Had he stayed back some distance, he would undoubtedly have seen the boy's markers. The thought crossed Tom's mind that he might be taking the risk for nothing, if no one decided that they were worth rescuing from the Cheyenne, or that the risk was too great. For a fourteen-year-old boy, he was growing fast.

"Noxa'e (Wait)!" A shout from behind.

Tom turned quickly to see the following warrior holding the last piece of cotton that he had dropped onto a branch, and was certain that he had done it both covertly and well. He was wrong.

The four Cheyenne in the lead pulled their horses heads around and rode back the short distance to the others. One warrior grasped the bridle of Tom's mule and hauled the animal towards him as it 'hawed' in protest at the rough handling. The man's other hand made a circle in the air and hit the boy hard on the head and drove him from his mount. Alice screamed and the Cheyenne added another hard blow to the first, knocking her also to the ground. In a thoughtless moment, Tom had regained his feet and leapt up at the warrior, flailing with his fists to avenge his sister's bad treatment, and perhaps his own. But before he could make contact a moccasin clad foot struck him hard in the chest and he was forced back onto the ground.

Alice's mule reared and pulled away but another Cheyenne caught the rein and held it back, just missing the girl with its flailing hooves. For a moment pandemonium reigned, as horses and riders were jostled by the frightened animal, until a warrior dismounted and calmed it, its eyes still wide and nervous from the commotion.

A high-pitched conversation in the Cheyenne language followed for some time. Tom crawled across to Alice and he comforted her as best he could. He could see that she was far from herself, and had been that way since yesterday. He wondered if she would ever be the same again, or if either of them would.

The man who had discovered the cotton thrust it forward at the leader with the feather-spiked headdress. His eyes flashed with anger as he complained about the ruse but it seemed to Tom that the others were blaming the warrior for his lack of observation. Horses moved erratically as the men argued among themselves and fingers were pointed back the way that they had come, and then at the boy. Tom felt the urge to use the situation for another chance to run, but decided against it. Had he been alone, perhaps he might have tried, but he knew that Alice could not be expected to comply in the mental state that she was in. He looked at her dirty face and distant, unblinking eyes.

"Alice!" He said in a low voice.

His sister turned to him and gave a smile, just the hint of a smile that belonged somewhere before yesterday.

"What time is it, Tommy?" She asked, frowning.

The boy shook his head, his eyes on the conversation of his captors.

"Don't know…"

"Gotta go check, see if the chicken's laid enough eggs for breakfast," she said. "Momma's waiting."

Tom shook his head, understanding that it was useless to protest the issue.

"Sure," he told her gently. "We'll go soon."

Conversation between the Cheyenne finished.

The boy's beating was intense and went on for some time, with three warriors bouncing him from one to the other using fists and feet to show their displeasure. Staying still and feigning unconsciousness did little to halt the blows that rained down on him, so he tried to fight back and at least maintain some kind of pride that they would not break him. That at least would give him some kind of satisfaction, but their anger at him knew no limits and at last he lay face down in the dirt, beaten and bloody.

Alice sat a little way off, her face pallid but showing little sign of expression. She was some distance away now, in a place where the world could not touch her, where only the past moved across her vacant eyes.

One Cheyenne had ridden back the way that they had come to find more of Tom's cotton trail, and assess from the distance between them how long he had worked upon the trail and how far back it might go. As Tom's ordeal ended, the warrior returned and spoke quickly with the leader, who had not participated in the beating. Sitting against a fallen tree and watching the boy fight back, he allowed the others to continue until satisfied that justice had been meted out to their pleasure.

They dragged Tom to where Alice sat, sad and scruffy with torn dress and still wearing the remnants of her makeshift foot coverings that her brother had made. She looked down at him, smiling with raised eyebrows and stroked his chin with her hand, his blood transferring to where she touched.

"Tommy, you've been in that mud hole again. Momma's not goin' to like it…"

Tom just looked up through half open, black and blue eyes, moist with blood and tears. He turned over painfully, only to see the Cheyenne leader walking towards them and feared a continuation of the violence that he had so far endured. The man hunkered down near the boy and looked intensely at him, shaking his head a little. He said something in Cheyenne that Tommy did not understand and slowly held out a leather water bag and unfastened the stopper, allowing liquid to fall in a stream and flow over the boys damaged face. Tom raised a hand and swiped the water over all his head and red matted hair, feeling the relief of its coolness, letting some find its way into his mouth. It was good, a soothing draught that helped to lessen the pain of the beating.

The Cheyenne turned up the palm of his right hand and swept it across in front of the boy. He spoke again in a quiet voice which went without understanding. Tom looked up at the man through swollen eyes, a savage that he had little in common with, culturally or morally, but somehow had a little more kindness than the others. At least that was his thought until he remembered that the man had stood by, and watched as others performed the violence upon him.

No food was given to the children that day. For Tom, the pain overshadowed the need for sustenance, although his need for water was almost unbearable. Alice did not seem to care and she just held on to the mule as it carried her through the trees, sometimes humming a melody from part of a tune that her mother sometimes sang.

Tom's head played a symphony of blows that refused to abate and he closed his eyes, hoping that it would go away.

***

A wagon rolled through the long grass, wobbling on uncertain axles. Every now and then one wheel confronted a stone or piece of ground that offered resistance and the vehicle slowed until the two tired horses that hauled it managed to overcome the obstacle. Over the top of the wagon a faded canopy was stretched across metal hoops to give shade and a modicum of living space for the two people on the driving box.

A woman in a visored bonnet maintained a loose rein and held out a long stick over the horses and flicked them regularly on the rump, to maintain an average walking speed. By her side was a thin man with dark clothing, trousers and long jacket, with a grubby white shirt, the collar of which was tightly buttoned around his neck. His attention was not on the animals that his wife drove, but on something that he observed through a small brass telescope, opened to full extension. He stretched out his free hand and pointed over to his right.

"Margaret! Margaret!" He exclaimed in excitement.

His wife followed his direction with slight interest.

"Prairie falcon, Falco Mexicanus," he expressed, "at the eastern extent of its range, by the Good Lord's grace. Never expected to see one this far east…"

Margaret nodded and went on with the task of driving the horses. She smiled fleetingly as her husband took out a shabby notebook from his pocket and began scribbling among the notes of other ornithological discoveries. Some way off, the object of his attention swooped into the grass and found a meal, a small rodent not fast enough to escape the sharp talons and beak of the bird of prey. The man tried to write but found the jolting of the wagon made it impossible. He turned to his wife.

"Time for water, I think, Margaret," he advised. "And see to the needs of the animals."

Margaret 'whoa-ed' the team and arched her back to ease the stiffness of the journey. She stood up on the wagon box and raised a hand to her eyes, casting a gaze along the horizon as her husband descended from his seat. She was younger than he by at least fifteen years, but her admiration for his sermons back home had cast aside any doubt that others had against the marriage.

"I still see no sign of the train, husband," she told him, sweeping the horizon once more. "Maybe we should go back and seek the trail that would return us to the fort?"

The man, a reverend, Joshua Morgenson by name, looked up from the bucket that he was freeing from the side of the wagon. He put the bucket beneath the water barrel secured above and scratched his beard, then pinched the bare lip where a moustache should have been.

"I think the train is near, Margaret," he advised. "It cannot be far, possibly just over the next rise, can you see evidence of dust?"

"I can see nothing but grass and the sky, and plenty of it."

Morgenson filled half the bucket with water and walked up to where the horses grazed on the dry foliage around them. He placed it in front of the animals and they drank eagerly.

"I am certain there will be a stream soon," he guessed. "The land cannot go on forever, and the Good Lord will provide."

The reverend took a scoop of water from the barrel and handed it up to his wife. She took it and swallowed slowly, not wishing to waste a drop, then handed it back for her husband to drink.

He finished and looked around at the open ground around them. A gentle breeze swayed the tops of the grass like ocean waves. Behind the wagon, a channel of open space showed where they had travelled, the wheels making deeper marks on either side. Morgenson looked up at the sun and shielded his eyes.

"Will be hot today."

Margaret Morgenson descended from the wagon box. She put her hands upon her hips and took another look around.

"I think we should go back," she suggested. "Maybe we can catch another train."

Her husband shook his head.

"We have no money for further passage with another train, even if there be one. If we go back, we will have to winter in Fort Laramie, and perhaps fall upon charity to see us through." He paused. "And I have no appetite for that."

Margaret looked concerned.

"Husband, we must face the fact that we are lost. Must we wander this wilderness until the water runs out and the animals die?"

Morgenson shrugged off the idea.

"Our Lord wandered the wild for forty days and forty nights, and he survived."

"We are not the Lord, Joshua," she advised. "And he had more resourceful relatives than we have."

Morgenson looked at her intently for a moment, and she wondered if a rebuke was advancing upon her. He returned the lid to the barrel, slamming it down hard.

"Then we must pray," he announced. "And ask for direction to the Gilbert Liberty Train or to the nearest water, whichever the Lord decides is the most prudent and convenient."

"Pray!" Margaret Morgenson asked. "Pray?"

The Reverend Morgenson looked around in surprise at the question and the way in which it was given.

"Of course," he answered. "Prayer is the solution to our problems; our faith tells us so. That is why the Lord showed us the way west, the way to a better life."

Margaret was flustered and she lifted her skirts and kicked the wagon wheel.

"Did the Lord show the way for you to fill that darn book with bird notes? With what swallow lays what coloured eggs and which darn buzzard flies in what part of the state, and when?"

Her husband was taken back with an outburst that he had never seen before, nor expected from his wife. He stared, unable to find the words. She wagged a finger at him.

"Because of your darn insistence to leave the train to follow birdsong and find its owner we lost our way, lost the Liberty Train, and sit here now in something that the Lord made to confound the human kind that he pretends to love so much!"

Morgenson stepped forward and held her shoulders, trying to calm her.

"Wife, just hear yourself," he advised. "Listen to the blasphemy that you are on the cusp of," he said. "The Lord will provide; we are good people of good stock and faithful stock. He will not see us perish for a cupful of water or a mile from the safety of the Liberty Train. Now come, kneel with me in prayer and see how He will deliver us from the wilderness and see us to the new country."

The Reverend Morgenson let her go and knelt at her feet, clasped his hands together and closed his eyes. He brought the knot of fingers up to his chin and began.

"Father who art above us. Deliver us, your children, from the perils of this wild land and the lack of water within it. Show us the way to a good drink and maybe a cold bath in this heat, Lord, and if you can spare a little for the animals, that would be fine. Forgive this woman for the doubting she shows, and show her that the way to the Liberty Train is a prayer away and sweep off the harsh words she uses to chastise her husband for his interest in the Lord's creatures, large and small."

He paused, concentrating on whatever else was needed.

"Lord, if the Liberty Train is too much trouble and we must return to the fort of civilised people, let us find willing charity without the need for financial exchange as my pockets are not deep, Lord, as you already know. And if we must winter in the fort, deliver unto us another emigrant train with religious people who will see the virtue of a free passage west." He paused once more. "We ask you this, Lord, as we hope to testify to your word on the other side of the Rocky Mountains at some stage, God willing."

He paused again.

"Amen."

Margaret fell back against the wagon, exasperated.

"Amen," she said, a little hollowly.

Morgenson rose from his knees, his hands still clasped in prayer but with his eyes now wide open. His face owned a frown that denoted the confidence of a righteous man. There was a rumble, a distant groaning of the Earth that was almost subsonic. Joshua Morgenson looked up into a clear blue sky and spread his hands.

"Thunder!" He exclaimed. "The Lord has heard our prayers and given us rain from a fine blue sky."

He looked around at his wife, who stood stock still against the wagon and raised a hand, pointing into the distance, her bonnet pushed back and eyes wide and fixed. Morgenson turned to follow her indication.

In the middle distance was a huge cloud of dust rolling upward, linked to the thunder that manufactured it. The reverend raised his arms to the sky again and he laughed aloud in satisfaction.

"Aaah!" He cried. "Tis the Liberty Train. Praise the Lord!"

Chapter Seven
Is It Monday?

William Standing still felt the sting of dissatisfaction. He cursed the army and Billy Cody for their lack of interest in his intentions. Both had reputations that were not worth the slick in his spit, and he wondered what incident might exhort them to deviate from the orders that they held in so much reverence.

The black horse loped along, making for the distant trees where the man hoped to pick up the track of the Cheyenne that held his kin captive. All around the rider was an ocean of swaying grass, too long and too late to trace clearly where horses had moved through. Cutting an oblique angle instead of a direct route, he zigged and zagged in an effort to find some sign where they had passed, but either the trail was cold or he had just not found it.

"God-damn," Standing said to himself, cursing his own lack of expertise.

Several times, he had dismounted to examine a possible sign of his quarry, but they all proved to be false, just the recent passage of a wolf or coyote that had slipped unseen ahead of him. Once, the shadow of a buzzard had skipped across close by as his attention was on the ground, and thinking it might be an ambush he jerked the Colt from his belt and flattened himself with the barrel aiming at nothing but sky. He had laughed at himself but it made him consider what might have happened had his impulse been correct, and resolved to be more observant. Who knew what dangers the long grass might conceal? He had heard from the old timers how Indians could pull down their mounts to their flanks in long grass, then when the time was right, kick them in the guts and get them up, mounting as they rose to attack an enemy.

Standing took the canteen from the saddle horn and drank a little, then grasped his hat by the crown and punched in the small depression to make a bowl. He let a little water fall into the hat and allowed the horse to take it up, far short of what was needed but enough to slake his thirst.

The treeline was now just a mile away. He took a long look and tried to decide where he might push a way through, had he been the Cheyenne. The problem was that there were many places where the timber provided gaps into the interior, all offering passage in the general direction of north, the way that they were heading. Standing decided that there was nothing for it but to gain the treeline and move along until he found some evidence of their passing. Surely, where the grass gave way to the woodland, open ground would retain the movement of many horses.

He mounted again and took a long look back, in the direction that they had come, until satisfied that he still had a good distance between himself and those that wanted him for a pendulum. Midnight responded to his urging and they rode quickly towards the trees.

As he had hoped, the long grass petered out where the big trees gave shadow to the ground below and discouraged growth. However, the ground was hard, giving little help to the unpractised eye, so he dismounted again and set his eyes for the slightest mark of a displaced leaf or broken twig that might be evidence of better signs. Just in case of the ambush he feared, he drew the Colt again, feeling more confident with a gun in his hand should they come at him from the brush.

It had crossed his mind several times, the notion of whether the Cheyenne expected pursuit, or if they were confident of evading it, if it proved the case. He guessed that they would expect the cavalry if they expected anything, and knew that they had little fear of just one man. How wrong they were, and how lucky they were that the military seemed to prefer the following of orders than the following of the Cheyenne.

Standing also thought of his own situation, and the task that he had set himself. It felt such a mindless thing to do, or expect of himself, but nothing in the last couple of days had seemed to make any sense. And yet, what else could he do, abandon those children to the will of the Cheyenne that had taken them, to a life that was hard to even think about?

He was not a brave man, he knew that. Sure, he could stick up a bank as long as the odds were in his favour and he had used common sense to work it out, and both times he had been successful. The first time was the easiest, as once the money was spent the Civil War had begun and he had managed to evade paying for the crime by joining the Army of the Potomac, and the law had no idea of his name anyway. He had considered himself lucky, and his luck held in the military, being raised to Sergeant for doing little but just being there and delivering messages with speed and despatch.

After the war, he had not intended to offend the law again, happy just to help out his sister and her husband as they tried to make a life on the land. It had been a good decision and he got on with Henry, and the kids, who of course knew nothing of the misdemeanours of their uncle. And there it would have continued, until the belligerent Bellfield turned off the faucet and dried up any land south of his until they paid him a price that most could not afford. Bellfield knew that, and it was just his way to move them on and take up the land for his own purposes.

Of course, the last bank he considered was only half successful, but then again it was only eighty dollars, and he had not shot anyone, nor could he with an empty side arm. It had been a close call that had added to his list the crime of horse theft, a hanging offence, and he knew it.

William Standing was not a religious man, and hardly bothered to dwell upon the social or ecclesiastical issues of his crimes, which he considered minor anyway. More important were the judicial and legal implications should he be caught. At least, that was his thinking before horse stealing imposed itself upon him, and that was a fault that preyed upon his mind somewhat, but his conscience allowed the idea that others had at least a little part to play in that.

Bringing himself back to the task he had taken on, he reflected once more on what he would do if and when he closed with the Cheyenne who took the children. At best it would be one against four or five, and that would be bad enough, but what if they joined with others along the way, and detected his pursuit? What if he became the hunted and they drove him back onto those that were coming up to put his head in a noose? Suddenly he felt himself a dead man walking, or riding, and the only advantage he had was a horse like a hawk's wing.

***

Marshal Deerbolt looked over at the rider at his side. He raised his voice over the drumming of horses' hooves.

"Mister Bellfield, we need to give these animals a rest. If they give out on us, we're out on foot with Indians around, and no place to go."

Bellfield's face was set on the distance, where his stolen horse was. But common sense was common sense, especially with the Cheyenne in a bad mood and looking for trouble wherever they found it. He pulled back the reins on his mount and the group of riders came to a halt. They dismounted, all of them, and were glad of the relief to their nether regions where leather had become uncomfortable. Small knots of men gathered to whisper and grumble, but knew where the next payday was coming from, and so kept their voices low. Two walked into the long grass to relieve themselves, but kept the distance to a minimum when the half jokes from fellow riders warned of possible horrors of ambush, or how a random arrow shot from a distance might find its mark and restrict their powers at a local house of disrepute.

Deerbolt kept his attention on Bellfield. He could see that this had become more than a stolen horse. It was as if Will Standing had taken more than a black stallion, and the action required much more than its return to set things right. Bellfield's eyes remained on the horizon, even as they rested, possibly hoping to observe the slightest of signs that they were close to completing their task. The Marshal wondered about suggesting that they abandon the idea, all things considered, but he had a fair idea of the tirade of abuse that such a thing would bring.

Of William Standing Deerbolt knew little, other than he had fought in the recent unpleasantness and worked for food and found on the Henderson place. He had heard the stories, but put them down to just that. From what he had seen of the man, he was a willing worker and until recently had caused no trouble in the town when he occasionally appeared there. What had prompted the events the previous Saturday were uncertain, but Deerbolt was sure he had a pretty good idea.

Bellfield turned to the Marshal with a hard look across his features.

"When we get going, we ride abreast, spread 'em out to look for where that horse thief went. We keep going until we do find his track, then keep going until we find him, and my damn horse."

Deerbolt was about to make his suggestions when one of the two who had walked off to make themselves more comfortable called back. When the rest looked across, he was kneeling and waving them forward to where he was examining the ground. The knot of people gathered around and looked for his discovery. The man pushed back his hat and pointed at a small section of open ground.

"Unshod ponies," he said, "can't tell how many, but more than one, heading north at an easy pace."

Bellfield pushed through.

"How long?"

The kneeling man shook his head and screwed up his face, thinking.

"Oh, maybe half a day, less, maybe."

"No sign of a shod horse?" Bellfield asked.

"Nope, just range ponies, only shod animals are a couple of mules they're trailing."

Alexander Bellfield beamed.

"Then we have him!" He exclaimed. "If these are the Cheyenne he's after, then we follow them. Somewhere along the way we must pick up his trail…"

Deerbolt spoke up.

"Mister Bellfield, we don't know if these are the bunch that Standing is after, and we don't know if he's still following. Lord knows, we only come across this by chance, and he's just one man."

Bellfield shook his head vigorously.

"It's him! He's still out there on the trail of those Cheyenne. He has to be. I know it! It's just a matter of time before we catch up."

Deerbolt knew he would waste his breath on more argument. He should have been more assertive before now, he knew that, but that was before they came across the remains of the Henderson place, when he thought it was just a chase after a horse thief and a robber of federal funds. It was now becoming much more than that.

***

Tommy Henderson wondered how long he had slept on the back of the mule, if it could be called sleep. Since the beating from the Cheyenne, he had slipped in and out of consciousness and the last hours had merged with half dreams of home. He had been tied to the mule with his head beside its neck and bounced along with the movement of the animal. He swallowed but there was nothing to ease his thirst.

Now, there were two Cheyenne following the mules, spread wide apart and always alert to the slightest movement from either of the children. One of the followers called to those at the head of the group and Tom looked over to see Alice, a slight smile of recognition on her dirt-streaked face.

"Is it Monday?" Tom croaked, wondering why it mattered so much, perhaps trying to figure out how long they had been captive and how long this torture would continue.

Alice just shrugged her shoulders and once more hummed those pieces of a tune that were becoming monotonous and out of character.

Water streamed down his face and he opened his mouth to catch as much as he could, letting the surplus streak down like tears through the dirt and blood on his face. Tom let his head slip back onto the mule, the strain on his neck becoming too much to hold against gravity.

They were still among trees, he could see that through bleary eyes, yellow shafts of sunlight searching through the timber for contact with the ground that banished dark shadows on all sides. Songbirds echoed in the distance while those closer twittered a warning as they flew off among the branches. Another woodpecker played its staccato drumming among the canopies above.

A second stream of water followed the first and Tom squeezed open one eye to see the painted hand of the Cheyenne that poured it. He was not surprised to see which of the warriors it was, and doubted any other would bother or care.

By mid-afternoon they had halted again and the children were dragged from their mounts unceremoniously and cast to the ground. One of the warriors was about to tie them but the leader stopped him with one word in Cheyenne. Tommy lay on his back, in the shade of the underbrush, just glad not to be bumping around on the back of the mule while Alice sat cross legged beside him. He turned to Alice and asked again.

"Alice, is it Monday today?"

His sister beamed for a moment, and then seemed to form a scolding expression. "Momma always sets school by Monday. I always have to do reading and writing on a Monday. Momma says I read real good, but sometimes I spell the big words bad." She laughed aloud. "Momma says when I grow up, maybe I'll go to a real school, with kids and real teachers and stuff…"

"You will, Alice," Tommy said, "you will."

A piece of dry, hard, cold meat was thrown between the two and Alice picked it up and began to chew eagerly as if it were a 'Thanksgiving' breakfast. Tom just wanted more water and it was not long in coming. Brown hands jerked him backward and pushed him against a tree, his back supported against rough bark. He stretched his swollen cheeks to allow him to see better and found the lead Cheyenne crouched in front of him with the hide water carrier. The man cupped liquid in his hand and spread it over Tom's face. He stared for a long moment at the boy.

"Hetsestseha hehpohenonoo'e (Now look)," The warrior said, shaking his thumb in the boy's direction.

Tom looked into the painted face beneath the feather-spiked headdress that fluttered with the breeze. It was the first time that he had been close enough to an Indian to observe the detail, his only other experience being in a dime novel that he had been given once at Christmas, unless the beating could be included. His upper face was stained dark blue, down to below his nose, with a yellow spot on his chin. Above the blue, a beaded band marked where the feathers stopped above his forehead and fell down over his eyes. The face was regular featured and almost handsome despite the frown that he now wore, deep brown eyes allowing a certain calmness to show through. Somehow, Tom had come to feel relieved when he was around, a certain feeling of defence against the warriors who were only too eager to show aggression. And yet, this man had sat by and watched others do their worst.

Tom had noticed that each of the warriors wore a long sash, wrapped several times around their waists, knotted at the back or side, and wondered what it was. It appeared to be of no regular use, but then again, neither was their headdress or other decorative items and he mentally put it down as something similar. Whatever else he knew that these people were, the boy could hardly deny that they were handsome devils, braided and beaded in all manner of ways for a culture he knew nothing of.

For some moments, the Cheyenne spoke to him and he listened, not understanding but trying to interpret the tone. It was not harsh or threatening, but almost natural and as if in conversation. He spoke without raising his voice but with high vowel sounds and expressed with hand movements which appeared to be a language of their own. Tom just watched the man's face and listened without making any attempt to reply, but allowed himself the reward of keeping an eye contact for his own self-respect, what little he had left to fall back upon.

The Cheyenne continued, often extending an arm into the direction that they had just come, then changing arms and indicating the way ahead with wide open eyes. He realised that the boy was not understanding and paused for a moment. He shook his head and the feathers above his eyes danced with the movement, then said one word, another that Tom did not understand.

Soon, the short halt was over and Tom could see that the journey was about to continue, to where he had no idea. The warriors rose from where they were sitting and the man with the fur headdress walked over to his horse, an animal obviously won in some manner from the cavalry, evidenced by the 'US' brand on its rump. It was a good-looking horse, a chestnut of good proportions and alert eyes.

Tom had experience of this man's brutality when he was beaten, and saw that he had little more sympathy for the horse that he rode. Reaching the animal, he thumped its head with the heel of his thumb and pushed it around so that he could throw over the saddle blanket and the roughly made buffalo bone saddle. The horse whinnied at the harsh treatment and raised up its neck in case of further mistreatment.

The boy leant towards is sister.

"Uncle Will always said people shouldn't be offhand with poor dumb animals," he told her despite her lack of response. "Uncle Will always said a horse will run itself into the ground to please the ass hole on its back kicking it in the slats."

He looked around at his sister's vacant expression, her eyes closed to his words.

"Course," Tommy continued, "he never said it when Mom was around."

Reaching around within arm's length, he found a handful of spiky burrs and closed his hand around them. The man who Tom had decided was the leader waved the children towards the mules in an indication to mount up. The boy helped his sister to rise and he took her hand and lead her over to where the animals were tied off. Slipping between the horses that belonged to the Cheyenne, Tom reached up and slipped the handful of burrs under the blanket on the horses back and pushed them in as far as he could. It was just in time and he was almost caught as the owner of the animal came around the rump of the horse and pushed the boy in the back to urge more speed.

Tom hauled his sister well clear as the Cheyenne leapt up onto the horse's back as if pulled by elastic and set his weight firmly into the skeletal saddle. Before he could turn the animal in the direction of his choice, the horse erupted in an explosion of kicking legs and flashing eyes, connecting with the other mounts around it and causing them to react in similar fashion. The Cheyenne struggled to keep their animals calm and away from the source of the eruption and pulled them clear.

For the rider with burrs beneath him, there was little he could do but hang on to the bucking horse as it humped and heaved to dislodge the discomfort on its back. The animal reared like a spring and hit the ground in a fog of dust and debris and broken twigs, then buckled its hind legs and set for another leap into the sunlight and dislodged leaves. Suddenly, a peal of laughter emerged from the other Cheyenne as they watched their fellow try to deal with the outrage of an uncontrollable horse.

The horse reared sideways into the trees and a low branch struck the rider in the chest and scraped along his body, thrusting leaves into his face and blinding him for a moment. Fighting free, he still struggled to find a way to calm the beast but doing so was no easy task. Another branch became an obstacle as the horse continued its bucking to dislodge the spikes on its back and the man that made it worse with his attempts to gain control. The laughter came to a crescendo when a third branch swept the Cheyenne from his seat on the horse's back, over its rump and down into the swirling dust that had been created behind it.

Now that the man was defeated, the chestnut horse calmed a little, but still moved erratically with the saddle and blanket dislodged and falling to one side, which kept the animal in an uneasy state.

Quickly, the downed rider rose and caught his mount by the rawhide bridle. He heaved himself up and set his teeth around one of the horse's ears and bit down until the animal calmed with the weight of the man, restricting movement.

As the Cheyenne laughed at the spectacle, so did Tom, despite his bruised face and aching body. Releasing the horse, the Cheyenne turned to the dislodged saddle and blanket. His eyes flashed as he found the object of his recent discomfort hooked onto the inside of the material and pulling them free, flung them at the boy and his sister, under little doubt as to who had engineered the problem. His face was twisted with anger, made worse by being seen as the object of ridicule on the part of his fellow warriors.

The Cheyenne drew a knife and took a step towards the children. The other warriors were still throwing mild insults at the man, but he ignored them, his eyes intense upon Tom, who stood watching with nowhere to go. The Cheyenne let his anger drop into a grimace of a smile as he raised the knife to his throat and made clear what he would like to do with the boy.

Satisfaction is a strange thing. At that moment, Tom felt his revenge completely liberated. As time went on, he often thought he had been perhaps a little excessive.

As Will moved along the treeline, his eyes on the ground, he wondered how far he was behind and if he stood a chance of catching up with the Cheyenne. It felt almost like every yard of advance had to be figured out, to be found and move forward, but check that he was not walking into some danger that waited to thrust itself upon him. There was an unease about those that followed him too, and it was a bitter apple, hoping that they would continue to follow but not catch up until the right moment, when he would be glad of their pursuit. He knew that it was a thin line that he was riding, and sooner or later there would be hell to pay, but who would pay it?

Standing hauled up gently on the rein and pulled Midnight to a halt as he saw something. Dismounting, he took off his hat and held it at an oblique angle to give shade. It was as sure as death and taxes that it was the mark of unshod ponies. A little disturbed by the passage of time and the elements, and the odd little critter that was out looking for lunch, but there they were, just as he had hoped.

Could they have tried the same trick as they did at the river, lay a false trail to slow down any follow up? Maybe they had, or maybe they were doubting pursuit; after all, as far as he knew there was no one else between him and them and to lay false tracks everywhere would delay them too. From their direction of travel, it was pretty clear that they were heading for the lands of the Northern Cheyenne, and that was still a way off, up into Montana.

Will Standing made the decision. He would cast fortune to the winds and follow the trail into the big trees and hope for the best. But before that, he would give the black horse a short break to graze while he climbed up through the lower canopies for a look back.

Since leaving the army, he had never worn spurs, so the climb was easier than he expected, except where a rotten branch gave to his weight and he slipped back onto the one below with a curse. Combatting the spring back of leafy twigs that contrived to delay him, he pushed through until he could get a good view of the rolling grassland that he had just crossed. Along the far skyline, a heat haze melded into a mirage. The ocean of high grass swept lazily with the slight breeze.

It looked clear, just the motion of the grasses and he was about to descend when something caught his eye, just a movement through the mirage, a slight difference to the distance. He squinted and tried to focus until he was sure.

He was sure. It was not totally clear, but there it was, a disturbance, a movement, a sure sign that they had not given up on him. He could not make out any detail, no definite shape, no distinct riders, but they were there and heading his way, an interference in the mirage that announced the chasers.

Standing slipped down faster than he went up and the black horse looked up as he left the underbrush. He thought for a moment, thinking that they may be a might too close yet, and decided to take a leaf from the book of the Cheyenne. Leading the horse through into the tress for a way, he threw the rein over a branch and went back to where he found he unshod tracks. Snapping off a leafy bough, he picked up some dirt and rubbed it where the light break contrasted with the bark, to disguise his action, then used it sweep over the tracks of both himself and the Cheyenne, careful not to be too heavy handed and make the camouflage a trail in its own right. To complete the work, he found broken twigs and dead leaves and threw them casually over the ground that he had cleared of his tracks. When satisfied, he made his way back to the horse, careful to step where the bushes would hide his boot marks.

Midnight whinnied as he climbed aboard, and once again he was following the Cheyenne to whatever climax providence had in store for him.

It was not an easy follow through the debris and the fallen leaves that littered the woodland floor. Here and there it was easy, but soon he was finding it more difficult as the Cheyenne appeared to have ridden in line abreast and made the tracking of single animals more difficult. He wondered if they were following some plan to put pursuers off the trail as they had done before, but decided that he was committed now, and would follow as best he could.

Then the trail petered out entirely. Standing dismounted and knelt to study the ground. How had he missed the trail so completely? He looked for disturbance in the leaf litter or a broken twig or an upturned stone kicked over by a horse, but there was none. They must still be heading north, of that he was sure, but how far was he off the marks?

It was getting late, but he had come some way. The sun was dropping below the canopies and light was fading. He felt lost, dejected and incompetent. Now, here, was not a good place for him to be, with no definite route forward, and certainly none back. Going on in the dark would achieve nothing, and might even make the situation worse. At least it would be the same for the chasers, unless they used lanterns, if they had any, and that would be a stupid thing to do with Cheyenne on the loose. He guessed there would be at least one sensible man who was coming up behind to hang him.

Will Standing slapped Midnight on the neck and threw the rein over a branch while he took off the saddle. The last shaft of light glinted on the branch and stopped the man in his activity. He stared at it for a moment until sure of what it was. In that second, everything changed, he was back on the trail again. Reaching across, he grinned like he never grinned before.

"Good boy, Tommy!" He said to himself.

Chapter Eight
Rolling Thunder

The Cheyenne and their captives left the woodland behind in the late afternoon and were back onto open ground, a prairie of mixed vegetation, grass and low bush. Somewhere up ahead and to the east were the Black Hills, just visible and blue in the fading day.

Tom saw the advantage of remaining in as low a profile as possible, while his sister continued to hum and sing her little tune, until one of the warriors became tired of the jingle and flicked her back with a whip or a bow tip. He still slumped over the withers of the mule and every step caused the pain in his head to return like a monotonous drum roll.

The horses and mules made their way forward at a steady walk. Tom closed his eyes and when he opened them again, he saw the Cheyenne at his side, the leader who had tried to communicate earlier that afternoon. His paint pony stepped in time with the boy's mount and Tom painfully twisted his head, ready for some new assault. He was surprised to see the warrior just watching him, as if the man were studying him intensely.

When the Cheyenne knew he had caught the boy's attention, he dropped the rein of his mount and brought his fists together over his chest and held them there. He said something in a low voice, something in his own language that Tom could have in no way interpreted, but felt he understood something of the meaning. It seemed to indicate a kind of respect, an admiration for one who would not be broken, no matter what hardship might come, and Tom decided that whatever the beating and whatever the abuse, it might just keep them alive.

***

The heads of the horses were low with the labours of the day and their shoulders rose and fell with the effort to haul the wagon. On the box seat, Reverend Morgenson stood, holding the first metal loop of the canopy support, his eyes on the rising cloud somewhere ahead. His wife slapped the reins to urge the animals to even further effort but it had little effect.

"Lord, let us catch the train before dark, or Heaven knows we might lose them again."

Morgenson looked down at the woman.

"Faith wife," he said confidently, "the Good Lord ain't found us just to lose us again. Can't be far now. You can see the dust that the wagons make up ahead."

Margaret was not quite so confident of her husband's relationship with the Almighty.

"Pretty hard to make out why he lost us in the first place, just for the sake of a scribbled bird in that book of yours. I told you we should not lose sight of the train."

The reverend blustered a reply and shook his head vigorously.

"Prairie Falcon, Margaret! I told you I had seen a Prairie Falcon, not just a scribbled bird. And at the eastern extent of its range and a good two hundred miles east of where the texts insist."

Another piece of uneven ground shook the wagon and almost ejected Morgenson from his perch, so to speak. He regained his balance and craned his thin neck forward, eyes wide and searching the land ahead for the first sign of deliverance.

Margaret set her face to a hopeful expression and wished the horses would respond quicker to her urging. She thought of what her mother had said when she announced her betrothal to the good reverend, that the man had beans for brains and expected too much from the Man Above and too little on his own willingness to earn a decent living. Her mother had been a little light on religion and a little heavy on port wine on occasion, but she knew a man shy of working muscle when she saw one and was never slow to tell them so. Her own father had been told so often that he had run off with the widow of a milliner and as far as Margaret knew they were doing well with a new business in St Louis. At least that was what he had said in the one and only Christmas card that she received some years back, which also casually asked if his wife was still breathing. But at thirty-five, a woman with little prospect of slipping from the shelf into the arms of a white knight must weigh herself on the scales of probability and perhaps consider the ecclesiastical considerations that the Reverend Morgenson had offered.

Married life back east had been a less passionate affair than she had imagined and put it down to his rheumatic legs and occasional facial psoriasis, but day to day living proved reasonable so long as the dinner was ready at seven and his ornithological interests were catered for. The latter often manifested itself during a meal or conversation, when a flutter of wings demanded his attention outside, lest it be a species he had yet to study or understand a little more.

Then, so casually, he had mentioned the subject of the Johnson Liberty Train to all parts west, a string of forty-eight wagons, soon to be forty-nine, with thoughts of sinners to be cleansed, babies baptised and presumably birds to be observed.

The wagon they purchased at a premium arrangement, with the previous owner stating that the vehicle had made the journey four times and still had in it another four, although why the wagon might return so often appeared lost on the reverend. Margaret's protests had gone unheard when the seller of the wagon extolled the richness of the fauna, particularly the winged kind all along the route, and one had to be careful not to step on the multitude of ground nesting birds that could be observed by the wayside.

All of that seemed so far away now.

There came a rumble like you find on a hot afternoon when the sky grows too weary and dark clouds rush to cool it down, scraping its skirts on the horizon and groaning with the effort.

"Horses!" Morgenson exclaimed excitedly. "I hear horses, and lots of 'em!"

Margaret heard them too, moving quickly.

"You think they heard us coming, and are trying to get away?" She said, sarcastically, knowing how some of the travellers on the train had tired of the reverend's constant shifting between the Good Lord and a lecture on the benefits of annual feathered migrants.

Morgenson dropped from the wagon box with some difficulty, but found the ground and rushed on ahead of the wagon, running past the horses that struggled over uneven ground. Just ahead, he could see that the plain dropped down into a wide gully, a mile across, the sides steep but manageable with caution for a wheeled vehicle. Stopping dead on the edge and looking down, Morgenson's face changed from one of hope to one of open-mouthed disappointment.

He stood frozen, looking down into the gully until Margaret arrived with the wagon and looked down from her seat. As far as the eye could penetrate the rising dust were the huge forms of buffalo, emerging from the cloud and then fading again, to be replaced by another, and another. Bulls leapt over cows that had lost their footing and swerved to miss another, lost calves raced between the spaces looking for their mothers and tried to avoid larger animals but often miscalculated and were trampled by heavy bodies that followed. Bearded bulls rushed open-mouthed and wild with excitement and humped and bumped another, then changed direction and looked for space. It was a congregation of moving flesh and dark hides, pressed together in an area that was too close for safety, erupting in a crash of bodies where one animal had caused a blockage for those coming on behind them.

Somewhere out of sight, a shot rang out and Margaret saw the blurred shape of a horseman, splitting the herd and riding between them. A big bull fell, its hind quarters rising, arching over its head and horns as the inertia carried it forward, chest and chin skidding along the ground in a disturbance of debris and dust. Somewhere else, another shot echoed the first and the herd changed direction as one animal, almost turning back the way that they had come, the buffalo on the perimeter forced up the edges of the gully and back against the tide.

The thunder of many hooves assaulted their ears, along with roaring bulls unable to challenge their tormentors, cows squealing for their lost calves and the echo of the rifle discharges.

From above, Morgenson could see the twisted shapes of dead bison when the frightened herd thinned and made open spaces for a brief moment, then as they closed panicked brown bodies leapt up and over the carcases like a waterfall of terrified beasts.

As the blur of disturbed earth cleared momentarily, and she could briefly see the opposite side of the gully, Margaret could make out where the other shot came from. A dark figure knelt on the far rim and was firing down into the buffalo with a long gun, the smoke visible before the sound reached her ears. The rifle was cradled in a forked stick for stability and had she been more familiar with firearms, Margaret would have recognised the definitive sound of a Sharps, point fifty-two calibre, the preferred method to destroy the buffalo.

Margaret Morgenson took her husband's small telescope from the bottom of the wagon box and focussed on the men at work in the gully. She could just make out the grizzled, unshaven faces, the rough clothing and the harsh way that they assaulted the bison at every move, bringing one down at almost every shot. It was a hard lesson to learn, how civilised men could have such a lack of pity or compassion for wild creatures. She saw it for what it was and wanted nothing to do with it.

Her husband also found the scene appalling. He had crouched down, almost unable to watch the horror as one bull after another was cut down by the Sharps rifle. Margaret dropped from the wagon and ran to the man, then pulled him away, unsure of the reception they might receive from such men.

"Husband, come away!" She told him. "We need to get out of the sight of these creatures, they are barbarous and cruel and we cannot trust to their Christian ways…"

The reverend turned and looked at his wife.

"I thought it for the Liberty Train, I thought we had made it back," he admitted. "Perhaps we could go down and talk to these men. Ask the way. To the Liberty Train, or the path back to Fort Laramie?"

Morgenson was clearly distressed. Margaret pulled him back.

"I do not think they are in a mood for talking or showing the way," she said.

They talked for a moment and decided to pull around and move back along their side of the gully, then when clear of the carnage and night came, they would head across to the other side and be clear by morning. It sounded like a good idea.

***

How many bison lay dead in the gully, it was hard to say. While they waited for dark, Margaret and her husband had pulled the wagon away from where it might be detected and lay under cover but able to watch the aftermath of the killing from above.

The bison had split into two groups, one heading up the gully and the other in the opposite direction, each making for safety as the last shots rang through the twilight. The creaking of poorly greased wheels announced the coming of a wagon, somewhere below. Another rough character drove two horses as it passed beneath them and Morgenson could just make out the faded and chipped lettering on the side in what light there still was. It was hand painted, squashed and squeezed in one line across the planking. 'Able and Howarth—Buffalo Hunters'.

As night fell, a fire was lit a little way down the gully and the three men could be seen, abandoning the stinking work of cutting off the hides from the bodies, taking the tongues for the delicacy that they were and packing them in salt for preservation. Some of the hides had already been thrown into the wagon, blood still evident and staining the dry wagon bed as it had many times before. Once the tongues and hides were taken, the carcases of the bison were left for the buzzards and the coyotes, attracted to the smell of rotting meat.

Margaret and Joshua Morgenson could smell the meat cooking, the hunters making the most of what choice pieces of buffalo they preferred. They could hear the harsh voices, the loud curses when one offended another and the coarse laughter as the third took one side or the other. A horse by the wagon below whinnied and one of the Morgenson's replied. Margaret hurried back and calmed the animal, hoping that the hunters had not heard. Her husband turned onto his side and raised a hand to reassure her that they had not.

It seemed an age before the three hunters appeared to settle down after their meal. Looking through the telescope, Margaret saw the appearance of a bottle and then another, passed around for some time to congratulate themselves on a good day's work and the rewards it would bring.

Some time passed and the reverend had nodded off into a shallow sleep and was awakened by Margaret, who had watched continually. While two hunters slept, a third was nominated to keep a lookout, duty for the procedure changed every few hours until dawn. However, the contents of the bottles had some effect upon discipline and the watchman had fallen asleep against the wagon wheel and the fire was becoming low with no one refuelling it.

"Let's go," Margaret whispered.

They returned to the wagon and were glad of the sandy soil around the top of the gully. The woman pulled the horses around, along the edge and away from the hunter's camp, looking for a way down which would cause the least noise or disturbance. When they felt safe to do so, and a suitable way presented itself, Margaret hauled the reins to one side and guided the team down towards the lower level.

The sound of the horses' hooves seemed louder than normal in the dark, and the slightest squeak or grating of timber from the old wagon appeared amplified to the point where they felt sure that they would be discovered, but hard liquor proved to be their ally where in any other scenario, the reverend would have condemned it.

The further they travelled across the floor of the gully, the more confident they felt. On the soft sandy floor, the horses hoof beats were muffled but the thin wheels dug deep into the ground. And then the wagon stuck fast, and the horses could not pull it out.

Morgenson looked behind to see the extent of the problem, He saw the rear wheels several inches into the dirt and beyond the struggles of tired animals. He grimaced and put his hands together in prayer, eyes open and tears almost ready to run down onto his cheeks.

"Oh Lord," he whispered to himself, "why have you forsaken us in this hard place?"

Margaret was a little more realistic in assessing the situation. She moved her head closer and spoke into his ear.

"Joshua, whatever the Good Lord has or hasn't done, one thing's for sure, he ain't going to come down and help push this darn wagon, so get your damn hide on the ground and put your back into it."

Without reply, Morgenson dropped silently to the floor of the gully and went to the back of the wagon. Margaret hooked her head around the side and waited for him to brace himself, then quietly shook the reins to urge the team to try again. As the animals did their best, the reverend pushed with one shoulder and felt his feet slipping on the surface. No progress was made after several minutes.

The man slipped around to the front of the wagon and shrugged his shoulders.

"It ain't going to work, Margaret!" He told her.

"The hell it ain't!" Margaret answered without pausing to think about her choice of words. "They got their darn wagon to move, why can't we?"

She calmed herself and concentrated on the problem, then looked down at her husband.

"We got to make the wagon lighter," she advised. "Clear some of the heavy stuff out, and give the horses a chance."

"But…" Morgenson was about to protest but knew there was nothing else for it.

As Margaret climbed under the canvas canopy, her husband moved back to the rear. The woman felt in the dark for any item that would help their progress when ejected. Several things were passed across and lifted down by the reverend, some of which he agreed with abandoning, and some he did not, but there was little point in argument under the present situation. He felt the smooth polished surface of one of his prize possessions, a large cabinet clock that was wound and quietly ticking, given him by the elders of his church upon his decision to move west. Mentally saying 'goodbye', he took the weight and put it gently on the ground with the pile of wooden stools, buckets and brooms.

Margaret threw down a blanket.

"Here. Cover them with this, and throw some sand over it," she ordered.

Morgenson did so, while his wife descended from the wagon and pulled the reins clear, intending to drive the team on foot to further reduce the weight. She looked down the gully to where the embers of the hunter's fire were just visible some way off.

"All right," she told her husband, "shoulder to it and push like you never pushed before."

Margaret slapped the reins and the horses began to move forward until halted by the weight that they were dragging. Her husband was putting everything into making those wheels churn out of the rut they were in. The woman held the reins in her left hand and with her right took hold of one of the spokes of the small wheel on the front axle, heaving as much as she could. Her feet slipped a little but found a purchase and she urged the team once more. She could hear her husband's grunts as he tried his best. He was not a strong man unless pointing from a pulpit but at a time like this, every little helps.

Then, inch by inch, slowly but surely, the wagon moved forward. Horses' hooves gripped better ground and after some hesitation they were on their way again. The reverend remained on the ground and kept pushing while his wife did likewise, but guided the team towards an easy slope that would take them up and over the opposite side of the gully.

They reached the top in the dark, barely finding their way and making it more by good luck than a definite visible direction. The team made level ground and pulled away. The front axle moved over the edge with little sound. Reverend Morgenson clasped his hands in the usual manner.

"Ooh, Lord of all mercy, Lord be praised at our deliverance from the work of this night…"

Then the wheel broke.

***

As the daylight gave way to the dark, the small party of Cheyenne and their captives had halted on the open ground. Before the light had gone completely, Tom saw the lead warrior take a pair of small binoculars from the leather pouch around his horse's neck. Such instruments were still uncommon, unlike telescopes of the period, and unknown to the boy, this wonder was taken from a fallen officer at Fort Wallace, some days before.

The man looked back towards the trees they had left behind that afternoon, and reassured himself that they were still free from pursuing enemies. Still denying themselves fire as a precaution, the Cheyenne wound themselves in blankets and sat in a circle, the children secured to each other by a strong rawhide cord between their feet and left outside of the group. An old saddle blanket was thrown over to the two, but when unfolded was barely large enough to cover both of them, so Tommy let his sister have the larger part and settled for less and his torn jacket.

Although not tethered to anything else, the boy knew that here on open ground there was nowhere to run, and even if there had been, he now understood the futility of thoughtless escape. All that he could hope for was rescue or wait for something to happen, something that would give a better than good chance of success. As for rescue, he had done all that he could think of and suffered for it.

As the night advanced, the children fell into what sleep was offered. Alice twitched and groaned in dreams that could only be guessed at and it took her brother longer to drift away. The Cheyenne conversed and discussed whatever issues were important, until one paused and looked into the distant darkness. He raised himself up by one arm and pointed with a free hand.

There in the inky black of the prairie night was a pinprick of illumination, the smallest smudge of red yellow that shone less than the stars above. All five of the Cheyenne stood and watched the place where it stood out against the night trading low conversation as to what it might be.

The binoculars were used again, to determine any detail of what the far fire might mean, but were of little use. As the children slept, two of the warriors mounted their ponies and headed out towards the light, delegated to find out what it might be. Upon this ride might depend the direction of their journey, and outcomes of the following day.

***

Margaret felt the tears run hot down her cheeks despite the cool of the night. Frustration and fear urged her and her husband to overcome the latest challenge that life had set them.

The big rear wheel had broken almost in two, halved by the axle hub with both parts escaping the iron rim. The bottom half lay on the ground flat, while the upper section, still attached to the hub and the axle had dropped into the soil, with broken spokes digging deep. The only advantages that the two had to disguise their efforts were the blackness of the night and two bottles of something that kept the hunters distracted and dozing some way off.

The woman looked down at the problem, her skirts torn and dirty and her hands upon her hips. They had tried to lift the corner to allow the horses to haul the wagon over the edge of the gully, where they would not stand out like a bee sting on a boil, but strength was not a major property of either party.

"Let us try again…" Joshua said. "The animals may have found rest by now."

Margaret knew it was hopeless just to keep trying, and a more intelligent way had to be found, and found by first light or they must take their chances with rough men across the way. She looked hard at the problem.

"Husband," she said, "If we can turn that upper part of the wheel, it would become a skid, like on a sleigh in winter."

Morgenson looked down at the broken wheel.

"But we cannot raise the wagon, we tried that."

Margaret agreed, but explained her intentions.

"But if we unhitch the horses, tie them off to the rear side of the top part, then get them to pull, it should haul the broken section above over, so that the smooth edge is on the ground. Then we tie it off so it can't move and we have a skid. At least we can get off this rim."

The reverend saw the possibility, but also doubted it. But then, what choice did they have? Within a half hour, the horses were taken from their hitch on the front of the wagon and backed around to the side of the broken wheel. It was not an easy thing to do without making noise and on several occasions, they had to check that the hunters still had not woken. A rope was fixed to the yolk between the animals and the other end fastened to the furthest spoke of the upper, secure section of wheel, and wound around the wooden rim to stop it slipping. Clearing away the iron tyre and the loose broken section, they were ready to get the horses pulling.

"Guide it around if you can, when they get to hauling," Margaret whispered an order.

Morgenson nodded and braced his hands on the wagon, just above the wheel.

"Ready?" She asked.

He nodded again and waited for the first effort. Margaret slapped the rein and the horses took the strain.

"Giddyap!" She urged, a little quieter than normal.

The rope tightened and the upper section of the broken rim began to move, slowly at first, and then a little more, the shattered spokes that held them captive edging free with the effort from the horses. Morgenson saw the movement and set his hands on the other spokes and helped guide the rim around on the axle. He felt the excitement of success and made more effort until together with another urging of the team, the half wheel was free and swung around with the smooth rim back on the ground, pulling the wagon around obliquely a little on the edge of the gully.

"Whoooa!" He called, not wanting the horses to pull the wheel back around to the original problematic position.

Morgenson's wife was elated that her idea had worked, and worked quite well. She smiled and wiped away what moisture still remained on her cheeks.

"All right," she said, untying the rope on the yolk and throwing the loose end back to her husband, "tie it off so it stays where it's at."

The Reverend Morgenson knotted the rope around the rim and the axle, securing the ends to metal rails above so that the skid would be immovable. To the east, the first light of dawn was breaking and Margaret saw the urgency of getting off that rim. Ahead of them, the ground dipped slightly into a low incline and she knew that if they could only make the short distance, they would be invisible from the ground below.

***

Providence is the trick of life that cuts the strings of one, while tying them off for another, with no never mind if it's the right thing to do or not. At least, that's the way it always seemed to Will, never finding evidence to prove himself wrong, and accepted the decisions that the trail offered and just went along with it.

Now, he was on the tying side again, thanks to Tommy. At least he guessed it was Tommy, knowing the ways that the boy had used to avoid a paddling from his father with a clever word or false evidence to cover his misdemeanours on occasion.

He had slept fitfully and rose as soon as light allowed him to investigate the tattered piece of cotton again. He was certain that it belonged to Alice, sure that he remembered the little roses printed into the fabric. From the way it was pushed onto the branch he guessed it was done quickly, but if he had done it once, maybe Tommy had done it again and was trying to show the way.

He saddled the black horse and heaved himself up onto his back without stopping to eat. Time was slipping away and he knew it, so he urged the animal on as the first beams of sunlight returned to the upper canopies. Shadows still remained in the woodland floor and Will Standing screwed up his eyes, looking for more of the paper chase that his nephew had initiated.

A short way along, he picked up a sign of unshod horses again as the light improved and it was reinforced by another strip of Alice's dress pinned to a broken bush. Direction was on his side again, but he still held the fears of what might be the outcome of the day when he caught up with the Cheyenne, if catch up with them he did. Standing also wondered if he had covered his own trail to well. Maybe he should have left a better trail for the chasers to follow, maybe he was becoming too clever for his own game and sticking his head up like a sore thumb?

He thought for a moment, then placed the strip of linen back onto the branch where he found it, making sure it was easy to find.

***

Light from the new sun flickered into the gully and onto the smelly wagon that was half filled with buffalo hides. The individual selected for picket duty jerked himself awake and realised that not only had he slept through the night, but he had failed to initiate the time for another to take over. But, what the hell?

Another stirred as the watchman broke wind and shuffled to rise.

"God-damn, Howarth," a waking voice said, "you fixin' to blow us the hell outta here?"

The last of the hunters opened his eyes, pushed back his grimy hat and raised his head from the saddle that had served for a pillow.

"What the hell happened to the fire?"

Howarth was on his feet and stretching away the night and the booze from his system with a little difficulty. He kicked sand at one of the others and laughed it off as a joke that was not reciprocated.

"One of you bastards git' a fire goin'. Later, we'll git' the rest of them hides up on the wagon and be on our way," he told them. "I'm sick of smellin' them buffalo."

"Sick of smellin you..." The recipient of the sand said, only to receive another.

Howarth stretched again and walked off down the gully to relieve himself from the excess of the night before. He stopped and as the sand was stained dark at his feet, he glanced across the open space to the opposite side. A glint of sunlight made him blink, but he was certain that he saw the top of a wagon, the last of a canvas canopy drop out of sight beneath the grassy rim a short distance away. He secured the stained trousers that he wore and turned back to the others.

"Hey, you see that?" He called back. "I thought..."

The arrow halted the sentence as it passed cleanly through his upper thigh. Up on the ridge above, the screams and challenge of five Cheyenne warriors made the two men by the dead fire jump for their rifles as more arrows cut through the air towards them, several burying themselves in the timber of the wagon.

****

Reverend Morgenson felt the wheels begin to slip as their efforts to free themselves from the edge of the gully made progress. Time had not been available to return the horses to their places in front of the wagon box seat and the whole vehicle did a slip-slide down the sandy slope on the other side at an odd angle.

Margaret hauled on the reins and pulled the animals to a halt, stopping the drift, but at least they were over the top and down out of sight of those below. They allowed themselves water and found an old saucepan to use for the horses to do likewise, although it took several fills until the animals were satisfied.

"Not much water left in the barrel," Margaret told her husband. "And please don't tell me the Good Lord will provide, unless you see him walking over with two pails in his hands, or pushing rain clouds in our direction."

Morgenson felt hurt at his wife's sudden lack of faith.

"Wife, I notice a certain…"

The scream from down in the gully cut off the words. Hardly thinking, both people threw themselves down on the ground and crawled towards the edge to see what had caused it. Almost opposite to where they lay in the long grass they could see the shapes of five horsemen, arrayed in colour and leaping over the cusp of the depression, skidding and galloping downward, the legs of their horses almost lost in the dust that they kicked up. Away from the old wagon, one man was isolated and down while the two others had found firearms and were firing wildly at their attackers. A chestnut horse carried the man on its back around the other side of the wagon and cut off any chance of retreat while paint horses reared and discharged their riders onto the ground, where agitated ground hid the conflict inside it.

Suddenly, a figure appeared beneath the wagon, crawling out and up and running away towards the open ground. Dust calmed and arrows cut the man down in mid-pace, two finding his back and exiting through his chest. He fell, breaking the arrowheads beneath his chin and widening the wounds. Two more arrows struck the ground by his head, missing narrowly, and he struggled to rise.

Several figures with painted faces hurried after the man and when close, used their bows to fling more pointed projectiles into his body, circling the man and keeping up the action until he was finished and thirteen arrows stuck out like a porcupine in every direction.

They then turned their attention to Howarth, who was still on the ground, trying to stop the rush of blood that exited from the wound that the single arrow had made. As three of the Cheyenne came close, the man drew his pistol and pointed it at them. They seemed unafraid, almost as if the weapon were invisible or they invulnerable to its discharge. He held it there for a moment, then threw it to the ground. His face grimaced in pain and fear. He looked at the warriors that were almost standing over him and threw out his arms.

"Make it quick! Make it quick," he pleaded.

Up on the opposite rim, Margaret and her husband watched the carnage of battle. They did not speak. There was little to say.

One warrior grabbed the boot of Howarth and began to haul him back towards the wagon, where the third hunter lay motionless on his back, another seven arrows expended upon him. The man screamed in pain as the rough ground dragged the protruding arrow against the flesh. Another Cheyenne reached down and ripped the stick quickly, making the fletching red as it was pulled through the leg.

"Oooh, Jesus, Mary and Joseph…" Howarth cried, suspecting he knew what was coming.

Chapter Nine
Rough Justice

Following the trail of the Cheyenne had not been easy, just as Will Standing had found. The Bellfield party spread out to make every effort to keep on it, in the hope that somewhere along the way they would find Midnight's shod tracks too. Bellfield was certain it would happen, and the way things were panning out, when you find one, soon you would more than likely find the other.

Long grass over hard, dry ground was a benefit for the pursued rather than the pursuer, but when the soft, sandy dust took over it became a lot easier. The trick was like joining up the dots, marking direction from one easy stretch to another and hoping for the best.

They reached the trees not far from where Standing had entered the woodland but his camouflaged tracks had been too well executed, just as he had feared. Riders loped along one after another, eyes on the ground and looking for sign.

With the light fading, and despite Bellfield's protests, Deerbolt called a halt to the day, promising an early start the next morning, as soon as the dawn gave sun enough to see by. Fearing little danger because of their number, a fire was lit and the riders huddled around, pushing in as close as they could with their saddles to feel its benefit, and using them as pillows with hats pulled over their eyes.

Bellfield ate quickly and stood by the trees looking inward. Deerbolt took a mug of coffee and handed it to him. He followed Bellfield's line of vision.

"If we pick up his trail tomorrow, we might finish this up by the day after, or the day after that," Deerbolt advised.

"If the Cheyenne haven't got to him first," Bellfield answered. "We need to get along faster tomorrow, get him, and get that horse back."

Deerbolt drank from his own mug and looked up at the sky.

"You know, you gotta give the man credit for going up against those Cheyenne, going after those kids on his own. Takes a certain kind of guts to go down that trail…"

Bellfield looked around at him, his face a picture of distaste.

"Takes a certain kind of stupid to rob a bank, to steal a horse, to prosecute a fraud, and who knows what else?" He said, tersely.

Marshal Deerbolt looked down into his coffee, knowing it was an argument he could not win, and he was not really trying.

"It was only eighty dollars," he replied, "I guess he could've taken it all if he'd been inclined…"

Alexander Bellfield turned full face and body towards the man at his side.

"That's why he's so stupid!"

***

The two Cheyenne had ridden towards the glow in the dark and dismounted when nearby. Leaving the horses some way back they crawled towards the edge of the gully and looked down to where the buffalo hunters were settling in for the night and passing around a bottle or two. They observed the wagon and its load and the carcases a short way off, still waiting to be skinned the following day. Two Sharps rifles were leaning against the wagon, in easy reach of the men. Taking in as much information as possible, the watchers crept back to the waiting horses and rode back to the others.

When they returned, Tom watched the excited Cheyenne talking among themselves, and knew something was happening. From their expressions, the boy could tell that it was probably good for them, but not so for him and his sister. Much happier he would have been if he saw fear and foreboding on their faces.

Alice was sleeping and Tom saw no sense in disturbing her. He wondered if fortune might at last smile upon them and give a good chance of escape, and knew it was only possible if the warriors were preoccupied with something else.

Well before dawn, Tom and Alice were rudely kicked awake and shoved back onto the mules, then the whole party made their way towards where a glow had been some time earlier, but was now gone. After a while, they halted and one of the warriors pushed the children to the ground in a similar manner as before and tied up their hands behind their backs and gagged their mouths with grimy buckskin strips.

With the first light, a reconnoitre was made by the leader. Good cover on the edge of the gully made concealment easy and he saw what the others had seen, and made his plans to assault those below.

When the attack came, Tom and Alice could only hear the gunfire, the yells and war cries of the Cheyenne, the drumming of horses' hooves and the occasional English word spoken in a way that was not encouraging. Some time passed and Tom tested the bindings around his hands but there was no give in the rawhide. He looked at his sister, but Alice remained passive, just looking at her brother as if in a dream.

Two Cheyenne returned to find the children where they had been left with the mules and kicked them to their feet, making them walk the short way to the edge of the depression while they rode behind. Tom noticed that one of the warriors had a dark red stain on his buckskin shirt, just above his left elbow, and guessed he had run afoul of a bullet.

Standing on the rim and looking down, Tom saw the horror for what it was, two men down, Americans they looked like, with their share of arrows protruding from every part of their bodies. A third was still alive and bloody, stretched across a wagon wheel with his legs staked apart and a fire being prepared between them.

Some kind of gibberish was emanating from the man's mouth in words that were hard to understand, but the meaning was as clear as a crystal stream. Tom looked away, not wanting to see more. Then somewhere to his right, down the gully, he thought he heard cattle.

A dust cloud was growing closer and larger and for a moment he hoped it was the cavalry, or maybe drovers who had come across the place by chance, but soon he saw the error of his mistake as buffalo filled the gully and were moving slowly towards them. He could hardly know that it was the rest of the herd that had been hunted the day before and finding no escape from the depression were heading back.

Tom had never seen buffalo before, although he had heard of them. Uncle Will had told him about them and how the big bulls fought each other for the cows, head to massive head and horns, combats that could last an hour, or the rest of the day. He preferred the sight to the one below and watched them come, hesitantly, when they became aware of more humans that might see them as supper, a robe to keep out the cold or a tongue to fill the menu of speciality dining.

The herd halted and milled around, their moaning calls betraying the anguish they felt, as would any wild things with the smell of blood and humans on the wind. But the Cheyenne below were engrossed in the pleasure of torture, seeing the man burn in the most sensitive of places, enjoying the ritual of a fallen enemy as a reward for the many ills that they saw as theirs to revenge.

The children were dragged down onto the lower level and pushed to watch. It looked to Tom as if the man was already dead, or passed out at the pain of his ordeal. The boy turned his head again, preferring to watch the buffalo than a man destroyed, but no sooner had he done so than the lead Cheyenne grabbed his chin and turned his head back to the horror. The warrior spoke to Tom in harsh tones in his sing song language and pointed with his free hand towards the hunter, as if explaining the man's crimes and how he had paid for them.

Then, the clock struck six 'o' clock!

***

Although the trail that Tommy had left was helping, it was still no easy task to make the progress that Will needed to make if he were to close the gap between himself and the war party that held the children. Along with the benefit of the small rag markers that generally showed the way, it told Standing more. It reassured him that they were still alive and at least one was in a good enough state of mind to think about rescue. Also, it told him that the spirit of defiance was still there and they had not given up. The whole truth was perhaps something a little different, but he had to go with what he had, and right then, it made him more determined to find them.

A woodpecker thumped its occupational hammering up in the trees nearby, a blue jay fluttered away excitedly and the man pulled back on the rein, listening for anything that might suggest he was not the only rider in the locality, either ahead or behind. He felt for the handle of the Colt's Walker in his belt but found the arrowhead and part shaft that he had taken from the cabin of his kin and kept. Why he had retained the arrow was uncertain, perhaps to remind him of the revenge he sought, or maybe to keep him focussed on his pursuit of the children and the responsibility that he had imposed upon himself. Never before had he put himself in such a cleft stick as now, with his head on the line whichever direction he allowed to close with first.

Satisfied that there was no apparent danger, Will settled the pistol back into his belt and urged Midnight on. A little further he found a part of Tommy's trouser at the bole of a tree and knew that the children were still together. He thought about Alice, and remembered how his little niece was almost a carbon copy of her mother, that wicked smile and the gentle hands that helped Molly with the baking every Sunday, mimicking each minor process and proud of the product they produced, and happy when the menfolk polished off the biscuits and gravy without hesitation. Will Standing wondered how she was coping with her ordeal and tried not to think of her future if he failed.

By a small stream that he could see was all but drying up, he let the black horse drink. The water was muddy but it hardly bothered the animal and at least it allowed him to retain clear water for himself in the canteen. The good part was that he could see where the Cheyenne had stopped, and even better he saw the hoof prints of two shod mules that reinforced his previous thoughts.

Of the children, there were no signs that he could find, but he guessed that Cheyenne heading out of harm's way would not bother to haul two mules for the sake of it. Having been going since the first blinks of dawn, Standing let the horse rest and graze for a while. He pulled down the Sharps long rifle from the saddle and checked it, slid his hand down the octagonal barrel and drew back the hammer to half cock, making sure that the block was clean and clear and the percussion nipple free of debris.

It had been some time since he had used the weapon, mainly due to having limited ammunition and even more limited funds to buy more. An elk had fallen to the gun the previous winter and it had provided for the family for some time, the meat hanging out in the cold and preserved until gone. He was a good shot and he guessed the elk's distance at perhaps eleven hundred yards. Good marksmen told of far more successful ranged shots for a Sharps, perhaps fourteen hundred, but Will Standing was happy with the lower so long as it filled bellies. He remembered the fat days when the snow piled up outside the cabin and he and Henry had swapped stories of the late unpleasantness between the states and chewed chunks of elk, when work outside was impossible.

Midnight shook off troublesome insects with a shake of his head, winged larvae emerging with the low tide of the brown water. It returned Will back to the reality of the present so he hooked the Sharps back over the saddle horn, mounted and returned to the trail, searching for more of Tommy's markers.

Standing had become fond of the black horse, its willingness to respond to the slightest urging, its tenacity and endurance, properties passed down from an Arabian mother and a Mustang father by pure chance four years before. Bellfield had seen the animal as a yearling and won it in a rigged game of chance from which he would emerge as the sole owner. Protests from the aggrieved loser came to nothing when the twin barrels of a shotgun were offered as a consolation.

Midnight slipped between the trees on a course that Standing directed and halted when another of Tommy's strips of material was found, then another and another. Will found the place where the Cheyenne had halted the day before and over by a nearby tree the small footprints of the children. Kneeling, he identified the signs of skirmish and knew them from what they were and who had come off worse. Over the turbulent ground were the prints of moccasins and he wondered what had occurred to cause so much violence, but guessed it might be Tommy's torn fragments of cloth as from then on there were no more.

From then on it was a hit and miss affair, with Standing finding sign and then losing it again and searching once more until something showed up. By mid-morning he realised that the trees were thinning and once more the long grass took over from the woodland. He rode forward slowly, looking for hoof prints, shod or unshod, but found nothing. He had lost the tracks.

Feeling time slipping away from him, he leant forward and put his hands firmly on the saddle horn. It was becoming hot again. He took off his hat and held it over his eyes to see the sun and deliberate the time, then blinked away the brightness and lowered his hat, squinting into the distance. He was certain it was what he thought it was, just a dark drift along the skyline, a mark upon the horizon that might be his signpost again. He was certain he knew what it was, a testament to something burning, a strip of grey beyond the long grass. Smoke.

***

From the northern rim of the depression, Margaret and Joshua Morgenson saw the explosion of horse flesh across the gully, and lowered their heads into the grass that scattered across the edge. Painted ponies and stolen cavalry mounts carried the riders down towards the buffalo hunters that were rising to the new day. Dust and scattered debris accompanied the assault down the incline and the first arrows found their marks, in the man who had walked away from the camp, and then the others, who were beginning to respond erratically with poorly aimed gunfire.

Poorly tied horses that pulled the wagon broke their tethers and galloped off, responding to the screams and gunshots. A warrior tried to cut them off but they were already too far ahead and he returned to the fight.

War cries from the Cheyenne cut the morning, the dawn light catching the flash of a feathered shield or a lance tip. The fight was over in a matter of minutes, the final drama being the hunter escaping under the wagon, but halted by an arrow that pierced his body, to be followed by more, aimed at a leisurely pace by dismounted Cheyenne.

The Reverend Morgenson's eyes were glazed at the scene below. He began to raise his head.

"Maybe I can…" he began to say, but his wife pulled him back down into the grass.

The Cheyenne turned their attention to the first of the hunters, who fought to staunch the wound in his thigh. The Morgenson's saw the man draw a pistol and aim, but turned it away at the approach of the warriors, perhaps in some hope of mercy, but it was in vain and the gun was kicked away. They heard the man speak, words that they could not quite make out, but appeared to be ineffective and lost upon his enemy. A warrior broke off the shaft of the arrow and another dragged him back behind the wagon.

From their hiding place, the Morgenson's could hear the sound of returning buffalo, keen to pass the carnage and re-join the main herd some way down the depression, hesitating to approach and suffer the fate of the previous day. Bulls pawed the ground and added to the general disturbance of earth and sand, while cows and calves milled around in anticipation of moving through.

Margaret noticed two white children thrust down from the opposite rim, a boy and a girl, ragged and dirty and treat roughly. She saw one of the warriors grab the boy and pull him towards the wagon.

Two of the Cheyenne had climbed the back of the wagon, throwing off the buffalo skins and searching for something else. Smoke appeared and pleading could be heard from the hunter but before too long, fire and screams betrayed his fate.

Margaret felt grateful that they could not see the other side of the wagon and what was occurring there. She could see the small girl but not the boy and wondered what his role in this might be.

One of the Cheyenne on the wagon found what he was looking for and held high a bottle. There were whoops from the others, yelps of excitement, high-pitched appreciation for the inebriation to come.

Then, high chimes announced the hour to be six and the whole group around the wagon froze, looking down towards the milling buffalo to see what was making such a sound, never heard before by ears that framed painted faces.

Margaret Morgenson knew exactly what it was. The alarm that Joshua set for his morning prayer sang out on the depression below, somewhere in the belongings that they had left behind to assist the horses to gain the top of the slope and over the rim. Covered with a blanket to camouflage their abandoned possessions, even the buffalo were spooked by the six bell chimes and their elastic aftershock, and moved away.

"Prayer time," Morgenson said, almost absent minded, "we must…"

Margaret pushed a hand over his mouth, wondering how she had married a man of such I concepts, and wished at that moment that she had heeded her mother's experience.

Down on the flat below, the Cheyenne were abandoning their pleasures at the wagon and approaching the pile of possessions that the Morgensons had left behind. Lucky for them, dust from the buffalo herd had drifted over their wagon tracks and lay over the blanket in a covering that was at first hard to spot. The ear of one of the Cheyenne was acute and he soon located the hard ticking of the polished wood clock that had been such a treasured gift to those above and watched its discovery. The blanket was torn away to reveal the Morgenson's belongings and puzzled Cheyenne looked down in surprise.

Picking up the large clock, they passed it around, not knowing what to make of it and pushing their ears against the glass covered face. Finally, the lead warrior had enough and threw the time piece to the floor with a satisfying twang of broken springs and unsheathed mechanisms. As far as they were aware at that moment, this was just more detritus belonging to the buffalo hunters and treat it with appropriate distain, kicking the buckets and baskets in every direction.

Some distance away, the bison still milled, waiting for a safe moment to circumnavigate the smoke and the smell of blood and men. It would be some time before they were free to do so as already a bottle was opened and another found. The deceased hunter was cut from the wagon wheel and hauled away while the fire that tortured him was fuelled to roast meat from the nearest carcase as a side course to the whisky.

Tom and Alice were pushed to the ground at the lower edge of the incline and tied together once more by their ankles. Alice had spoken little lately and just seemed to stare right ahead, barely bothering to turn her head when he spoke to her. Tom sat upright and found it helped to watch the buffalo a short way off and wondered why they just remained there, with little grazing or water, as if time was standing still until they could return to a normal existence. He had little idea of the trauma that trampled even the wildest mind.

Presently, half raw, half cooked meat was thrown to the children unceremoniously and they ate, Tom feeding his sister with some difficulty. Compared to the usual fare, this was good eating and while the Cheyenne worked upon the whisky the watchers on the rim slipped down to the wagon to satiate their thirst from the barrel on the wagon.

It was a stiff pickle that the Morgensons were in, with horses tired and thirsty and a wagon that was twisted on the slope and reduced to three wheels, with a skid for the fourth. Any kind of escape from their situation, even with four good wheels, would have been futile, at least Margaret knew that. The reverend seemed not to fully understand their plight, shocked at what he had already observed and finding it hard to visualise the depths of brutality that some congregations found easy and every day, especially when they owned the moral high ground by force of arms.

Margaret looked at her husband and spoke in a low voice.

"Maybe if we stay calm and hidden, they will go back where they came from. I see they have white children with them but I fear we can do no good for them right now." She looked at the blank face of the reverend. "I think the wagon is gone, broken for good and all and we can't use it any more if we are not to die of thirst or worse. Once those people are gone, we should ride the horses to the nearest civilised parts and maybe then we can send help for those kids. Do you understand?"

Morgenson nodded. Down below a series of inebriated cries grew ever louder and more aggressive. It continued until mid-afternoon when the whisky ran out and two Cheyenne fought roughly for the last dregs of the last bottle and then threw it away. Not enough to make them all drunk, the liquor had invaded their senses and loosened the will to act as their culture had once directed.

Once the whisky was gone, there was no reason to stay, and slowly the party gathered what they could use from the wagon and set it alight after pulling off the wet hides and casting them onto the ground. The smoke began to bother the buffalo that had now retreated back a little way down the gully and it made them uneasy. Then in single file the Cheyenne crossed to the far side of the gully and found an easy way up onto the ground above. The children were back on the mules and followed by a lone warrior who lowered his lance in a gesture that kept them moving at the speed he required. Behind them, the wagon blazed and the smoke rose in a plume of grey, weightless bright embers floating through the atmosphere and some finding landfall on the bodies of the dead hunters.

***

"Ten silver dollars for the first man to find that horse thief's trail!" Bellfield told the men around him.

The riders close by spread out more and continued along the perimeter of the trees, where they met the grass. All eyes were on the ground, dazzled slightly by the offer that had just been made and which increased their perception. For a quarter mile they moved along the edge of the woodland until a pair of sharp eyes spotted a broken branch, some way from the trees, almost hidden in the grass and with a fresh break at the stem. The man dismounted and looked closely at the leaves, wilting a little but quite fresh.

Leaving his horse to graze, he moved directly towards the trees and found a patch of hard ground, clear of tracks but almost too undisturbed. He bent over and observed the random scatter of debris, almost too random.

"Here!" He called to the others, who turned and spurred their horses back towards him.

Marshal Deerbolt was the first to be at his side and examining the ground. He screwed up his face and tried to make something of the other man's suspicions. Bellfield came across and also dismounted, then listened to the reasoning of the signs on the ground. He stood and thought for a moment, then made up his mind.

"All right, let's go in here and see if we can pick up a better trail."

All but the man who put the signs together mounted and turned towards the woodland. He looked eagerly at his disappearing leader, then called after him.

"Mr Bellfield, you said…"

Deerbolt had caught the man's horse and held out the rein. He looked down at him and with a twist of his mouth shook his head as if he should know better.

Riding faster than was wise between the trees, all of the rider's eyes were on the ground, spread out beyond the widest part of the trail. They had gone some way when one called out and held something high above his head. When the group gathered again, they could see it for what it was, a small slip of cotton fabric, white with a pink rose pattern that was fading and ragged.

Riding on in the same direction, they found the next one, then the next, and then Tom's trouser grey.

"I guess that these must be from the Henderson kids," Bellfield deduced, "looks like Standing is right on the line, if that's what he's following."

Deerbolt thought about it and was not too sure. If Standing was following the cotton trail, why would he leave it for them to find? Had he missed it altogether and gone off on a tangent to nowhere? Surely this must be the path that the Cheyenne were taking with the children, so where the hell was he?
A little further and it became clearer. Though the hard, dry earth and ground litter made tracking difficult, the signature hoof prints of Midnight were found in the mud by a drying stream. Marshal Deerbolt stared down at them while most of the others made noises of excitement, and wondered why a hunted man would allow such marks to remain.

***

The horses of the Cheyenne made easy work of the incline and soon the party was making its way over grassland again. As before, two warriors came up behind the children, their heads still fuzzy from the whisky, and bellies full of buffalo.

Reaching the rim, the riders moved steadily away from the depression behind and at last the patient bison began to move along behind and below them and skirted around the burning wagon to find the rest of the herd somewhere ahead. The noise from the moving animals was considerable, drumming hooves and the roars and bellowing of the bison as they found freedom from the temporary confinement.

A whinny from a thirsty horse caught the ear of the second rider in the line and he glanced to his right, searching for the origin of the sound. He pulled his mount to a halt and frowned into the middle distance.

"Ahasestse'o (Wait, listen)," he said to the others.

The group halted and tried to find the source of the sound that the man's sharp ears had picked up above the light breeze. The leader turned to the warrior behind him and shrugged off the idea until another whinny proved him right. As one, the Cheyenne turned along the edge of the gully and rode quietly until they saw the top of the canvas canopy that covered the wagon.

Advancing from their mounts, the leader silently signalled one warrior to stay with Tom and Alice, then led the others forward, cautiously until sure of what lay ahead.

Peering through the long grass that hid them, Morgenson and his wife could see the Cheyenne advancing. They slipped back towards the wagon, unsure of what action to take. The reverend took his wife by the arm and looked her in the eye.

"We have company, wife," he said, in a confident voice. "Better put on your bonnet and dust off your dress. We must show ourselves in good order."

Margaret looked at him incredulously, wondering what he intended to do, but his face was set and adamant and she knew how fortitude took over his spirit when a sermon was about to spring forth.

"Joshua," she said firmly, "those are wild Indians, and they have just killed people for whisky and wild ways."

Morgenson put a finger to his lips and hushed her up.

"They are the Lord's children, and this is why we have travelled so far, to acquaint them of the light and the lamb." It was the sermon that Margaret feared was breaking. "Now, put on your bonnet, the sun is quite warm, and dust off your dress for our guests."

She thought for a moment that maybe he was right, that fortitude and bare cheek might save the day. What alternative did they have? She rose and did as she was told, pushing the horses aside to find her bonnet, tying the ribbon about her neck. Morgenson followed, found his stovepipe hat and put it on, resembling the late demised president as he pulled the book from his pocket. The two of them watched as the Cheyenne halted in a line, some yards away from them, watching the performance as if it were acted out for their benefit, which in fact it was.

They sat their horses with shields over their chests and lances at the port, their feathers and fur caps catching the breeze. Tom could hardly believe what he was seeing, sitting further back on one of the mules and wondering what state of madness the man might be suffering, and wondering if he knew to whom he was addressing. Alice sat silent, wide-eyed, as if waiting for something.

Morgenson took a pace forward. He held up the book and spoke in a tone of ecclesiastical depth, while Margaret just stayed by the wagon taking her cue from her husband.

"Brothers!" The reverend called out to the Cheyenne. "Welcome." He waved his free hand to the wagon. "As you can see, we are pilgrims come upon hard times and our wagon is of little use, but we can offer you water to drink if you would care to dismount from your animals."

The warriors watched as the bearded man continued, amused at his way.

"Here I have the book, the book whose words will transform the sword into the ploughshare…" He thrust it towards them and Margaret realised that it was not the Bible but her husband's bird notes. "I see that you have children, white children who are surely Christian souls and must be redeemed…"

The Cheyenne were urging their mounts closer as the reverend spoke, the man still unaware of the volume of bird identifications that he presented, but still preaching from it as if it were more powerful a volume.

Two Cheyenne dismounted and walked past the preacher, hardly giving him a second look, then one climbed up onto the wagon box, disappeared under the canvas and began rummaging through the Morgenson's remaining possessions. Margaret risked a slow movement to observe what the warrior was doing but dared not make a sound. The reverend had followed with his eyes as the Cheyenne passed but continued with his earnest sermon.

From his horse, the leading warrior levelled his lance towards Morgenson and laughed, his feathered bonnet undulating with the movements of his head. He spoke a few words to the other Cheyenne by his side, and they both indulged in mocking the preacher openly, but still Morgenson continued. Margaret swallowed hard. She could see no good in this.

"My friends," Morgenson went on, "you have slain your brothers and the Lord has seen it. He loves more the sinner who has mended his ways and beaten the sword into ploughshares. He is…"

The first arrow pierced his abdomen just above his belt and he fell back against the wagon, his stovepipe hat falling from his head and rolling onto the floor. The warrior beside the leader loosed a second and it took the preacher in the right shoulder, and a third in his left side as he turned, reaching up to where the second struck him.

"Ooooh!"

Morgenson fell back and Margaret screamed, her hands to her mouth. The Cheyenne inside the wagon, uncertain of what was happening outside, scrambled through the Morgenson's belongings that littered the wooden floor, and leapt to the ground, close to where the woman stood. A knife was in his hand and he stabbed forward without any particular aim and caught the preacher's wife in the throat, just catching her carotid artery and bringing blood. It was a lightning strike that took Margaret by surprise and she clutched her neck and fell to the ground, her mouth moving but words left unformed.

Excited 'whoops' and cries escaped from the mouths of the Cheyenne warriors as those astride their horses dismounted and joined the others in rummaging through the contents of the wagon while the owners lay on the ground beside it.

The last of the Cheyenne that were with the children let go of the mules, eager to obtain his share of the spoils and kicked his horse hard in the sides to encourage it to move swifter. Dismounting before the horse had halted, he leapt the preacher's body, ignoring the man and joining the others.

Tom watched from his mount. It was becoming too common a thing to be horror-stricken at, except when he thought of the same happening to his family a short time before. He glanced at his sister, whose face had not changed, her expression still blank and almost calm.

The boy let the thoughts of escape fight their contradictions in his mind. They were free, with no Cheyenne holding them. The warriors were intense in their ransacking of the wagon. What if he reached over and took Alice's mule by the rein and turned back into the gully, over the flat and up the other side? 'Never underestimate a mule', Uncle Will had told him that, 'there were cavalrymen who preferred mules to horses, with their stamina and strength'. Tom swallowed and wondered what would happen if they tried and were caught once more. There was no doubt that he would take another beating, but what if they succeeded and the mules gained ground on the Cheyenne ponies, if the warriors decided that they were not worth the trouble to follow?

Before he knew it, Tom's mind had made the decision for him and he reached over and took the leather rein of Alice's mount. He pulled it around and kicked the mule hard, returning along the rim of the gully and looking for the best way down.

He could see the bison, still moving along below, without hindrance now that the hunters were gone.

"Hang on Alice!" He called over, and Alice automatically grabbed onto the mane of the animal to avoid falling off.

The two mules were at full gallop but already behind, the lead Cheyenne had seen it unfold and in one leap he was on his pony's back and giving chase. A short way behind, the others followed, approaching their animals so fast that their horses shied and made mounting difficult. Soon it was a chase with all in motion along the ridge. Tom was about to pull the mules head around and down into the gully when a strong brown arm appeared and the hand took hold of the reins and hauled back the animals in an upheaval of loose ground.

Chapter Ten
Wild Men and Wild Horses

It was impossible to know what caused that smoke and Will Standing guessed it meant no good for someone. Almost without a second thought, he urged Midnight into a gallop, a stride that ate up the distance and a pace that refused to accede to exhaustion. The second thought that Will did have was beaten by the chance that he might retrieve the children, although how he might do that he put down to providence, and if there was anyone up there above the clouds, that they would have observed his natural kindness to animals and forgive the other parts that were less to his credit.

It was a hot day and the drumming of hooves on the hard ground was monotonous but he had to catch up if he stood any chance to fulfil his undertaking. The horse's head was high and the bit jangled in his mouth as the gallop proceeded. Standing squinted towards the smoke and knew there was some distance to go. It hardly seemed to come closer and for a moment he felt it might be a mirage, but it was not, and a second later, it bloomed grey and dark against the sky.

Twenty minutes without slowing and Standing held back the rein. There was only so long that the black horse could be expected to travel at that speed so he stopped, dismounted and checked his canteen. It was half empty, but once more he pushed in the crown of his hat and poured in the rest of the water, offering it to the panting Midnight.

"You need it more than me, fellah," Standing said.

The horse assaulted the hat and finished the water within seconds, then snorted away the mucus in its nasal passages as if wanting to be away again. Will Standing knew that the horse would run, he had no doubt of that, but an exhausted animal on dangerous ground made no sense at all, so he would give time to the animal and hoped he had not over exerted it.

So many times during the Civil War he had seen willing horses blown to pieces by cannon shells, through no fault of their own and with no animosity to those who fired the missiles. It always seemed all right if men decided to take the risk and blow each other's heads off but why should they expect a horse to do likewise, with no reward but a chew of hay at the end of it if they survived? And yet, what was he doing right then, expecting Midnight to put itself in the middle of a Cheyenne war party just to please the man on his back?

Climbing back aboard, Will clicked his mouth and the black horse erupted into speed again, clearing the occasional tight grass clump with ease and continuing the pace almost without pausing. The smoke grew closer and darker and when about a mile away, he halted once more to check the Colt in his belt and ease the broken arrow that had become uncomfortable with the jolts of riding. He felt the need to reassure himself even knowing that he had already done it more than once. Then, finding a box of the cartridges from Mr Bridey's store, he took a handful and shoved them into his trouser pocket. When the time came, he did not wish to be found wanting and fishing for ammunition.

As a last check, he let the hammer of the Colt down onto the empty chamber, so that when next fired it would be in earnest. Placing it back into his wide belt, he lifted the loop of the Sharps from its place on the saddle horn and once again checked that the action was smooth, first levering the hammer into half cock, and then full to reveal the block that had opened wide to take a cartridge. But with only five cartridges, he had no wish to waste them and would not insert one until needed. The side arm would be his main defence at close range and he settled it into his belt again, making it as comfortable as possible and yet easy to find.

He had never shot a man before, and hoped he might avoid it this time. Even the war had spared him that and he was glad of it. Sure, he had used a weapon to do bad things and might even again, but it was never his intention to kill, if only for a good night's sleep's sake.

Standing's approach to the smoke was careful and he held Midnight back, although the animal still seemed keen to run. As he approached the gully, he could hear the crackle of fire, the bellowing of the bison and see the dust cloud that they were creating, melding with the grey and black smoke. Reaching the rim, he looked down. A little way to his right, a wagon burned and the big animals were giving the horrors of it a wide berth and moving steadily to his left.

Of the creators of this picture, Standing had little doubt, the remaining unburned arrows sticking into the timber told him that, and a cold stream of tingling fear ran down his spine. Will Standing was not a brave man, he knew that, and would make no apologies for it.

Midnight danced nervously on the edge of the gully, bringing up the dry earth and vestiges of grass. Something was bothering the animal and it spread to its rider.

"I know, fellah," Standing told the horse, reaching down and slapping the dark neck to reassure the animal. "I feel the same way."

He drove the horse gingerly over the rim and felt the animal's forelegs slip down finding purchase on the sandy gradient. Standing leant back to keep his centre of gravity and gave the horse its head to make its way down. Moving slowly towards the burning wagon, he could clearly see what remained of a human form, lashed to a wheel that was partly in flames. All around were abandoned buffalo skins that were a direct contrast to the moving group of big bulls that were just passing a short way off.

One of the bulls halted and shook its big shaggy head for a moment, jet-black and woolly and easing down dramatically to the red brown of the back and sides. Standing could see the curved horns that half emerged from the curly hair of the skull and wanted none of them. If they did not bother him, he would damn sure not bother them.

From the marks of what was left of the arrows in the wagon side, Standing could clearly see that this was the work of the same party that he was chasing. A buzzard flew off, frightened from its meal on one of the bodies and took the man by equal surprise, making his heart pound even more than it already was. He pressed on around the remains of the carnage and Midnight's long, black legs stomped the blood-soaked earth. With one hand on the Colt, the man's eyes darted this way and that, aware that any moment he might be into something that he wished he were not. He tried to determine how long it had been since this tragedy had occurred and guessed not more than a couple of hours or so, maybe less from the way that the flames were charring the timber on the wagon and the stench of burning flesh.

He was close, he knew it. That black horse had proved itself and eaten up the miles and the minutes to be right behind those Cheyenne and the children that he had promised himself to recover.

More bison passed by and he kept an eye on them too, just in case he got too close for comfort and initiated a wrong response from an angry bull. Buffalo bulls could be sensitive when cows were around and he had enough to be concerned about without one of those big 'shaggies' down on him.

Now he had circled around the burning wagon, keeping a distance from the heat and the smoke, between the flames and the passing bison. A bull roared a challenge some way off but he doubted it was aimed at him. Others answered and cows lowed in response and hurried to pass with trailing calves. Smoke melded with the dust and debris kicked up by the passing animals and Standing wiped his stinging eyes with the back of his hand. Then through the haze he saw a movement through the dust, on the opposite side of the gully and up on the far ridge. Just a shadow through his watery eyes that might only be a trick of the light through the ground disturbed by the buffalo.

He rubbed his eyes to gain clarity and saw it again, cleared and sharper as he stood in the saddle to find height and a better view. It was up against the sun and he squinted through the dusty clouds that obscured his vision.

Two mules with riders raced along the rim, alone for a moment before others followed, more riders on fast ponies and feathered bonnets, lances primed and held behind circular shields, bodies bent forward with the speed of their mounts and chasing the mules. Within seconds, as Will Standing went for the Colt in his belt, the mules were seized by their reins and drawn to a violent halt on the edge of the ridge. He could clearly see the mules and their riders now and realised it was the children.

With their attention on the escapees, the Cheyenne had no knowledge of the rider below, camouflaged as he was behind the moving mass of bison, the dust and the smoke.

Tommy's mule was pulled around by the head and as he turned, he saw the figure below, a black horse emerging from the dust carrying a rider that he knew well. His eyes widened and lit up with hope.

"Uncle Will!" He called not thinking that it might not be the best way to encourage help.

At the shout, all five warriors turned their attention to the ground below and immediately identified the black horse and the rider. The lead Cheyenne growled an instruction to the others while he maintained a grip on the mule's reins and as one the warriors yelped a war cry and put their horses to the slope, descending towards their enemy with lances raised. Pulling the mules behind him, the leader followed and dragged the animals over the rim and down towards where the bison were still moving across.

Standing saw the advance upon him and looked quickly back to where he had descended, realising that it was easier coming down than it would be going up and time spent in the effort might prove fatal. The Cheyenne were already pushing a way through the bison, which were milling in disorder at a new assault. He could see the mules descending too, led by another warrior urging his horse a little further up the gully in an obvious attempt to cut him off.

Either direction down the gully was hampered now with the frightened buffalo. For a second, Will thought it was all over and feared to use the Colt in the confusion lest he hit one of the children, or their mounts which would cast them into the mountain of surging black and red muscle and fearful horns.

Midnight pranced nervously, turning on the spot, led by both the jerky movements of its rider and the closing perils that threatened to engulf them. 'Buffalo, buffalo, buffalo', the word flashed across Will's brain. He turned the horse towards the burning wagon and reached for one of the bison hides that had not yet burned, dragged it out and threw it over his head and that of the black horse, then touched Midnight's ribs with his heels and urged it into the herd, dropping over the saddle horn and down over the horse's neck to disguise his profile.

Worried animals churned around and began to calm a little as the Cheyenne slowed their ponies, trying to locate the black horse and its rider. Turning down the gully, the herd still milled in the uncertain nearness of humans. The noise was deafening with bellowing and the stomping of one-ton bodies all around, mingling with the dust and displaced earth.

Standing pulled the robe well over his head and let the horse drift with the current of the buffalo, wide-eyed and uncertain of the proximity of such creatures that it had never known before. The Cheyenne poked and prodded with their lances where they thought the fugitive might be but it only succeeded in encouraging the beasts to change direction and make investigation harder.

Several times, a Cheyenne came within easy reach of the man and the black horse, but dust and confused animals and the buffalo robe that covered them maintained the defence against discovery. Standing peeped from under the hide and tried to manoeuvre in the same direction as the buffalo, letting them make the progress. How far he would have to go in this manner he had no idea, other than the trick was working, and a desperate man would maintain that discomfort, if he had any sense.

Occasionally the head of a bull might come close and sniff the horse, but the scent of the hide that covered them masqueraded for the truth and allowed them to pass.

Will looked out again from under the hide and saw the warrior who led the mules through the dust and bobbing bodies. He was coming closer and within a minute was almost by his side, reins in his teeth and lance held high with a free hand, searching around for a sign of the white man. The Cheyenne moved along and still dragged the mules and the children behind him. Standing could only see Tom's feet and legs and he wanted to reach out to touch and reassure, but held himself back in case it might have the wrong effect.

Then, Midnight coughed and whinnied with the dust in his nostrils.

Above the din of the moving buffalo, the Cheyenne heard it and swung around, trying to find the source of the sound. He pulled the head of his horse around roughly and urged it through the buffalo, pushing away Midnight among the surge of brown bodies, then turning again to maintain his general position, waiting for another chance to pinpoint the enemy. Standing took another look beneath the robe and found Tommy looking down directly at him. He put a finger to his mouth.

The Cheyenne turned his horse again and looked through the dust at the animals closest to him, Midnight among them. He raised the lance and was about to strike randomly.

"Uncle Will!" Tommy shouted and waved a hand in the opposite direction.

The Cheyenne dragged his animal's head around sharply and followed the direction of the boy's hand, kicking the horse in the sides and advancing it through more milling buffalo to where he thought Tommy had seen the man.

Alice remained in a state of strange torpor that Tom found hard to penetrate. All through the last few days she had been drifting in a kind of distant world of her own, hardly seeming to understand the situation that they were in. And yet, she clung to the mule as if this were an everyday event, making little sign that she was aware of her surroundings or the dangers that they were experiencing.

Like the horse, Standing was smothered by the lack of clear air and fought to breathe, but kept one hand over his mouth and nose to fend off the discomfort, trying one side over another where it felt easier. Risking a breath when he felt it possible, he tried to acquaint himself as to the position of those who searched for him and gradually discovered that they were well behind and Midnight had carried them both to a place where they were beyond immediate danger.

After some time, the lead Cheyenne realised the futility of the search. He called to the others a little way off.

"Noheto! (Let's go!)" He called, and the others gave up the hunt and moved back up towards the rim and their original direction of travel.

Reaching the top of the ridge with the mules, the Cheyenne turned to look back down. He watched the last of the clouds of bison surging away to find the remaining herd members and his face betrayed the dissatisfaction of not dealing with the man who he now knew would follow.

Tom felt the dual emotions of hope and disappointment. But now he knew that they were not alone and with Uncle Will close by, he felt the proximity of family once more and a chance that they might yet get through this. But Uncle Will was only one man and the Cheyenne were five, and he had seen what they had done to others.

For a short time, the Cheyenne followed the edge of the gully, Then the leader turned away, leading the others, the mules and the horses that had once belonged to the Morgenson's. He cast one more glance over his shoulder and gave thought to the one who followed, but that battle was for another day.

***

Leaving the claustrophobic woodland was a relief for the men who followed Belfield. But open ground meant hot riding and resting the horses more frequently. Away to the north, the faded blue of the Black Hills was just visible on the horizon. Belfield took the telescope from his bag and extended it to look forward, across the waving grassland.

"Anything?" asked Deerbolt.

Belfield still rolled the optical instrument over the distance, then moved it back over to where he had recently looked.

"You know, we've been going since early," the Marshal continued, "we lose horses out here, we're in big trouble."

Belfield dropped the telescope and looked around at him, a harsh expression on his face, but he saw the weariness in the others and had no wish to press too much and lose them.

"Thirty minutes," he said. "Thirty minutes."

They dismounted and Deerbolt moved to Belfield's side, who was once more looking over the grassland with the telescope.

"You know, there's a little grumbling from these men," he explained. "Wondering why all this over a horse?"

Belfield turned on him.

"Not just any horse," he growled, "my horse, and my money that's paying them and filling their bellies. You remind them of that. And do you have any advice to give me, Marshal Deerbolt?"

Deerbolt shook his head.

"I guess not."

Thirty minutes passed quickly and the men mounted up once more. The member of the party who was owed the ten silver dollars approached Belfield nervously. When quite close, he spoke in a quiet voice.

"Mr Belfield, you said about ten silver…"

But Belfield was already riding away and ignoring the man.

The trail had gone cold some time before but they maintained their direction, spreading out abreast once more and looking for some track that would give away a definite route to follow. After an hour, a slight parting of the long grass betrayed where Will Standing had put Midnight to the gallop.

"He's moving fast, not long past, but no sign of him yet," Belfield said, looking through the brass telescope again. "Damn, that horse can run."

The man paused on one spot for a moment, then handed over the instrument to Deerbolt. He pointed up ahead.

"Out there, just on the horizon."

Deerbolt put his eye to the small glass button and looked through.

"See it?" Belfield asked urgently. "Just a mark, something?"

The Marshal looked again and found it.

"Smoke," he agreed, "dust, smoke, maybe something burning."

***

Will Standing let the horse move out of the slowly moving herd. They were some way from their original descent now, so he risked a glance under the buffalo robe. All that he could see were the bison, the dust and the rim of the gully that was descending in height as they moved forward.

Cautiously he lifted the hide from over his head and back across his shoulders. The black horse also felt the freedom of movement that the removal gave and threw back its head and whinnied its approval. There was no sign of the

Cheyenne and Standing knew that he had been lucky. It felt just like the relief of a robbery gone right, or a horse lifted without being identified, and he was well aware of both of those things.

So now things had changed some. Now the Cheyenne knew he was following and unless they were a little light on their brain pans, they knew that he was kin to those kids. That said, they probably knew that he would still be coming and making every effort to deal with him in their own inimitable way.

Will finally threw off the robe and found himself and the horse patch-covered with buffalo blood. For the first time, now not distracted by what might have been his last moments on this Earth, he could smell the scent of death, but had to admit that he had been thankful for it.

He left the horse below while he climbed the slope to the level above and looked across the grassland. Of the Cheyenne and the children there was no visible sign. He wondered if they would still keep to the north, maybe head for the Black Hills where they could throw him off the track or maybe lay in wait and ambush him. Either way, it was not good.

What he had hoped for was a level sighting of the Cheyenne, when he could use the Sharps and take maybe a couple down to even the odds a little. If he could knock down an elk at a thousand yards, he could sure as hell knock down one of them, maybe two if he could load fast enough. He decided that the game was one of degrading the odds. If he could degrade the odds in his favour, his chances improved, if they degraded the odds in their favour, then it was all over. Moreover, he had only five cartridges for the long gun, and with there being five of them, he had no room for a miss. He worried a little about if it came to close quarters. There was still his Colt, with five rounds in the cylinder, but ejecting and reloading was slow, too slow. This was not the Confederate Army coming on slowly and conveniently in ranks that gave the opposition the time to aim properly. He had seen it but thankfully had not had an order to take part.

It was an aversion that he had to overcome. Those Cheyenne would not show a moments concern to put an arrow in him, or worse, and if it came to the choice of them or him, he was damn sure he would do his utmost to ensure the former idea.

He worried about the children and what would happen to them if he failed, not aware of the detail but pretty sure he had a fair idea. It was something that crossed his mind often. Will knew that he had pressed his luck too often and that any moment he could make that fatal mistake that could see it run out.

Certain that he had escaped for the moment and everything seemed clear, he hauled the black horse up onto the flat. He mounted and rode along the rim, hoping once more to pick up the trail and continue after them. He guessed that they had gained an hour on him, perhaps a little less, but he needed a sign to make up the time.

Keeping himself sharp, just in case they waited for him along the way, he followed the rim until he found the tracks of unshod horses. A little further along, he saw the wagon, now devoid of horses. Moving carefully forward, he halted and dismounted, taking the Colt from his belt and advancing towards the place where the warm breeze fluttered the canvas awning. He found Morgenson, still alive with three arrows in his body. The man found speaking difficult and Standing knew he had not much time left in this world.

Morgenson opened his eyes and looked at him, his lips cracked and dry. Standing had no water left so he looked along the wagon and saw the barrel. He also saw the woman, her hands clutching her throat, also living but breathing with difficulty through gurgling sounds. He flipped the lid of the barrel and found the dipper but had to go well down before he found water.

Filling the dipper, Standing realised that water would be the last thing to give the woman. He saw the blood emerging from the wound in her throat and knew her time also was close. He went back to the man in the dark clothes and with one arm raised his head a little, allowing water to trickle down into his mouth. Morgenson opened his eyes once more, glazed and distant though they were.

"Be you a Christian man?" He asked, in a broken, croaking voice.

Will Standing swallowed hard and took a quick drink from the dipper himself.

"Oh, I guess so," he said, wondering if it was the truth.

Morgenson opened his eyes wider.

"Am I to die today?" He asked.

Gurgling noises grew louder from the woman a short distance away. Will found it a hard question, but a lie was useless.

"I believe you are, Sir," he answered. "I am sorry that there is little more that I can do, other than see you safe from the predation of wolves and such."

Morgenson seemed to take the truth.

"And my wife?"

Will shook his head and took off his hat to shield the man's face.

"I think that her time is short also."

"Is she in pain?" Morgenson asked. "I think that she is in pain for I can hear it and can identify it as such."

"I think maybe she is, Sir."

Morgenson grabbed his hand and looked up.

"Then as a Christian man, you must ease her burden, release her from this world and put her in the bosom of the next…"

"Sir, I can't…"

Morgenson tightened his hold on Will's hand, and his eyes intensified their hold on him. Standing paused for a moment's thought.

"All right, Sir," he told the man. "I will do what I can for her." He took a breath. "Sir, may I know your family name?"

The preacher frowned.

"We are the Morgensons, late of the Liberty Train which we have become separated from."

Will Standing eased his hand from Morgenson's loose grip and went over to his wife. She remained with her hands around her throat, staunching the slow seepage of blood that had become substantial, her eyes wide but unblinking. He knelt down beside her. She eased her gaze towards him as out of her sight he took the Colt from his belt and removed his hat.

"Ma'am. Your husband is all but gone and I am sorry that I cannot do much for your situation. There is maybe something that I can do to ease your suffering and your husband has asked me to do so."

He moved the barrel of the Colt up to the side of her head.

"It will be quick, Ma'am, and I hope that you bear me no ill."

Standing pulled the hammer back to full cock and the cylinder moved around to present a live cartridge. He put his free hand on hers.

"I have your family name, and will see you both safe under."

He pulled the trigger and wept for some time.

***

Tommy was surprised that he received no further abuse from the Cheyenne and guessed that the appearance of his Uncle Will had set their minds on other things. He realised how close his uncle had come to being caught and going under at the hands of those that presently held him and his sister, and was glad that he had been at least a little responsible for helping him avoid that fate. It had been a close call.

Once on the flat again, and moving quickly, there was no more of the chatter that the warriors had indulged in along the trail. It was as if they now had something else to concern them. But why the concern for one man? The boy wondered if maybe Uncle Will had not been alone after all and they knew something that he didn't, or maybe their confidence in their security was not quite as they had hoped.

The party now moved in single file with the children's mules in the centre of the column. Behind came two warriors with the Morgenson's horses and ahead three more riding in silence.

Tommy glanced across at his sister and called her name. She turned to him and made the slightest smile, as if recognising him from some distant memory.

"That was Uncle Will, Alice," he said quietly.

Her head turned a little as she bounced on the mule.

"Uncle Will?" She seemed to be searching for the name.

The lead warrior turned in the buffalo bone saddle and scowled back at them from beneath the feather bonnet.

"He'kotahe! (Quiet!)" He grunted.

The boy knew what it meant. There was no need for translation.

The sun began to drop in a burst of red and gold. Often the Cheyenne leader pulled the field glasses from the bag around his horse's neck and scanned the ground that they had crossed. It grew dark but the war party continued to ride through the night, stopping only infrequently to rest the animals. Tom and his sister were exhausted but the Cheyenne seemed not to tire and now probably had more to think about.

The boy wondered what might come next. He asked himself how Uncle Will could possibly have any chance against such people if it came to a confrontation. What had happened earlier seemed to have made it quite clear that one against these five was a lost cause and he himself had felt the brutality of going against them. So, what chance did Uncle Will have?

At first light the landscape had changed as the rocky skirts of the Black Hills were reached. Big timber accentuated the slopes as the party climbed higher through boulder strewn ground. This was Sioux country but the Sioux and the Cheyenne were allies and travelled each other's territory with trust. This rocky high country had once been owned by the Kiowa, the Crow, the Pawnee, and even the Cheyenne but with the expansion of the Lakota Sioux in the seventeen hundreds, it had been theirs by force of arms. To the Lakota they were 'He Sapa', and to the Cheyenne, 'Mo'ohta-vo'honaaeva'.

Tom guessed that they had covered forty miles since the day before, or maybe more, even at the steady walk of the horses. As the sun made itself known behind the treeline, they halted. It had been some time since food was available to the children, just a hank of half raw buffalo meat that was thrown to them back in the gully, the same fare that the warriors consumed with excited enthusiasm from the nearby carcases. The boy also felt the need for water, his bruises hurt and his head ached. Alice seemed oblivious to any need but her drawn face showed the lack of attention that any girl of her age should receive.

The animals were hobbled and given access to the fresh green grass of the slopes, better fare than what little was available on the flat below. The children were once more hobbled too, with a rawhide thong that bound one of Tom's legs to his sister's. The boy saw the lead warrior approaching, his spiky feathered headdress standing out from the more traditional pattern of the others. In his hand was the skin bag from his horse's neck and the water pouch.

Kneeling, he lifted Alice's head by her chin and dribbled water into her mouth, which she allowed without protest. Capping off the flow, he threw the pouch to Tom so that he could also drink. The man then looked at Alice's feet, in a poor state despite the remnants of her previous bindings. He then ran a hand up her leg and pushed aside the remains of her torn dress to reveal her bare legs up to the crotch. Tom saw it and misjudged the gesture, reaching forward in a brave but futile attempt to push the man off his sister.

The Cheyenne pushed back, catching the boy full in the chest and heaving him away with a harsh word. The warrior turned his attention back to Alice and pulling a hollow bone from his bag, scooped out a fatty substance that clung there, rubbing into her inner thighs where the rough blanket that served for a saddle on her mule had worn the skin red and sore. Tom realised his mistake.

"I'm sorry," he said. "I thought…"

The Cheyenne looked at him, and answered in a gentler voice than before. He chopped his palm above the sores, twice in quick succession and Tom understood. Then, the warrior took a pair of moccasins from his bag, which were far too big for the girl's tiny feet. He released the cord that bound the girl and applied them anyway, and tied the cords tightly to where the deerskin ended just below her knees. Alice looked like some strange cultural doll, with overlarge feet and a strange expression. He could not help the gulp of a laugh, coughed up on a breath of expended air.

The Cheyenne saw it and his mouth turned into what Tom saw as almost a smile, not firm but just a twist from that stern expression that he almost always held. The man pushed the water sack back at the boy and jerked his head up to invoke another pull of water. Alice was also given another drink and then the Cheyenne returned to the others, joining in an animated conversation that rose and fell with the emotion of argument.

A short time later another of the warriors came over to the children and gave more of the buffalo meat for them to chew over until the low thunder in their bellies were satisfied. They ate without considering the manners that their mother had once insisted upon and Tom wondered if this might be the first signs of becoming the barbarian that she warned of if such courtesies were not conformed to.

They had been in the same place for an hour when the lead Cheyenne walked back to a stand of boulders that they had passed on the way up. Tom watched as he leant forward against the rock, supporting his chest against it while peering over the top, the pair of stolen binoculars to his eyes.

***

Far from ever shooting a man, Will never in a month of Fridays expected to have to shoot a woman, and a pretty one at that. He pulled a hand down from his temples and swept away the sweat and tears that had accumulated there. Still sitting beside, her with his hat over face, he felt the hollow in his gut that he had felt back at the cabin, but this time his anger and disgust was for himself.

Midnight whinnied in impatience and he looked up and across to where the horse stood in the shade of the wagon, between himself and the dead preacher.

"I know, I know…" he said to the horse, as if it spoke his language.

Standing had expended the cartridge and returned to her husband, only to find him also gone, and hoped that both of these people had arrived at the place where their religion told them existed, above these damn dry plains. Then he had returned to sit by the woman, ashamed of his involvement in the inevitable.

How long he had sat there, he could not say, but long enough for the horse to complain. His thoughts turned to the responsibility of the present, see to the horse, put these people in the ground, and take back the children. Simple to say, and maybe he was shooting high.

Checking the water barrel, he found two inches in the bottom and releasing it from the metal hoops that secured it, dropped it to the ground and used his hat again to convey a drink for the horse. What was left he added to the space in his canteen but it only filled to halfway.

Ransacking the wagon he found a shovel, a priceless item for any migrant, and finding a place that looked reasonable he began to dig a sizeable space to plant the two of them. The ground was sandy and not difficult to move, but the task was hard in other ways and the work slow. Three feet down, he decided it was enough, and breaking off the arrows from the man, he hauled him in the canvas canopy to his final resting place on this, his previous plane of existence. The hole proved a little short in width, and as he fitted the woman in, he found that the two were pressed together closer than he had anticipated, but concluded that as they were married, such mild indecency would be overlooked by the Almighty.

Before returning the ground to its original place, Standing tore boards from the wagon box and lay them over the couple to deter wolves and other predators from disturbing them. In doing so, he found the reverend's telescope and put it in his pocket. He also found the small bird book on the ground, with notes that he found confusing, in a language he could not understand.

Also under the seat, he found five tins of food, four of beans and one of tinned pineapple that the Cheyenne had obviously overlooked due to his own involvement in their hasty searches. Food had run out for him some hours back and he was already running on the grumbles, so this was a good find. He had heard about pineapples, but never seen or tasted one and he determined to do both at the first opportunity. According to popular conversation, the fruit was grown in Hawaii by ladies that lived in mud huts and wore grass skirts, with nothing above that but their own embarrassment. Where Hawaii was, he had no idea, other than it was in the middle of one ocean or another.

He filled in the grave until it was level and finding a broken board, took a knife from his saddle bag and roughly carved the name 'Morgenson' at one end, hoping that he had spelled it correctly. He stuck the board in the ground and made sure it would stand. All of the general prayers of his childhood he had forgotten, remembering only the dark one that was spoken over dead soldiers during the war, full of expletives and disrespect for the deceased and the afterlife that was common for those situations. He decided that those words were not fit by the grave of a lady and discounted the thought, and so just tipped his hat by way of a permanent farewell. Finally, he took one more look at the broken wagon and saw it for the sad sight that it was.

The telescope was also a new innovation. During the war he had seen officers with them, and also field glasses but had never been of sufficient rank to own or use one, nor ever really needed to. Pulling out the brass sheath had been a mild puzzle but he discovered the idea quick enough and he used the implement to look back across the gully and the distant plain for any sign of pursuit. There was none. Now close behind the Cheyenne, he felt a little exposed and disappointed, knowing that he had left a trail easy enough to follow over the last day or so.

"God-damn!" He said to himself. "What the hell I have to do to get myself hung?"

Even though the sun was going, Will Standing found no wish to sleep or rest. All he wanted was to put the day behind him and look to tomorrow. It was easier said than done and the guilt pursued him beyond the wreck of a broken wagon. As half of the night passed, he halted, took off the saddle and let the horse graze. In the dark, with only the stars watching, he sat on the saddle and accepted his guilt, his elbows resting upon his knees and eyes somewhere on the ground, wondering if maybe he would soon be in it.

Morning was an hour away and the black horse was walking steadily on. The trail of the Cheyenne had been fresh and easy to follow from the wagon until the light was gone. Will could see the hills in the gloom of the twilight before dawn and presumed he was not far from Dakota territory, guessing that was their chosen destination, where he could be more easily discouraged from following or erased permanently from their concern. He had previous worries about tracking the Cheyenne through woodland in case of an ambush, but then they had been unaware of him. Now it was different.

As dawn opened up the land to the naked eye, Standing saw the environment changing. Green was overtaking the longer dry grass of the high plains to ease into the lower slopes of the Black Hills, and spotted with a maze of rocky outcrops and boulders. Higher, he could see the pine covered landscape that surrounded the seven-thousand-foot peaks that dominated the summit.

Pulling back on the rein, Will pulled out the telescope, glad of the novelty of long vision. He scoured the slopes in the hope of seeing the party that he followed, letting the telescope move slowly across due to its narrow field of vision.

He thought he saw something, just a dark movement that cast a long shadow against grey rock but the view had moved too quickly to halt, and he rolled it back a little way. He held his breath to steady the telescope but Midnight changed weight on his feet and shuddered.

"Whoooa!"

Standing checked again in the place where he thought he had seen the movement and a few moments later found it. Observing him from above, he could see the headdress that he noticed in the gully, the feathers extending out from his skull like the quills of a porcupine or a lady's pincushion. Beneath was what he could see of the face, the eyes covered by a binocular and held there.

Will Sanding felt the world shrinking to just here, where he sat on the black horse. For some seconds, they watched each other in silence. Standing felt the need to show his intentions, that he would not give up and had the means to show it. Dropping the telescope from his eyes, he pulled up the Sharps rifle from its loop on the saddle horn and held it mid-barrel, resting the stock on his knee. He knew that the Cheyenne would understand, knew that he would be aware of the Sharps and its reputation at a thousand yards. It was maybe a futile gesture. He guessed the distance to the Cheyenne at well over fifteen hundred and well beyond risking a shot, even had it been a bigger target, so it remained just a warning, and one they might respect.

He returned the telescope to his eye once more but the man had gone. Standing moved the view to try to find him again. Then, there he was, back at the same spot behind the rock, but this time he was not alone. The Cheyenne had returned and climbed the rock and was holding up a boy, Tommy, by the scruff of the neck. Tommy struggled but he was held tightly, his legs searching for foothold. A brown hand reached up and pulled a feather from his head covering and thrust it into the boy's hair, a symbol of who now owned him.

Will saw it for the threat that was being given. Let the children live and be owned, or die on the sharp stones below. He thought for a moment, wondering what to do next, then returned the Sharps to its place on the saddle horn and pulled the black horse's head around and rode slowly back the way he came.

***

It was smoke. Down in the gully was the proof. It was a sight from hell, burned bodies and buffalo meat rotting on the bone, covered with buzzards and the odd coyote devouring the carnage. All around were the hoof prints of bison, now long gone and glad to be so.

Bellfield led the way down after finding a gentle slope and took out a handkerchief and put it up to his face, to filter good air from bad. Deerbolt followed, taking a Spencer rifle from its sheath beneath the stirrup flap. The riders spread out to view the scene and it was not hard to make out what had happened there.

"Is Standing one of them?" asked Bellfield of one who had risked closer examination.

The rider had dismounted and held the rein of his shying horse tightly.

"Don't look so," he answered. "Buffalo skinners, looks like, from what meat's left on 'em."

"Damn!" Bellfield said, disappointed.

Deerbolt rode close to him.

"Maybe a good thing, those Cheyenne took him, they'd have the horse too."

Bellfield saw the logic.

"Quite so. But where the hell is that damn mongrel?" He said, turning to the others. "Take a look around, look for shod tracks."

The smell was becoming overpowering in the heat and the party distanced themselves from the immediate area.

"Hey," someone called, "there's an old clock over her, other stuff too."

Some of the riders scrabbled up the opposite side of the gully and paused at the top. One of them shouted across at the others.

"Something else up here, a wagon, more tracks!"

Soon, they were all back up on the opposing rim of the depression. Bellfield and Deerbolt dismounted and walked past the grave of the Morgensons. They examined the wagon and looked around, finding the blood of the owners. Deerbolt picked up the small book of birds that Standing had put back on the ground where he found it. He shook his head.

"See! See here…" Bellfield called, pointing to the ground where Margaret had died.

Deerbolt joined him and shrugged, wondering what the other had found.

"See," Bellfield told him. "See the blood around here? Those tracks?"

"So? I see them," Deerbolt agreed.

Bellfield smiled a smile of some satisfaction.

"Those tracks around the blood, they are not moccasin tracks, they are boot tracks. See, the heel marks?"

"I don't..."

Bellfield stood back a pace.

"We need to see the bodies!" He shouted over at the group of mounted men. "These people were not killed by Indians, they were killed by the horse thief, Standing!"

Marshal Deerbolt was amazed at the way that Bellfield had interpreted the scene. He took in a long breath.

"Mr Bellfield, I'm not sure that your thoughts on this are making sense. You saw the hell down there that those Cheyenne created. It just doesn't make sense."

Bellfield turned on him, pointing to the ground and the evidence.

"You can see those tracks, boots over moccasins, and blood as confirmation, now let's have those people up out of the ground. It is our responsibility to know the truth." He twisted his body to address the others. "Dig 'em up!"

No one found the order to their liking, but Bellfield paid the dollar, so dig them up it was. They took turns after finding the shovel propped against a wheel and before long found the boards that covered the Morgensons. Removing them, everyone stood around in morbid curiosity, their eyes fixed on the tightly packed couple.

"Look real pretty, don't they?" Someone said.

Alexander Bellfield seemed to show no shame as he told the diggers to drag them out. Then he moved in to examine the wounds of the disturbed deceased. Rigor mortis had not yet set in so the bodies flopped over on the ground with the late reverend's arm in a sensitive position near his wife's rear part. Someone turned over the dead man.

"This one sure died from Indians," another ventured. "Look at them arrow stubs, sticking out of him like hat hooks on a church porch."

"But this woman did not!" Bellfield grunted. "See the bullet mark, where it went in, and the big hole where it came out. The powder burns and where it all but set alight to the poor wife's bonnet?" He looked up at the gathering around the grave. "The bastard all but took her head off. Gentlemen, we are now chasing a murderer. A woman killer!"

Anyone watching the gruesome scene that Bellfield had instigated would undoubtedly have been shocked. Now, dust worn and tattered with the long ride, together with the drawn expressions, one might have thought they had come upon a surreal incarnation of the place where lost souls reside. The skirts of Bellfield's expensive long jacket had become ribboned and frayed and his face streaked with grime. It was the same for all.

Horses were tired and wilting in the heat and had not been watered for some time. Grazing had been scarce and occasional and the animals were fast losing condition.

Hardly surprising then that at this latest incarnation of the man's will, a couple of men refused to go further. It started when Bellfield ordered the re-interring of the Morgensons while he sat astride his horse, waiting to be off once more. The two men defined for the duty refused, adding that they were not there to play either the mortician or the grave digger just on his say so, and were returning to a Christian place, and if he did not like it, he could go to hell and stay there.

A shocked Bellfield told them that they were fired and could whistle the 'stars and stripes' for their months outstanding pay, but as their horses were his, they must walk back and risk all on shoe leather, and if they decided to steal those horses, they were no better than the man they hunted and he would order them shot down like the thieves they were.

Deerbolt tried to calm the situation and asked consideration from all sides, making it clear that no one would be shot while he was the Marshal. Bellfield then told him that such employment might easily be terminated should support for the project be reduced in mind and spirit.

As the argument proceeded around the grave of the two unfortunates, the reverend's internal juices groaned as his bodily functions deteriorated and the whole group jumped for the sky and would have stayed there had gravity not been invented. To say the incident caused a fluctuation of courage would probably be exaggerating.

Before long, reason was seen. Deerbolt and a deputy took on the responsibility to see the Morgensons off once more in their search for infinity and although the task was performed without the care that Will Standing had taken, they were laid to rest for the final time, minus the boards that had covered them to deter predation, or the board that carried their name. Time was pressing.

The two itinerants went on their way, plus their horses, after Deerbolt convinced Bellfield that it might be prudent not to shoot them or explain why they had disappeared. Indians would be the perfect excuse, he agreed, but with the passage of time, someone was bound to talk and if Wyoming became a state, as was likely the following year, a circuit judge might not be poor enough to bribe.

So, the wagon was ransacked for a third time, with diminishing results and what remained of the Bellfield party continued on their way.

Chapter Eleven
A Sorry Sight

Down among the big stones, the Cheyenne could see the figure approaching. He was certain it was the same white man from the buffalo gulch and wondered how he had evaded them. He watched for some time, his eyes mainly upon the big black horse that the man rode, far too good for a 'white eye'.

The animal was something he had never seen before, not the range ponies or the stolen cavalry mounts that many favoured, or even the southern mustangs with their famous stamina. Cross bred horses of all of these had been prized by the Crow and stolen on raids but none had any of the dash and beauty of this animal and he wondered how it had been achieved, unaware that Arabian stock was the catalyst.

To this Cheyenne, the horse had now become the prize, the object of his dreams, the magnificent creature he desired that the women would sing songs about, with he on its back and rushing to battle with the wind chasing them. Soon, he would make the horse his.

Focussing again on the rider of the black horse, he saw the bedraggled creature that he was, tall, but thin and bent over the saddle horn. He saw the man pull up his mount to search for something and put it to his eye, and then found himself trading eye contact. They stayed that way for some moments, then the Cheyenne saw the rifle, the Sharps long gun that spoke long after the bullet was heard or received, so far did it shoot. The man braced the rifle on his knee and stayed that way to make the point that he welcomed battle.

It was a test that the Cheyenne must deny. Since Fort Wallace, their mediocre weapons had no ammunition to fill them, and many had been thrown away, relying on more traditional skills to produce the same effect. Going up against a long gun with only a lance would invite the inevitable and was stupid unless numbers were vastly on your side and another might take the impact of a round meant for you.

The Cheyenne ran over to where the children sat on the ground and cut their tether with a knife, then hauled the young boy towards the rock that he had used to support himself in his observations. In one movement he grabbed Tom by the loose fabric of his jacket collar and thrust him over the rock so that his legs dangled into thin air and scrambled to find purchase on the stone. The warrior pulled a feather from his headdress and thrust it into Tom's thick head of hair. The point had been made. Both antagonists watched each other for a few seconds, then the boy saw his uncle turn the black horse away.

For the moment, the white who followed was held at bay and with him the long gun. The Cheyenne knew it was not over; he had travelled too far, followed on their tracks, overcome distance and the wilderness to give up now. The time would come and the horse would be his, of that he had no doubt.

***

Midnight carried Will Standing some way back, almost to where the yellow of the plain met the green of the hills. At noon, he halted and dismounted, feeling that he was far enough back along the trail and out of range of the binoculars that the Cheyenne had. To make sure, he had used every stand of trees and rocks that he found to cover his retreat, but now knew where to pick up their tracks, up along the big boulders and along that line of evergreens that he had memorised in his mind's eye. He would give it time, maybe until mid-afternoon when he was sure they would have moved on, and then retrace his steps and hope that Midnight would pick up the lost time.

He had felt disheartened when he had seen Tommy held above the rock, fearing that similar threats might be put to him if the situation arose once more. Standing wondered how the boy felt, used in such a way, helpless and lost and counting upon him as their only hope. He wondered about Alice and how she fared, having only a fleeting glance of her at the gully.

Standing knew his disadvantages, knew that the weight of stealth lay with the Cheyenne. This was their country and they knew it better than he ever could. But why did they not take him? They had the advantage of numbers, and the possession of the children. He knew that they had firearms, taken from the buffalo hunters, so why did they not just come at him and finish it?

It was a guess but the only conclusion was the long gun. Buffalo rifles used cartridges with plenty of black powder grains for a long shot, but those hunters killed the animals from horseback where the guns could be less powerful and the cartridges cheaper to buy, and were probably army carbines with somewhere around a fifty-grain cartridge. Such firearms had the reputation of having a trajectory like a rainbow, good up to five hundred yards, but a bitch over that.

Drawing on those who hunted him had seemed like a good idea at the time, but Will Standing felt that maybe he had mistimed things to the extent that they would not be there when he needed reinforcement. And how did he know that they would be willing to stand if and when the time came? Did they want his neck that much? Instead of evening the odds, maybe he was doubling them.

By mid-afternoon, Standing guessed it would be safe to return. He doubted they would stay in one place for long, unless they intended to lay in wait and finish it, but he had little choice. The Cheyenne seemed to have some place to be and wanted to be there soon with the spoils of their raid on Fort Wallace, so he had to take the chance. Just in case, he decided that he would make it back to the foothills and sit out the night there, then find fresh tracks in the morning.

About to follow his strategy, he climbed up on Midnight's back and pulling out the telescope, took a look back to where the long grass swayed into the distance. Far out, too far to make a distinct observation, he saw a flash, maybe the sun glinting on polished metal, the barrel of a rifle maybe. He stood in the stirrups to gain height but it did not help, and yet he knew what it meant.

"Well, it's about God-damn time!" He said to himself.

***

After the incident at the rocks, the Cheyenne mounted up and instead of climbing higher, followed the contours of the slope they traversed. There had been heated conversation again and Tom could reason clearly that Uncle Will was the subject. He tried to understand from the occasional sign language that he caught what their plan might be, but he found it too complicated to follow and kept an eye on their direction to see if he could fathom it out.

Around mid-day, they halted. The leader once more came to the children and gave them water, but no food. Tom still ached from the beating he had and found any contact with these people difficult, but decided, if only for his sister's sake to ease the burden of their situation.

When the warrior offered Tom the water bag, the boy pointed to his chest.

"Tom," he said, and pointed then at the Cheyenne.

The man looked quizzically for a moment and then spoke in his own language.

"Hotoa'oxhaa'astaestse," the warrior said, slapping a fist on his chest.

Tom shook his head and tried to pronounce the name but failed so miserably that the man grinned. It was the first time that the boy had seen this in any of the Cheyenne. The man stood and put a palm over his head, raising the palm higher, then lowering it and doing the same continually. Tom tried to figure it out.

"Big, bigger, high, taller…"

The Cheyenne then hunched over and curled his fingers, and put them on either side of his head to mimic a bison. Tom tried for the second word.

"Buffalo, bull…" he said aloud and pointed at the warrior. "I think you are called High Buffalo, Big Buffalo, Tall buffalo, or High Bull."

The Cheyenne just shrugged, left it there and walked away. In fact, Tom had been close, for the leader's name was Tall Bull.

***

In the army, they called it Corporal's law, when every darn thing went against you despite your best effort to make it right. It felt that way now for Will Standing, pressed by those up ahead, and now those who hunted him. But was that not what he planned? Suddenly everything was closing in like the jaws of a vice, and he in the middle. Even the sun seemed to delay the time until dark as he did not want to get too close to the hills before dusk.

He moved slowly when approaching the lower slopes again, keeping to as much cover as possible until he felt that night had given him the benefit of invisibility. He dismounted and walked Midnight up the slope until he found a place that felt at least a little secure, open ground to one side and a finger of evergreen trees to the other. He decided that this was perhaps the best of both worlds, if at some stage he needed cover or the open ground to give Midnight his head in a pursuit. A low rise further down would shield him from any unwanted guests, so he felt that he had chosen the halt wisely. As always, a fire was out of the question, but he risked taking the saddle from the horse's back. He had ridden without one before and it held no worry for him should the necessity arise.

130

Sitting with his back against the saddle he stretched out his legs and looked up at a half-moon, surrounded by a million stars. He reached back and decided to eat something now that the excitement of fear had subsided, but before he touched the saddle bag, he heard something in the trees, a crack of twig or a hoof beat, or both.

Slowly he hunkered down and felt for the handle of the Colt, sliding it through his belt and over his abdomen. Blurring his eyes into the evergreens to detect the slightest movement, he heard it again, closer and more distinct. It was only yards away.

The branches parted and a figure appeared.

"You look a sorry sight, sonny," a voice said.

It was a fair comment considering Will Standing's appearance, dark stained with blood and dirty with dust and sweat, with several days of beard growth to add to the general neglect.

"Then slide out into the open where I can see you…" Standing said, wondering if they had caught up with him at last.

"Aaah, you can put that cannon away, sonny, I ain't figuring to do no harm."

In the half light of the moon, Standing could see the form of a man emerging, hauling a mule and a horse. The mule was packed with cargo of some kind that was hard to make out. Standing watched for more, but he seemed to be alone.

"Who are you?" He asked.

The man seemed to proceed with pulling his animals from the timber with little concern for Will's pistol that was aimed in his direction.

"Wilson's the name," he said, turning to face the other. "Elisondro Wilson if you want my full title, but I answer most times to just Eli, it being a condition imposed upon me by my late father, who appeared to like the name without consideration to the likings that his son might favour."

Will could see the man clear now that he was closer. He was an older man, totally dressed in skin clothing, fabricated from the hides of one deceased creature or another and wore a fur cap which Standing felt too hot for the current climate. His hair was long and his beard considerable and grey, adorned with a moustache that blended in well. He stood just a yard away and looked down into the eye of the Colt.

"I would consider it well if you would allow me the benefit of a cordial conversation, seeing as how I have not spoken to a white man these eighteen months or so, or maybe more; I tend to lose the time up in these parts."

Will Standing felt uneasy, but he seemed harmless enough, and certainly cordial in his manner. Still, he let the Colt drop to one side so that he could reach it quickly. The man kept talking as he dropped the load from the mule and unsaddled the horse.

"A white skin is considered unwelcome round these parts," he went on, "unless he has some way to redirect the disadvantage. It is a situation that I have pondered on for some time and I think..." He turned to the prone man on the ground. "Am I talking too much? You must advise me when I am talking too much."

Will made a small laugh. He found the man's language strange and almost comedic.

"No," he said, "but keep it low, there may be Indians around."

Wilson dropped his saddle to the ground and looked across.

"There be Indians hereabouts, you'd be short your hair by now. I can smell 'em, hear 'em, understand 'em, and on occasion I have loved 'em, when I was a younger man, of course, but that's another story."

Wilson looked around to intensify his next question.

"I see you are on your own in this area, it is not an advisable manner of travel, if you take my word for it. I have seen many go under for such a mistake."

"But you are alone out here?" Standing asked.

The man stroked his beard and raised his brows. He pushed back the fur cap and fell back against his saddle, resting on one arm.

"Been up here a long time, but I'm I' old and the cold is getting through to old bones. Figuring maybe I should winter in a warmer place, that's if they'll have me."

"You a trapper?"

"Trapper, hunter, trader, I do most things that will sustain a body through a lifetime. And what better place to do so but these mountains?" He looked across at Will Standing. "What brings you up here?"

Standing hardly knew where to start. It now seemed confused and without direction.

"Chasing children," he told the man. "Days ago, the Cheyenne hit my sister's place, killed all but two and took 'em captive, a niece and a nephew. Twelve and fourteen. I was told they attacked Fort Wallace and broke up to raid all the way back to where they come from. Trailed 'em all the way across Wyoming to here." He paused. "Is this still Wyoming?"

Wilson shook his head.

"Wyoming, Dakota maybe," he said. "Either way you're on a hiding to nothing. Your chances of getting back those kids on your own are less than poor, if that."

"What will happen to them if I don't?" Will asked.

Eli frowned.

"Oh, if you want the truth it ain't pretty," he began. "The girl will be sold to one of the young bucks, or traded with the Sioux, but either way she'll be a slave until puberty and then, well you can guess the rest. The boy, if he's strong, might last a while depending on his age. At fourteen, he'll be too old to forget his white ways and turn wild, so they'll work him hard, put him with the women and whipped into menial stuff."

"Then I have to get them back."

"You can try, and good luck with that," Wilson told him.

In truth the fate of the children was something that he had often considered. He had heard those things before and never doubted the reality of it.

"Do you get by with the Cheyenne?" He asked. "You trade skins with 'em? And kept your hair?"

"I do that, on occasion," Wilson confirmed.

"How?"

"Oh, I carry a couple of bottles every now and then, along with other trade things. They don't shut me down because they know I'll turn up again some time with another couple. It gets me through." He paused. "I trade elk hides, lynx, beaver maybe, but never buffalo. You hunt buffalo in these hills, you won't last long."

"I've seen that already," Will agreed.

"I trade with the Crow too, and the Cheyenne don't like that, but a bottle usually forgives the misdemeanour," Eli said. "Good thing you don't work a fire, all the same, not around here. No sense in advertising."

Will drew the arrow from his belt, and handed it over to Wilson.

"I keep that to tell me I'm on the right track."

Wilson looked at it with hard eyes. He blinked and looked up.

"Sonny, you've set yourself a mark you can't hit," he explained. "This is no regular Cheyenne you're after, this is the mark of dog soldiers."

"Dog soldiers?"

"The Cheyenne have six societies, all with their own ways. Some are political, some deal with stuff like maintaining the religious ways, and then you have the dog men. They are the first line of attack and the last line of defence for a clan, great warriors with reputations for never surrendering, never giving up. Women and kids look up to 'em like knights in armour. Damn handsome devils and the finest horsemen you ever laid eyes on." He looked at the fletching on the arrow stump again. "They carry a long sash, wrapped around their body, and if they get in a spot they can't get out of, they pin it to the ground with a sacred arrow, not unlike this one, like telling the enemy that this is it, no surrender, no retreat. You're lucky you're still alive, sonny."

"Do you have any advice on how I should proceed?" Will asked.

Wilson nodded.

"Go home, while you still can."

Standing glanced back down and across to where the high plains stretched out in the darkness. He had done so several times.

"Something back there stopping you?" Eli asked.

"It's a long story about a quick decision."

Midnight had stepped over to the new arrivals and Wilson looked across.

"Damn fine animal," he said. "A young buck would cut off his waterworks for a ride like that."

Will agreed.

"I guess that's why I'm still breathing, thanks to that horse."

Standing fished back into the saddle bag.

"You hungry?" He asked. "Only got cold beans but you're welcome to those."

Eli Wilson grinned as he was thrown a can. He caught it and proceeded to attempt the opening with a knife drawn from his belt.

"After Lord knows how many months of elk, beans is a welcome departure."

Will Standing followed his example and they devoured the beans with relish, cold though they were.

"Mister Lincoln still president of the country?" Eli asked.

Standing shook his head.

"Lincoln was shot. In the head. Back in sixty-five," he told him. "You been up here that long?"

"I guess so," Wilson answered, without surprise of the late president's demise. "Damn shame, unless you hailed for the other side."

They finished the beans. Will thought about it for a moment, then said…

"You ever eaten pineapple?"

"Pine what?"

"Pineapple, it's a fruit or vegetable, I guess, grown by ladies in grass skirts on an island in the ocean. I have some if you want to try it. I have never had any myself before but I sure would like to."

Will fished for the tin.

"Pine…apple," Eli asked. "You mean apples grown on pine trees?"

Will shrugged off the question as he struggled to cope with the sealed lid.

"I don't rightly know," he said, "but from the picture on the tin, if one of those ripened and fell off, and you were under it, you'd sure have a headache for the rest of the day."

He managed to unlock the contents and offered over the tin for Eli to scoop out some of the irregular pieces. The man put them gingerly into his mouth and his eyes lit up with the result.

"Lord, something that good can't be no good for your innards…"

Standing too had his first taste and agreed. He changed the direction of the conversation.

"You ever see white captives with the Cheyenne?" Will asked.

A sad expression folded Wilson's face into a frown.

"I have," he answered. "But Indians got their own ways, just like a Christian white. There're things that an Indian sees the whites doing that they'd never understand and the other way around. Both end up in the same direction, mostly. The Cheyenne hates the buffalo skinners, but I seen Cheyenne and Sioux drive a whole herd off a cliff, buffalo jumps they call 'em, then fill their bellies and leave the rest for the coyotes and the wolves."

"All right for the coyotes and wolves, I guess," Will said. "They ever treat captives well?"

"Oh, I guess," Eli answered. "An Indian is the product of his fathers, just like other folks. Whites are the same. They all have their whims and preferences, depending on their moods at any given time. And they see no fault in living life in this place just like their kin did, stealing horses, taking captives and such, all for reasons that go back thousands of years. They condemn whites for stealing their land, and rightly so, but the Sioux took land from the Cheyenne way back, the Cheyenne from the Crow, all going round in one big circle. But they have their own morals, their own ways of thinking, and I for one can't find much fault in it."

They finished the pineapple and laughed at the unusual taste that both had been introduced to and the tin was emptied quickly. Slowly the conversation died and a kind of sleep passed the time until first light.

Elisondro Wilson was the first to wake as the dawn broke. Standing fell into sleep later, with much on his mind, and so responded to a gentle kick from his strange visitor. He shook himself into the advancing twilight and looked around, making his first task to check the distant plains with the telescope.

"Always believed in waking early," Wilson said over his shoulder, busying himself with his horse and the mule. "Never had much mind with wastrels that slept late and wasted a day. Course, winter is different from the warmer months and just keeping a body from freezing is work in itself, least that's what it feels like from my perspective, old as I am."

Will Standing saw no sign of the chasers and laughed to himself, amused at Eli Wilson's views on the world around him. He continued.

"The Almighty never intended Christian men to sing on Sundays when there's traps to be checked and beaver skinned. Prayer never took a horse to water or milked a cow, no matter how many times you say it. All I see in religion is the employment of rascals that are big on bluster and short on anything else, and when my time comes, I want none around my tombstone."

Will glanced over to him, a question on his face.

"Is it Sunday?" He asked. "I kind of lost the days…"

Eli turned to face him and shrugged his shoulders.

"How the hell do I know?"

It grew lighter and they shared another tin of cold beans. Wilson had packed his load back on the mule and was tightening the straps to keep steady. Will faced him on the other side of Midnight and was employed in a similar manner.

"Well, I thank you for your company, Eli, and the advice. Where to now?"

Eli slapped the mule on the rump.

"Ooh, I'd like to see the Canadas. Getting too crowded around here. Time was I'd never see a white face for five or six years, now I come across one every ten, fifteen months. Hope to get over the line by winter, find somewhere warm, then set out fresh by spring. They say beaver's still good up there." He paused and looked solemnly over at Will Standing. "If I was you, I would accept the inevitable and leave things be. Tragedy has ways of making more tragedy."

It was hard advice.

"I guess I've come too far to give up now," he said. "And those kids know I'm here so how can I give up on 'em?"

Eli nodded, knowing further discouragement was useless.

"Well, if you fight 'em, do it on the flat, where you can make a chance with that long gun. Don't fight 'em in the timber, or they'll come at you from all sides and you won't see 'em."

"I will remember that."

"And if you see a riderless horse coming at you, shoot him," Eli advised, "and if you put one on the ground, put another in him to make sure. Dog men don't die easy."

Standing tightened his lips to acknowledge the words. Eli was almost finished with the strapping.

"I seen dog soldiers go up against the Crow once," he said, the first beams of sunlight creeping across the open spaces, "No one can lick 'em on horse, or few on the ground close up, why I…"

He cut off mid-sentence. Will Standing looked up from tightening his own girth, waiting for the culmination of the story. Eli was looking across over his shoulder. Will turned to see what had caught his attention. Up on the rise, a hundred yards away, sat four mounted Cheyenne, their painted faces and feathers catching the sunlight. Each sat with a shield and lance presented forward, but Will could see the tips of bows and the stocks of stolen rifles. It was a moment that froze both white men.

"What now?" Standing asked.

"Just keep working," Eli said, "Don't make a move for a gun, just mount up and maybe we can talk our way out of this."

"What?"

"I told you I have had an intercourse with the Cheyenne. I know the one up on the left, Chases the Otter is what they call him, knew him before he went up with the dog clan. He was a mean bastard then and I don't guess he's changed much, but he likes a bottle when there's one available."

"You have one?"

"Nope." It was a disappointing answer. "But maybe I can convince them that I might have soon. Might just be a chance I can lower the tone a little, make like we want to trade something for those kids, these elk pelts are first order. All depends on how they woke up this morning." He paused. "The one with the fancy hair piece is called Tall Bull, they all look up to him, so maybe I can appeal to his better nature. Don't recall the others."

"I can't pay you for those pelts…" Will told Eli.

The trapper shrugged.

"Can't pay you for the beans," he replied.

The Cheyenne just sat their mounts, as if waiting for others to make the first move. Will guessed that if it were not for Eli's presence, he would be dead by now.

"There were five, I'm sure of it," he said, "so there's another somewhere, probably with the children."

Eli Wilson climbed onto his horse. He looked down.

"Mount up, but stay well behind me. If anything kicks away, ride as fast as that damn horse will carry you, and remember what I said."

"I will."

Eli rode slowly towards the four mounted Cheyenne who were some feet above him on the low ridge. Standing followed behind and halted halfway, placing himself so that he could see everything and yet have an avenue of retreat.

"Haaahe (Hello there)," Wilson began the talking, but there was no response from any of the Cheyenne. "E-peve-voona'a (It's a good morning)."

"Hene'eenoseoneve (Know me)," he said, slapping his chest. "God-damn my poor Cheyenne."

"Mahatamaahe! (Old woman)," Tall Bull said, looking down at Wilson.

"What's he saying?" Standing asked.

Eli turned his horse around gently, so that he was sideways on to both the Cheyenne and Will Standing. He jerked a shoulder.

"Oh, just the normal insults," he said, turning back to the warriors above and to his left.

There was an exchange of conversation which Standing could not understand nor interpret. Then Eli looked over to the rider on the black horse.

"He says you have the luck of a chased rabbit on ice and if you keep following you will find it gets thinner as you go," Eli said, then lowered his voice a little. "I take it you have had close dealings with them before today?"

"I seen 'em a couple of times," Will answered. "Tell them they killed my kin, but all I want is the children they took. I want no trouble with them, just the kids."

More conversation followed as the trapper did his best to interpret Standing's request. It went on for some time. He turned back to Will.

"Tall Bull says he ain't got nuthin' against a trade, but it's against his principles to go back to the women without a respectable haul. I told him he could have the elk skins but he said he has enough of those and I can shove 'em in a place that I find hard to interpret."

Standing swallowed hard, wondering where this was going, but at least they were still talking.

"He says he likes your horse," Eli went on, "he knows it's something special, that's why he's willing to parley, and he might consider something along that street if you're willing."

Will leant forward in the saddle.

"What do you think?"

The trapper dropped his head to one side. Up above there seemed to be impatience between the warriors.

"It's a risky 'hard to say'. I wouldn't want to be afoot in this country with a couple of kids strung along. Once you've got traded, it all depends on what mood they got up in this morning." He looked directly at the other white man. "They got their own ways. Once a trade is done, all bets are off and throwing the die for the next one. It's a hard choice, sonny."

"Then I'm back where I started," Will said. "Tell him it's not my horse, so I can't trade it."

Wilson laughed.

"I kind of figured that one out already."

He returned to the Cheyenne and turned them into words that Tall Bull could understand. The warrior exploded in a peal of laughter and replied.

"He says his horse belonged to somebody else too, afore he took it off 'em," Eli said.

Tall Bull called down again and the trapper listened until he was done.

"He says, 'what about that long gun on your saddle horn, he'd maybe let you have one of the kids for that, and you can choose which one', although he'd prefer to keep the boy."

Will Standing shook his head.

"Amounts to the same thing, doesn't it? If I agree, he'd know I don't have much ammunition for the damn thing, but he would have the advantage over me before I got a mile away. And anyway, it's both or none."

"I would consider your response," Eli said, "sounds kind of like an ultimatum, and I doubt he'd take kindly to that."

"Tell him," Will said.

Wilson paused in thought for a moment, then looked at Will again.

"I tell him that, seems like we're done, but maybe we were done before it started," he said. "Truth is he's never taken his eyes off that black horse since we first talked."

"Tell him," Will insisted.

Eli nodded and pulled down his fur cap.

"All right. Now when this is finished, I'm letting go the mule and kicking this horse in the slats and making for those trees. I ain't got a fast ride like you got, so I look to cover for my survival. I have two Remington pistols beneath this coat and a Spencer carbine to boot. I would advise you to use the ground and make speed your deliverance, and I wish you luck." He grinned. "Now, I'm goin' to tell him to shove his lance up his ass, so git!"

Will Standing decided to wait for Eli to make his move first. He gingerly moved his hand to the Colt's Walker in his belt and felt for the smooth grip. The trapper waited a moment and seemed to be summoning the will to begin. Then he turned his head slowly up to the warriors above and shouted something that they found hard to ignore, initiating a shriek of response and four painted horsemen exploded in attack.

Midnight shied at the sudden noises and half reared as Eli Wilson did exactly as he had intended, releasing the mule and spurring his horse towards the timber. Will's Colt was in his hand and he fired into the oncoming war party without aiming, hoping it might deter them as he pulled the black horse's head around.

Already down on his level, the Cheyenne gained speed and a lance caught the trapper in the side before he had gone far, and unseated him from the horse. The mule was rolled over in the advance of the charge and struggled to rise but was hampered by the load on its back, its legs thrashing aimlessly to find some purchase.

Eli Wilson turned onto his back as the warriors passed, and he managed to find his Remingtons under the folds of his coat. Throwing his head back, he fired up at the warrior leaping his horse over him and hit with both shots in the belly of the animal, which fell heavily on the ground almost beside him, throwing the rider. Wilson turned onto his side and aimed again at the rising warrior but a fifty calibre from a stolen carbine finished the issue and it was all over.

Already the other three Cheyenne were pursuing the black horse and its rider, who had gained ground. The fallen warrior took the trapper's horse and gave chase after the others while the mule still kicked in its attempts to get back on its legs.

Will Standing rode out onto the open ground and towards the long grass that he had so recently crossed. Midnight galloped as if running on air and proved why the animal was so prized. His head moved in unison with the blur of his legs and covered the ground with the ease of the wind. The man on his back bent over the withers and tried to make himself weightless to help the horse, the Sharps rifle thumping against his leg.

Somewhere behind painted horses and shrieking warriors raced to catch them. Will heard a gunshot and the whine of a bullet pass somewhere near, but out of his vision, Tall Bull admonished the shooter for risking the horse.

For almost fifteen minutes the pace hardly slackened, and Will felt the foam on the horse's neck wet on his face. He risked a look back and saw the Cheyenne had already slowed to a halt some way back, either resting before continuing or giving up. He doubted the latter, but hauled back on the rein to give Midnight a breather.

The horse danced to a halt and Standing looked back. The Cheyenne were almost a mile away on blown horses, but watching him still. Now, it was his turn. He dismounted and unhooked the Sharps and the hessian bag behind the saddle. Reaching in he found a cartridge, then fished for a percussion cap. Pulling the hammer to half cock with the lever beneath the trigger, he pushed the cap onto the nipple, drew back to full cock and inserted the cartridge as the breech opened. He returned the lever to its closed position and the block closed, snipping the end of the cartridge and allowing black powder to spill into the pan. He blew away the excess and flipped up the sight, screwing the adjuster and estimating the distance. He guessed just under the mile, perhaps sixteen hundred yards. Will slowly thumbed the screw and hoped against a misfire.

The Cheyenne had seen him dismount and slowly urged their tired horses forward again, ready to make up the distance. Midnight shied.

"Whoaa! Easy."

Standing walked a little way from his animal and knelt onto the ground, parting the long stalks that might hinder his aim. He pulled the Sharps into his shoulder and held it tight, knowing the effect of the recoil. He gauged the distance now at coming up to fifteen hundred and readjusted for fourteen. That far, it was hard to make out individual riders and he hoped to go for the leader, but reducing the number against him was more important so he decided upon the one on the left, who seemed less animated than the others and a fuller target. On they came, dark shadows against the background.

Will looked down the barrel, lining the front sight with the back and the target. When he thought that the distance was accurate, he pulled the trigger and felt the thump into his shoulder. The ignition of the cartridge was deafening, black powder grains impelling the bullet forward and over the long grass at the oncoming Cheyenne.

The bullet hit the man clean in the chest, left of centre, smashing the bone breastplate that he wore and shattering his scapula as it exited. The rider went backwards over his horse's rump and fell in a heap in the grass, his shield and weapons scattered around him.

Behind the four Cheyenne, the fifth warrior had heard the sound of battle and was bringing up the mules carrying the children, unwilling to miss the action. Tom had seen the body of the trapper and wondered who he was, seen the thrashing mule and heard gunshots and the whoops and shrieks of the attacking Cheyenne.

Will had seen his first man go down. He dropped the long gun and started to reload, but time was not on his side as the oncoming warriors whipped their mounts into the gallop before the next round could be fired. Looking down, Will's nervous fingers fumbled with the percussion cap and then the cartridge, snapping up the lever to cut the end and allow black powder into the pan. He looked up again and could only see two mounted warriors, and a riderless horse to the left coming on. He immediately thought it was the mount of the first shot, but could see that animal way over to his left, fleeing from the commotion. They were closing and he shifted the sight to line up one of the mounted Cheyenne, but remembered Eli's warning. Gritting his teeth, he held his breath and fired, dropping the light-coloured horse in its tracks as the body overtook the head and did a somersault into the ground. As the horse fell, he realised that Wilson had been right, as the rider of the horse had dropped to the animal's side, hooked a leg over the withers and could shoot him easily from under the animal's neck.

The rider hit the ground and the horse on top of him, smashing bone and flesh. The animal rolled and returned to an upright position, its belly on the ground and legs splayed in all directions. An arrow zipped past Standing's shoulder and he knew that he was now in bow range. They were close.

Will reached for the Colt, but the smooth grip was not there, lost in the long grass when he had dismounted. He looked around to see that the black horse had run a short way off at the noise and the commotion of combat, too far to reach with safety. As more arrows hit the ground close by, he decided to run to the downed horse for cover and made good progress despite hunching over to make his profile smaller. As he closed with the animal, he saw the rider, still alive and reaching for an army carbine a few feet away. It was too far and the Cheyenne drew a knife. Standing beat him to it, picked up the rifle, drew back the hammer and shot him dead.

The third Cheyenne, with the children had caught up with the others. Will smiled to himself. At least he had lessened the odds, and now it was only three to one, but he knew it was all over. He had nothing left and nowhere to go.

Chapter Twelve
What Days May Come

The Bellfield party advanced with torn clothes and tired animals. Once more the grassland stretched ahead of them and the ride was monotonous and long. Those blue hills now seemed darker, closer and they were two men light and apart from that Bellfield at the end of their tether. Water had been scarce for some time and they travelled dry and hungry, with hardly any let up from their leader and only the loss of a month's pay keeping most going. And even those felt the comfort of a good night's sleep overcoming the means to pay for it.

"Mr Bellfield," Marshal Deerbolt said, pulling level with the man. "We can't go much further. The pack animals are empty, we got hardly any water left and we still haven't seen a hair of Will Standing. It's over."

Deerbolt pulled up his animal and it stood with drooped head.

"I suggest we make the hills the end, find water up there and give it up. I'm sorry about that damn horse, but we go any further we might not get back."

Bellfield had hauled up and looked open-mouthed across to the other man. He spoke slowly and intensely.

"Deerbolt. You are fired. You are no longer the Marshal of Dogwood. You yellow son of a bitch. I heaped up the votes for you and I can heap them down again. You want to go back, then go back, and good riddance to you."

The Marshal heard the words. He was almost past caring.

"Sir, you could die out here. It has become foolhardy and I believe you are headstrong beyond your ways. That black horse has become all in your mind and I think you should be free of it and look to turning back."

There was agreement behind from most of the others, who felt the same way.

"Then damn you all!" He grunted. "I will go on alone!"

He pulled his horses head around and put his spurs to its side and it moved slowly forward. The rest remained halted, with horses at rest. Then a shot rang out across the plains, then another. Belfield turned in the saddle and pointed towards the not-so-distant hills.

"Do you hear that?"

***

Will Standing watched the Cheyenne horsemen moving towards him. He was torn and worn and covered in blood and dirt and sweat. He had nothing left but the knowledge that he had failed the children, failed everyone and must now pay the price.

The warriors were in no hurry, he knew that and knew it would not be quick. He could now at least see the two small figures on the mules and wondered what they had been through since he last spoke to them.

The sun was high and probably around mid-morning. He wondered what day he was dying on and could not remember. Saturday, Sunday, Friday, maybe. But he would not go down easy, he would not make it easy for them. One last glance over at Midnight. The black horse was some way off and looking over, the light catching blue off his dark hide. 'Lord, what a fine animal'. Standing smiled at the thought.

He bent over wearily and found the knife, pulled the sash from around the waist of the dead Cheyenne, stepped over the horse and found the stump of the arrow that he had kept from the cabin, still in his belt. Wrapping the sash once around his own waist, he pinned the other end to the dry ground with the broken arrow, just as Eli told him the dog soldiers did when there was no hope left.

He called out, "Come on then, let's finish it!"

The Cheyenne fanned out twenty yards ahead of him with the children and their mules some way back. They sat astride their ponies, feathered and fit, almost naked and devoid of their clothing, as was their custom when formally arrayed for battle. Tall Bull heeled his animal forward a little ahead of the others and dropped his head to one side. He held the position for a moment and then reversed his lance and stuck it point first into the ground. He started to speak, turning his horse sideways to his enemy and riding a short distance, then returned the opposite way, parading in front of Will Standing as if admonishing him. All of the time he was spreading his palms as if in some kind of explanation that he could not understand.

145

Tall Bull cast a hand back to the children and then pointed at him, and then over to where the black horse stood. He pulled the horse's head around and came a step closer. All of the time, Will waited for the inevitable. Then Tall Bull galloped off to where Midnight stood and slipped down from his own horse, took a knife and sliced off the saddle, letting it fall to the ground. Pulling one of the grey feathers from his head piece, he slipped it into the bridle and secured it, then sprung in one fluid movement onto the horse's back with a piercing yell. Midnight reared at the forceful physical commands that he was unused to, but settled as the Cheyenne rode him back. Again, Will was treated to a parade from Tall Bull, again the admonishment or whatever it was that he hardly understood.

Gunshots. One of the Cheyenne pointed across the plain. Tall Bull turned on the back of the black horse to look. It was a group of riders, the smoke from the discharge of their firearms visible as white smoke. He made one last gesture to Will Standing, then with a scolding gesture galloped back to where the mules were with the children on their backs. The Cheyenne halted, reached over and pulled Tom off the animal and dropped him to the ground. Another warrior did the same for Alice, then as he made one final yell of defiance, Tall Bull led the Cheyenne and the mules off towards the Black Hills, leaving the children behind.

Will ran over to where the Sharps lay on the ground where he left it, together with the remaining three cartridges and the caps. He grabbed them and then ran over to where Tom and Alice lay on the grass.

"Uncle Will!"

Tommy stood and ran towards his uncle, dragging Alice behind him. Standing dropped to his knees and pulled them to his breast, the tears of relief staining the crust of blood and dirt on his face.

"You kids OK?" he asked.

Tommy was crying from the emotion of freedom and seeing his uncle. He nodded, unable to find the words. Alice seemed distant, as if none of this was happening.

Will Standing stepped to one side and pulled down the lever of the Sharps long gun, revealing the breech. He blew away the debris from the previous shot and went through the loading procedure, slipped in a cartridge, then replaced the percussion cap. He guessed the retreating Cheyenne at almost a thousand yards and fixed the rear sight at eleven hundred. He lifted the gun and put it into his shoulder, then lined up on the man mounted on the black horse. He waited for a moment and put his finger on the trigger and was about to pull.

Standing looked up. Tommy's hand was across the breech and holding back the hammer. He looked intensely into his uncle's eyes. Will could not quite understand it but the indication was clear. He smiled a little and jerked his head upwards to acknowledge what was being asked of him.

***

A hammering of hooves announced that the chase was over. Will Standing looked at the weary faces of those who had pursued him and now sat their horses above him, Bellfield looking out after his black horse that was now a Cheyenne war pony. Deerbolt dropped from the saddle and took the Sharps rifle from the man on the ground.

"Those kids all right?" He asked as he did so.

Standing nodded.

"They're alive."

Bellfield exploded.

"Bind him!" He ordered. "Somebody bring a rope, we'll hang him from the first tree we find!"

Deerbolt turned to look up at the bedraggled Bellfield.

"Nobody's hanging nobody," he told him. "If there's justice to be done, we'll deal with it in Dogwood. Wyoming will likely be a state by this time next year and we don't want it tainted by a lynching that none of us can justify or condone."

Bellfield thrust a finger down in his direction.

"You are the elected Marshal, now do you job. That man is a fraud, a horse thief, a murderer and more!"

Deerbolt gave a cold stare.

"You fired me remember. Now if you want to go get that damn horse of yours, there he is and you're welcome to do so, and nobody here is stopping you. Right now, my concern is returning those children to the civilised places and seeing them safe."

He pointed out to where the Cheyenne were still visible on the lower slopes of the Black Hills. Will Standing was too far gone to have worried about the crimes aimed at him. He hugged the children, and showed some concern about Alice.

"We have to take you back, Will," Deerbolt said. "Robbing a bank and horse thieving is something we just can't forgive or forget. Do I need to put you in chains?"

"I guess not," Will answered, promising not to try to escape, after all there were the children to consider.

"Will, don't fret about them when we get back," he promised. "My wife can't carry kids, and she'd be well fixed to look to 'em for as long as it takes."

Standing thanked him and felt assured. He hugged the children to him again, tightly. Smiling, he looked the children's faces.

"Look," he told them, "I gotta go someplace for a while, but I will come back for you, you know that?"

Tom nodded, with tears in his eyes. Will continued his promise.

"You go with Mr Deerbolt and be good kids till I get back. I know things have been hard, but you're back now and sometime soon we'll set things right. All right?"

There was little more to be said. Deerbolt saw the state of the children, ragged and rundown, who were smaller versions of themselves. He pulled over the depleted pack animals and gave one to Will and the other for Alice and Tom. He saw clearly the concern that Standing carried.

They made a slow ride to the hills until they found water, lay up for a while and then headed back the way they had come.

Bellfield sulked all the way back and spoke hardly to anyone, especially Deerbolt. No one was sorry that the ride was ending and looked forward to the sight of home on the horizon. They passed the old wagon that marked the demise of the Morgensons and all of the riders missed the single Prairie Falcon that swooped overhead, some way east of its normal range.

The return of the column when it rode through main street was welcomed with some interest. It passed the bank which now had eighty dollars to make up on its books, and Mr Bridey's store, where some said it had all begun. Whispers about the absence of a black horse were rife and the rumours were many about what had happened, expanded upon by those that were there.

The return coincided with the fourth of July and that night the town celebrated. The Longhorn drinking emporium did good business until well into the next morning and Miss Annabelle's laundry, which also doubled as an establishment of horizontal refreshment, suffered likewise.

For Will Standing, the single iron boudoir in the Marshal's office should have been his home until the circuit judge got there sometime in August. But with the current emergency it was decided to move him by an iron cage wagon to Fort Laramie, along with six armed deputies, furnished by Bellfield.

Chapter Thirteen
The Outlaw, William Standing

The cage wagon proved the most uncomfortable journey that Will Standing had experienced since being caught drunk and returned to his company two days after Fredericksburg in an army wagon. It had cost him a stripe, but he had won it back after delivering an urgent message to General Mead some months later. But, all things considered, he weathered it in the hope that at least the food might be better in an army establishment and the company more to his taste and satisfaction. He was wrong.

It was some weeks before the circuit judge was to appear, so Will had the time to reflect on his situation. He had no money, and due to his current limited travel arrangements, could hardly steal any, so hiring a lawyer to defend him was somewhat difficult. So, he set about going through it in his mind, adding his pluses on one side and his minuses on the other in the hope that one might outweigh the other, and it did. The only problem being that the heavy cup dropped on the minus side, the only satisfaction being that the court had little idea of the extent of his sins prior to those that were at that time being considered.

He worried about the kids and asked for writing materials in order to contact Deerbolt back in Dogwood, to be reassured as to their wellbeing. He was as far as he now knew, their only kin within a thousand miles. Henry had folks back in Virginia somewhere but he never mentioned them much or who they were, and so that side of the family remained a closed book. After a few days, one of the guards took pity on him and pushed what he had asked for through the bars. As his spelling needed attention, it took him some time to complete the task, which unfortunately proved a waste of time as he forgot the absence of revenue to cover the postage.

***

And so, the day came. Another Indian scare had come and gone, amounting to nothing much more than rumour, and the delay of supplies to the fort which included hard liquor. Not that it bothered William Standing much due to his present incarceration, but it did make the guards particularly short tempered, and were willing to take their frustrations out on any unfortunate that could not resolve them. This added to more delay until at last a defining moment came when Standing was advised that the day after tomorrow would be the date of his trial as the judge had now arrived, and after a little relaxation, would receive him then.

Along with his other charges, he was now considered a murderer. How this ever came about was a mystery to him, unless Tall Bull could be called as a witness to do him down, even though it was as far as he was concerned, self-defence.

It was nine-twenty when the iron door rattled open and he was chained, hands and feet, and made to hobble across the to the adjutant's office which had become the temporary court room. The place was the usual army building, log structured with less than professionally plastered walls inside and hung with poor reproductions of the late president and other military dignitaries.

Seating was considerable and Standing assumed that the whole of the regiment had been invited. At the far end had been placed a substantial desk, raised a foot by sawn logs to give a more judicial feeling to the procedure. Already in place on wooden forms were those who had assumed an interest in the case, including Alexander Bellfield, who had smartened himself up since the last time Will had seen him but still wore the same unfortunate grimace, which followed Standing to his seat at the front of the room, opposite and to the left of the desk.

Hardly had the defendant been shoved into the chair than a door at the back opened and the black coated figure of an elderly man entered with half rim spectacles and side whiskers that ran down the side of his face to the corners of his mouth. He hurried in as if late for dinner, took a quick and formal glance at Will Standing, then stepped up onto the dais that held the chair high enough to match the desk. Everyone stood, and so did the defendant, hardly wishing to set his case back even before it started.

The judge sat down, followed by the rest of the room. Books were shuffled and a gavel dropped with remarkable echo onto a wooden block.

"This court is in session. I am Judge Nicholas Flanders, presiding," he informed those present. "I apologise for the informal surroundings for this hearing, but with the current emergency it will have to do. We will take it for given that everyone here is obliged to tell the truth, the whole truth, and nothing but the truth or be fined one thousand dollars if the bastard is found not doing so."

A rumble of varying opinions went across the room and the gavel struck again.

"Now, as I understand it from my notes, we have the defendant William Standing, who is accused of the crimes of bank robbery, fraud, horse stealing and downright murder," he read, then through fumbled words, went on "and a few other things, such as loss of gambling and financial issues, which he attributed to Mr Bellfield, which I don't quite understand."

The judge looked around the room.

"Mr Bellfield, are you here today?"

Bellfield stood up.

"I am, Sir, and I can confirm that this man is the worst kind of…"

He was cut off by the weariness of judicial patience.

"Yes, yes, Sir. We will come on to that, but first we must deal with the main issues. William Standing, stand up."

Will stood and jangled the chains for effect.

"William Standing, do you plead guilty, or not guilty?"

The defendant looked at the judge, a question on his countenance.

"Well, Sir," he began. "I guess if you ask, did I rob that bank, I gotta say I did. If you ask, did I steal that horse, and a damn fine horse it was too, I gotta say I did. Now I don't kind of understand the fraud, seeing as how I just asked for a name on a paper, and as to the murder part I would sure like to know who it is I'm supposed to have done in, and when and how. I sure can't recall that one."

The judge looked at his notes.

"The deceased indicated here is a Mrs Morgenson. Late of somewhere east by all accounts, her origin is a little hazy. It is said that you shot that fine lady in the head by all accounts."

Will Standing's eyes widened. He threw up his hands.

"Now, now, Judge," he protested, "I did no murder on that woman, it was…"

Judge Flanders pressed down on the gavel again.

"Yes, yes, yes, Sir. This is not the time for detail," he said. "Now be seated and be quiet until spoken to. Now, to finalise the charges, did you indeed shoot that woman in the head, yes, or no?"

Standing felt the anguish of truth, with the weight of the law pressing down on him like a bar room bouncer.

"Yes, I did, but…"

The gavel again. Bellfield smiled to those around him.

"That is all we need to know, for now. Now sit and be quiet, or I will try this case with you back in the hole."

Bank robbery was bad enough, and horse stealing a hanging offence, but murder was something else. The fraud part and the other stuff bothered Will little, but he knew he was up against it, with no defence but his own testimony, and who would believe that?

"First witness, Mr Alexander Bellfield." The judge used the gavel to usher him to the inverted chair just to the right of his makeshift bar.

Bellfield had brought in his legal man from Dogwood, a man whose normal employment was land grabbing, rental increases and water manipulation on behalf of his master, by the name of Thaddeus Woodruff.

"Mr Woodruff," said the judge, "are you ready to question the witness?"

"Yes, Sir, Judge," he said walking over from his seat.

"Now, Mr Bellfield, you are the injured party in this case?"

"I am," He admitted. "Unless you consider the late Ms. Morgenson, who I have to admit is more injured than I am."

The reply drew a peal of laughter from those on the benches and it was halted by another gavel crack. Belfield enjoyed the part of comedian and smiled along.

"So, this whole sorry state of affairs began with the accused, William Standing, robbing the Dogwood Bank on the Saturday morning of your monthly horse race?"

"It did."

"Eighty dollars," Standing called out. "I took eighty dollars, that's all…"

Another gavel strike.

"William Standing!" said the judge. "If you call out one more time, I will find you guilty of all charges and send you to await the unfortunate outcome at the court's convenience. Do you understand?"

Standing remained silent.

"Please continue, Mr Woodruff."

"So, in your own words, Sir, please tell the court what happened on that Saturday morning."

Bellfield took a deep breath.

"Well, the race had all but finished, and that black horse, my black horse, had beat the others hands down, or hooves down whichever you prefer, and as always happens, the people gathered around waiting for the celebratory drink that I always accord them."

"And was William Standing among them?"

"No, Sir. He was robbing the bank…"

"Allegedly, Mr Bellfield, he has not yet been found guilty," the judge reminded him. "Allegedly."

"I believe Mr Standing has already pleaded guilty to horse theft and robbery, your honour," Woodruff replied.

"True, true, Mr Woodruff, but let us keep to the guidelines until we have tried the case," he ruled. "Please carry on, Mr Bellfield."

Bellfield did so.

"So, there was a pretty hoo-hah going on when I saw Standing steal that black horse and ride off on him, and just prior to this he obtained my name on a receipt for the money he just robbed."

The judge glanced across into the face of the accused.

"Why did you steal that horse, Mr Standing?"

"Well, Sir," Will began, "mine was a ways off, among them as was looking for who robbed the bank. I knew that horse could run and so I just took the opportunity to see how fast. I ask you, Judge, if you was in my predicament, what would you have done?"

It did not quite satisfy the question.

"And why did you commit the offence of bank robbery in the first place?"

"Necessity, I guess, Judge," he answered. "My sister and her husband were short on the money to pay the water rights. I only took eighty dollars. I could've took more…"

Judge Flanders raised his eyebrows.

"Very commendable of you, I'm sure," he said. "You mentioned water rights?"

"Well, Mr Bellfield over there, he—"

"Might we carry on with the witness, please judge?" Woodruff cut in and the judge acquiesced.

"Well, the Marshal," Bellfield paused, "the ex-Marshal, organised some people and we chased that thief clear to the Black Hills, where he was caught and apprehended. It was decided not to hang him right there but to commit the man to the justice that we will expect when we hope to become a state shortly."

"And the unfortunate Mrs Morgenson?" Flanders asked.

"Ah," said Bellfield, his eyes dropping to the floor in mock reverence. "Along the trail, we found a broken wagon belonging to the Morgensons. There appeared to have been some interaction with wild Indians, but the woman was obviously despatched with a firearm, with Standing's boot marks as proof."

And so it went on, not going well for the accused and he knew it. One after one, Bellfield's men bolstered their boss's story and heaped the worst upon him. The judge gave him the opportunity to speak and he did so, but every time he opened his mouth it seemed like he was adding to his own guilt.

At noon, they stopped the proceeding for lunch. Bellfield and Woodruff had brought their own victuals and found a shady corner of the parade ground to eat, followed by a reasonable red wine and as much of a cigar that they could smoke before resuming.

Towards the end of the day, Justice was becoming weary and Judge Nicholas Flanders sat back on the chair and was about to make his final summing up. He put down the gavel onto the block and asked if anyone had anything more to say. William Standing had a fair idea what the end product was going to be and had already weighed up the possibility of making a run for it, maybe exiting through the window and over to the stables in the hope that a mount might be available but the shackles put that idea to bed so he would have to think again.

Then a voice piped up somewhere behind and the prisoner turned to see who it was. Ex-Marshal Deerbolt was waiting to speak, his hat held respectfully in his hands.

"And who are you, Sir?" asked the judge.

"My name is Deerbolt, Your Honour, I was the Marshal in the town of Dogwood and I was with the group that followed after William Standing when he stole Mr Bellfield's horse."

"Come forward Mr Deerbolt," the judge said, "consider yourself sworn in."

Deerbolt walked towards the front of the room and took the witness chair. He glanced at William Standing, then at Bellfield who was eyeing him with displeasure.

"Please Mr Deerbolt," Flanders told him, waving a palm towards him, "tell us what you know of these events."

The witness fiddled with his hat for a moment and the began.

"I know of William Standing, Judge, don't know him well. About all I know of his prior days is that he was in the army during the war, and after that turned up to live with his sister, and her family, fed and found, I guess, up around one of the homesteads near Dogwood." He paused for a few seconds. "Now I can't defend what he done, the bank and the horse he stole, but there's more to the story you don't know."

There was nothing said by anyone, and he looked to the judge for confirmation to continue.

"Go on, Mr Deerbolt."

"What I do know is that same morning, the Henderson place was hit by Cheyenne, the Henderson's being his kin, and all were gone under except the two older children, who were taken off by those raiders." He turned back once more to Judge Flanders. "Seems like they were part of the same bunch that hit Fort Wallace some time back. Anyway, when the accused got back that day, the whole cabin was burned and the rest of his kin butchered, including a baby. I guess that set his mind a little to what to do next."

"And what did he do?"

"Set on after those kids, Judge, and kept after 'em till he won 'em back. My wife and I are at the moment seeing to the children until we see what finishes here, or we find kin to take 'em on."

"Very commendable, Mr Deerbolt," said the judge. "And do you know about Ms. Morgenson?"

"Only what I seen with my own eyes, Sir," he answered firmly. "I don't believe Standing did for the woman as it looks. They were hit by the same party that did for the Hendersons, and others. She had a wound on her windpipe which I guess was a slow way to go, and it looked to me like somebody helped her through it."

The judge paused a moment for respect, then turned to the prisoner.

"Mr Standing, are these explanations correct, the way Mr Deerbolt puts them?"

All of the guilt for Mrs Morgenson had returned. He had tried to put it behind him and the return of the children helped, but it would always be there. Standing looked up at the judge, his face drawn with the memories. He just nodded his head in agreement. Flanders sat back.

"I will adjourn these proceedings to ponder what has been said here. We will resume in twenty minutes and anyone found returning inebriated will suffer the detention of the military in their own inimitable way."

He banged down the gavel once more and retired.

Twenty minutes passed, and a little more. Then Judge Flanders returned and took his seat. Most everyone else had also retaken their places. William Standing was brought back inside. He had been allowed the short period of waiting under guard outside in the open to see the sky that had been lost to him while at the fort.

For some moments, the judge sat quietly, looking around the room. And then…

"William Standing, approach the bar."

Will heaved himself up and with the irons around his feet jangling, walked himself before Judge Nicholas Flanders. He was glowered at.

"There is no doubt that you, William Standing, are a felon of considerable design. You admit to the theft of a horse, to financial disregard and to the crime of bank robbery." He paused. "However, I find the issue of murder unproven, thanks to the intervention of Mr Deerbolt, who I take to be of good character, being an ex-law officer of this territory, and I think that you should be very grateful for his despatch in this matter."

"I am, Sir."

"I have also taken into consideration your actions with regard to the return of white captives taken by Indians, which were your kin, and I commend you for it."

"Thank you, Sir."

The judge leant forward and pushed his head closer to the prisoner.

"I understand from the testimony of Mr Deerbolt that you were involved in the late unpleasantness between the states. Were you discharged honourably?"

"I was, Sir."

"And might I ask which side you served under?" asked the judge.

Standing stood up straight. "The winning side, Sir."

Flanders sat back and looked at him. His eyes widened a little.

"William Standing, it had been my intention to sentence you to ten years penal servitude, but my conversation with you has shown me the error in that decision."

He looked hard at the prisoner, then smashed down the gavel for a final time and raised his voice with the final judgment. Will was detecting just a hint of a Virginia accent.

"William Standing, I sentence you to twenty years in the Georgia Penitentiary!"

Chapter Fourteen
The Georgia Pen

The day after the trial of William Standing, he received a visitor, ushered in by a corporal who remained there. It was Deerbolt. Told to keep a distance of six feet from the prisoner, he complied and sat on the stool that was placed for him.

Standing looked through the crossed bars and thanked him for his testimony, which at least had left his neck unmolested. He asked about the children.

"You don't need any fret over the kids," Deerbolt said. "My wife Edith is all over 'em. Like they was her own. That Tommy is a real case, ain't he?"

Standing smiled and said that he sure was, and if not for him, things might have worked out a lot different. He asked about Alice, and Deerbolt shook his head.

"We don't know what they had to go through since them Cheyenne turned up, and it doesn't do to dwell on it, but I think it took her hard. Edith said she says an odd word but she's not like she should be at her age. Doc Sanders says to give it time and she might come out of it, but who knows?"

"I can't pay anything, you know," Will said. "And my only worry is those kids."

Deerbolt shook his head.

"Don't matter, what it gives my Edith is more than money, but it ain't right for us to keep them when there's proper kin somewhere."

Will folded his arms.

"All I know is, Henry had family in Virginia some place, but that's all I know. I don't recall him talking about 'em much."

"Well, we'll give it a try," Deerbolt told him. "We get anywhere, I'll mail you, let you know where they are."

The meeting finished without a handshake as it was forbidden.

Some days later, William Standing, the notorious villain, as the newspapers put it, was placed in a cage wagon with two others and taken to the rail head. Conversation with his companions proved limited, one being Mexican and the other a Pawnee scout who had got drunk and stabbed an army mule in the tender quarters. There was some dialogue, mostly reduced to single words, which did little to pass the time.

The journey by train was long and tedious but thankfully he had lost the benefit of his two companions, their accommodation being rendered somewhere else. Chained in the caboose, with federal deputies taking over from the military, the only change of scenery came when needing to visit the outhouse. On these occasions, he was taken to the rear platform and chained to the outside railing, and left to enjoy the view until the moment had passed.

The deputies proved even less conversationalists than his previous fellow travellers, and despite his attempts at interaction, they ignored him completely. Food came irregularly when the locomotive halted at various small townships for wood and water, and usually consisted of what he thought was meat, but he might have been mistaken, in a condition that he often suspected was still moving.

His seating arrangements were nothing but the bare boards of the caboose floor and the chains caused sores around his wrists and ankles, so sometimes he found the food useful to act as a balm. Sleep was difficult and he grew used to the constant flow of tree tops which passed by in a blur through the windows a foot above his head.

Sometimes, when the train stopped for fuel, the guards would take turns to stretch their legs on the boards of the station platform, returning frequently with some pretty girl that they had met and promised a glimpse of the prison bait sat on the caboose floor in chains, ragged and dirty and unshaven with his elbows braced on his knees.

Dismounting from the train was like Christmas, with the return of sounds and smells and scenery that seemed to have disappeared from the Earth over the last few days. But you can have too much of the real thing, as he was walked from the halt to his destination, still chained and accompanied by deputies, the latter now riding on federal mounts, a bay horse and a black, but nothing like the one he knew.

It was eight miles to the Georgia Pen and the big gates looked as uninviting as a bankrupt whorehouse. The fields on either side were filled with convicts, working away their sentences by hard labour and backbreaking toil, collecting cotton, he guessed and watched over by armed uniforms. Inside, he lined up with more new inmates and stood there until several more joined the intake, walked there from another direction, all in much the same state as he was, drawn and smelling like something the cat might bring in, and then take right back out again.

There were now eight or ten guards who paraded up and down the line until the warden appeared on a small, raised platform made of wood. He was tall but portly and gave his name as Elmer Paul, and proceeded to tell them all what they already knew, that to step out of line would invite violence of the most intense kind, and no one would know a thing about it, or care. Then each man was stripped, placed against a wall with his hands akimbo and doused with buckets of cold water from the guards until they smelled fresher. Next came the best part, as each received a brand-new suit, pleasantly shaded with blue and grey hoops, but on inspection the garments proved that they had previously been used and heavily patched to the point where it was hard to find an original, untouched area.

William Standing observed inmates of every creed and colour, white, black, Mexican, even Chinese who had come to judicial grief by challenging their supervisors on the railroad. Lined up in their new finery, they were marched along to their dormitory blocks but as the line decreased in number, Standing was led aside roughly and pushed against the wall. He wondered why he had been singled out.

Elmer Paul appeared.

"It's the box for you, you murdering horse thief!" Paul grunted, giving a nod to a guard who hit him hard in the stomach. "Twelve months in the box!"

Although he could never have proved it, Will guessed that money had been exchanged to put him in that cold, dark place known as 'the box', and it was not hard to figure out who that might have been. There were no windows and only a chink of light managed to peek through the grill on the bottom of the door. This would be home for a year.

As his eyes became used to the dark, he found that the cell measured five feet by six, and six high, so he could barely stand and could touch either side with his hands with little effort. Time and tedium played with his mind and he lived the trail again, following the Cheyenne, old Eli Wilson, and the Morgensons. Sometimes he heard the sound of singing, way off along the high walls, the songs of the cotton fields or the Mormon choirs, and he thought he was dreaming or imagining things due to his condition.

He had been in the dark for five days, and fed with rancid beef and bread with green edges, which at first he denied himself, but soon looked forward to the sound of the grill, opening just enough for it to be pushed through. In the dark he could see little of it, and learned to mask the taste by imagining he was in a fancy restaurant with dark red drapes and real cutlery, like his sister told him were plentiful back east. Water came once a day in a flat pan that spilled as it was given and he had to lick the wastage from the floor to slake his thirst. Waste was disposed of through a hole in the floor at the far end of the cell and did little to enhance the meals.

On the sixth day the grill opened, just a little wider than normal, and Will crawled over to receive the offerings, but what came through was a surprise, a collection of things he had almost forgotten, cold cooked bacon, sausage and fresh biscuits, and an apple. He grasped the apple to his breast and held it there, hardly daring to bite into it lest it be another trick to torture him with. After some minutes he risked a small bite and felt the juice run down his chin and onto his beard, together with the tears that he could not hold back.

The identity of his benefactor puzzled him and it was always on his mind. At least twice a week the gifts came through the grill and he decided that they were worth the wait and dumped the usual prison fare down the hole.

But the regular improvement in his food hardly helped his mental state and he often woke to find himself calling to others who could be in hearing range, and listening to see if they might reply. They never did.

***

The hours passed and became a year and forty-one days. With no warning the creaking iron door was flung wide and even the dim light of the outside corridor hurt his eyes. He fell back against the far wall, fearing what might come next.

"Come on out!" A voice said, not challenging or harsh, just normal and every day, like he was being invited to a social.

Like an animal, he edged into the light, shielding his eyes and twitching with doubt. An arm reached in and took his, gently and eased him forward.

"What day is it?" Will Standing asked.

"It is Thursday," the voice told him.

"And the month?"

"September, moving into to October, eighteen hundred and sixty-eight, and the sun is shining outside."

There was a copper disc on the wall that had once held a candle and Will caught a glimpse of himself in the reflections. It was like an old man with long whiskers and it reminded him of Elisondro Wilson the trapper. He had not thought of him for some time, nor the face that stared back at him.

"Good Lord, is that myself?" He asked, his voice trembling, his eyes blinking.

It was hard to stand high, to his normal height and the looped fabric hung on him like rags on a washing line. He grunted and shook his head.

"Am I to go back in there?" He asked.

"I think not," the other told him. "We have another warden now, and on seeing your time in the box is overdue, he said to release you immediately."

"How did he know?" Will asked.

"Because I told him."

What might be said about an animal finding release? Not to the freedom of the wild, but to a larger cage, and one with light and colour and clean air to breathe and others of its kind to consider. That was the condition that the outlaw, William Standing now found himself inhabiting.

That night, in a solitary cell with the moon shining through a single window, he slept a sleep he had not known for some time. And yet the ghosts returned to challenge him, wild men on wild horses and worse.

The next day was difficult, as it would be for someone unused to normal things, and normal ways, if those things could rightly be said about the Georgia Penitentiary. He was given scissors and a small mirror to cut his beard and for the first time in many days he looked into a face that he remembered. It looked older. He was allowed a large half barrel with tepid water to wash off a year's grime and once gone it revealed the sores and boils that would bother him for some time.

A new suit, this time just a plain grey, and underwear that had arms and legs and a flap at the back for convenience. This was luxury living.

His new accommodation was still a prison cell, but when morning came his barred door opened and he was chained by the legs and ushered by a guard along an unfamiliar route to a door which led into the large courtyard. Sunlight was like some strange assault on his senses and he stepped out and to one side to feel its warmth.

"Move along," the guard told him, and across the wide yard, under a canvas canopy, shackled convicts were walking in line, advancing slowly to where food was given.

Standing obliged the order and took his place, his eyes wandering over the new faces, the new smells, the new environment. As he moved up the line, he was given a deep plate containing some kind of cereal, softened by warm water, and a lump of bread. Finally, at the end there were tin mugs, filled with water, clean and warm in the sun. After collection the breakfast was taken back to the inmates' individual cells and consumed there, which suited Standing well. He had not yet acclimatised to the proximity of so many people.

This became the routine for all meals, rain or shine, hot or cold and to Will Standing it did not matter much. After his initial time at the institution, there could be little that was worse and the last thing he wanted was another minute in the 'box'.

Some days after his release from the box, he was taken, still chained, before the new warden. One guard remained outside of his office, while another entered with him, both armed and wearing what appeared to be some kind of official uniform to distinguish them from the inmates and confirm their authority.

Standing clanked through the door and stood there, until the man behind the desk opposite lowered his spectacles and looked up at him. There was little warmth behind the eyes.

"I am Warden Cherry," he began. "You are as I understand it, William Standing?"

Will said he was.

"You have recovered from your time in that hole?"

Will said he had, although it was not really true, but it was a kind of a self-respect sort of thing, not admitting that they had broken you, but it almost did. Cherry broke his eye contact and took off the spectacles.

"I do not condone that kind of treatment, nor do I find the overlook of your time there good practice," he went on. "But that does not mean that I will allow behaviour that breaks the code of this establishment and I will punish anyone that does. Do you understand?"

Will said he did.

"Now I have looked at your record and I see that you still have almost eighteen years to serve. In that time, you will work as the state sees fit, in labour that is yet to be defined. Work well and you will receive good treatment. If not, then the responsibility is yours and you must take the consequence." He paused for a moment. "William Standing, you are convicted of bank robbery and horse theft and other things so you will be confined in a cell, had you prospected less serious misdemeanours you would be entitled to dormitory population and less manual labours in the fields. Do you understand?"

Will said he did, and the visit ended. Soon, he discovered the manual labour that was to last nine years. It consisted of breaking rocks with a fifteen-pound hammer in a walled yard adjacent to the main building. Twice a day, the two big wooden doors would open and a wagon brought stones from somewhere nearby. The ten assigned to the hammer duties would pause their work and proceed to discharge the wagon, then continue breaking. Once a week, usually a Friday, the wagon would take a return load of smaller stones, the product of the ten, and these were then used by a chain gang to improve dusty tracks in the area.

All of the work was overseen by a series of armed guards who patrolled the chained convicts and allowed little down time outside of the ten-minute official water break every hour.

Will always kept to himself, never caring for socialising much other than a nod to other miscreants that he passed in the day. Two weeks into the back breaking work, the water halt was called mid-morning, and Will thought he recalled the voice, but said nothing. Interaction with the guards was forbidden unless instigated by them, so when one of the uniforms called him across to where he had been working, he wondered what the issue might be. They were some way from the others when the guard pointed down to the broken rocks that Will had serviced that day.

"Are you recovered from that hole?" The man asked.

It took Standing by surprise.

"Look down, man," he said in a low voice, "as if I am admonishing you for your work."

Will did so, and nodded violently as if taking criticism.

"Was it you…"

"Yes," said the guard, a small, thin individual with a dark, thin moustache and goatee.

"I don't understand but I thank you for it."

The guard checked to see if anyone watched them, but no one cared. He pointed more to the rock pile.

"This is the South, William Standing, and you are in it. Most here are from the south, and you are from the north. The land is still policed by the federal military and the people do not like it. You would be well to keep your past to yourself." His accent was definitely southern.

"And why would you care?" Standing asked.

"Because I also fought for the north, and will not see a wearer of the blue wallow in the filth that you had to."

"Then I owe you a lot," Will told him, "possibly my life, not to put too fine a point on it, and I thank you for it."

"I was glad to do it," the guard said, "now go back to the rest and curse me for wasting your water break."

The man who had kept him alive, he found later, was named Thomas, although what his Christian name was, Will never found out. At first, their contacts were infrequent and often without much conversation lest it became obvious and the connection broken.

With the indulgence of time, William Standing became familiar with the everyday workings of the Georgia Pen, how to make the hard work easier by pretending to need the outhouse, slipping and feigning hurt limbs and the like, distracting the attention of the prison trustees on the food line so that another could steal extra bread, and so on and so forth. Everyone seemed to have their well-practiced ways to survive and improve their lot and he was no exception. He learned the routines of others, including the guards, who often seemed to be just as incarcerated as the convicts, and also had their own means of distraction.

The guards were housed in their own dormitory, in single cots with sheets changed at least once a month. Also, once a month, on Saturday nights when the warden was off duty and with his family, ladies from a house of nocturnal business would be sneaked in to while away the time with paying customers while their comrades slept uneasily beside them. Those convicts who occupied the dormitory were grateful to he who filed a key to their door and for a plug of tobacco were allowed to put their ears to that of the guards and listen.

A few months into his sentence Will had become familiar with his own routine and looked forward to the days when the wagons came. It was good to see the horses and it reminded him of times past, some good and others not. When possible, he gave the animals a friendly slap and ran his hand over their noses, a regard that they seldom received from others.

On one occasion the wagon halted and Will called up to the driver, an ageing guard with whiskers as old as he was. He knew it was a risk, but could not help himself.

"Boss, that left animal's got a knee strain," he advised. "You keep pushin' him, you'll be pullin' the damn cart yourself by Thursday."

The driver had looked down on him.

"You keep your darn ideas to yourself, you damn stone stomper!"

However, a different animal hauled the stones the next day.

Christmas day was a given holiday, the only one, and by chance the guard who had been assigned to his block was Thomas. The man stopped by Standing's barred door and pushed through a newspaper. He smiled as Will took it and leant against the iron. It was some weeks old, and Will was no scholar, but it was a newspaper and a welcome distraction.

"A mite late with delivery," Standing said, grinning and thumbing through the pages.

"Better late than never," Thomas agreed. "News is always behind down here, anyway."

Will nodded his agreement with a smile as he worked through, looking for something interesting. He stopped, inserting his head into the folds.

"Something interesting?" asked the guard.

Will nodded again.

"Looks like a…" He handed back the paper. "Can you read this for me?"

Thomas took it. He put on a pair of spectacles and pointed to the page.

"Yes."

Thomas began.

"It's headed, The Fight at Summit Springs'."

"That's the one," Will confirmed.

"Following the abduction of two white women by Cheyenne of the dog clan," Thomas read, "a contingent of the Fifth Cavalry under General Carr pursued the Indians to a camp near the area of Summit Springs. After a heroic battle in which only one soldier was injured in the ear, one white woman was rescued alive but according to the facts that this journal has accumulated, another was found deceased. It was discovered by interrogation that the unfortunate was killed by Cheyenne women who carried a jealous intent towards her and finished her with a tomahawk. A three-month-old child is at this time unaccounted for. The female found alive could speak no English, and it was determined that she was the

German wife of a nearby farmer, who had recently emigrated to the US. Upon her abduction, the farmer followed the hostiles up the Spring River and then returned to give the alarm. Also involved in the battle were army scouts, Mr North and Mr Cody, who accounted themselves wondrously. Many Indians were killed, including the chief, Tall Bull, and many wagons of stolen property were relayed from the battle field. Mr Cody assumed custody of the Cheyenne chief's horse. It appears that the much-feared dog soldier clan has been all but broken…"

Will Standing was sitting on his cot and he fell back against the wall.

"Tall Bull. It reads Tall Bull?" Will asked.

"That's what it says," Thomas replied, "you want more?"

"No."

Thomas pushed the paper back through the bars.

"You know these people?" He asked.

"Some of 'em." He laughed. "Billy Cody sure gets around."

Over time the two got to know each other well, taking care not to make the relationship overtly obvious. Standing told Thomas some of his story, and left out the parts that poked his conscience. Thomas's story was equally strange and proved the idea that it never goes the way that you intended. He had left home in Atlanta to fight in the Civil War in eighteen sixty-one, as had his brother, but his heart had been with the Union. He had kept correspondence to his family to a minimum and left much untold and untrue. His brother was killed by a sniper's bullet at Bull Run and his mother of a broken heart. So, when the war ended, he abandoned the family home and assumed his brother's name as his own, and sought employment at the penitentiary. Permanent jobs in the south were hard to come by and if he had remained with the Union Army, sooner or later his life might be forfeit on home ground.

And so, nine years of breaking stone came to an end when Will Standing broke an ankle. This time it was for real. Thomas dragged him to the medical room, where a drunken doctor set it as best as he could and as luck would have it, he didn't make a half bad job of it. In those years, Will had thought of escape many times and thought of the children. He had expected news of some kind but he had received nothing, and wondered why. They would be nigh on their twenties by now, he thought, and all but forgotten him anyway. But some things just won't go away.

Shortly after, it was a bad time for Will Standing. Thomas had managed to get him a job in the farrier's shop, after the appointment of yet another warden, and two weeks after, his friend had whistled his way back to the dormitory, and put a shell from a Schofield pistol in his temple. It came as a shock, but Will knew the pressures of conscience.

Eighteen seventy-seven. Now pushing forty, incarceration was certainly better for him, and working with the horses passed the time quicker and with more satisfaction. They were just haulage mares and given no never mind by most people, but Will found that they all had their own ways and responded to what little respect and fondness he could give them.

Reforms had come and he no longer wore the chains that he had come to hate, and even the food improved to the point where he felt it pointless to steal more of it. To say that he was trusted was pushing it a mite, but he had been in the pen for a long time and was almost considered part of the furniture. He caused no harm and gave no trouble, other than the occasional curse, which was returned.

His work in the farrier's shop honed his skills with horses and iron and although he was subservient to the civilian blacksmith, his advice became the standard practice. Still, the children appeared in the flames of the furnace but he saw their faces as they used to be, still young and without the advance of years. Why had he heard nothing?

The years were ticking by, and by eighteen eighty-five he had only two to go, but those two years seemed a lifetime. For a while he had traded good humoured insults with old 'whiskers', who drove the stone wagon, and expecting him to bring over the wagon for repairs one rainy morning, was irritated by the fact that he did not arrive at the appointed time. The parts were made ready for installing and the furnace primed but still no wagon.

By the time the weather cleared it was known to all that the man, already in his late seventies, had driven his last wagon and succumbed to some unknown cause the night before. Having no kin, it was decided that the state would pay for his burial, providing that the prison would plant him in the place reserved mainly for convicts, a short distance from the walls, out of sight of a sensitive public on the edge of a wooded area.

A formal hearse was out of the question, so it seemed only right and proper that his last journey would be via the wagon that he had cursed for so many years. The farrier's shop made swift and complete repairs and within a day was ready to carry the deceased to his final resting place. Will watched as the old man's makeshift coffin was placed aboard the wagon bed with appropriate reverence as the rain clouds were gathering and a storm approached to herald his send off.

Thunder clapped above like a cannon shot and the senior guard who had been given the duty of driver looked up at the first lightning bolt. He stepped back under cover as the rain began to hammer down.

"You take him, Will," the guard told him. "I ain't stepping out in this. You take him and come right back."

The order surprised the convict that was William Standing. This would be his first time beyond the gates in eighteen years. He stood wearing nothing but his prison grey and his underwear and knew that he would soon be soaking wet, but the chance to look outside was worth it. Without reply he walked out into the rain and climbed up onto the wagon box. Four armed riders took a corner each, the rain sluicing from their oilskins. One of them looked back at the original driver, who waved a hand as authority for things to go.

"He's only got two years to go," he called out. "He ain't going nowhere."

The rider waved Will on and he slapped the reins and urged the horses forward, large bursts of rain exploding on their backs. As the wagon approached the huge, heavy wooden doors of the main gate, they were heaved open and William Standing passed through, trying to remember if the surrounding area had been like this when he first entered.

They moved along the short, cobbled road that led to the main track, crossed right over onto muddy grass towards the burial ground. The grave was pre-dug and Will hauled the horses to a halt some thirty yards from it, so that it gave space to turn the wagon. Three of the four guards dismounted and pulled out the coffin, but called for the services of the other as the weight proved difficult in the driving rain. Around the grave, soil was already being washed back in and the temporary padre waiting by its side urged them to hurry by thrusting out a hand from under his dark oilskin.

Will smiled as he saw them slither in the wet, and was surprised that he had not been called to assist, but the guards hauled the coffin on and as they reached the grave, the edge partly gave way and a pall bearer went with it. The coffin was dropped as his companions sought to save him, and Will could only guess at the discomfort of the corpse. It was quite a scene and he decided it was worth the wet.

The horses of the guards had been tied to the wagon side and one snorted at its dislike of the weather. Then happened one of those moments, when against everything that the mind warns against is discarded and the body is already in motion and discounting the cost. Will glanced down at the nearest horse, saw the big brown eyes blinking away the rain, and shaking off the water that streamed from its mane. In a sliced second, he had untied the others and jumped on its back, felt the smoothness of the saddle and the hard flesh that pressed against his calves. One yell and he scared off the others while the guards struggled in the mud thirty yards away.

Chapter Fifteen
The Man on the Horse

September 1885

Which way to go was a guess. With no sun to show the direction, he took a chance and galloped the animal through the rain and the thunder and shielded his eyes at the lightning. He knew that if caught, it would be another ten years added to the two remaining so he must shake off any pursuit at all costs. The rain would be an ally and cover his tracks and deter dogs and any other attempts to find him, but he knew he was now no spring chicken and time would not always be on his side.

Standing decided to make a long circuit around the penitentiary. Like all chasers, they would figure that his mind be aligned to a straight line of escape to put as many miles between them as he could, but his mind worked differently and knowing theirs, knew better.

Some hours of riding went by and both he and the horse were blown. He found a stand of oak trees and pulled the animal inside as the rain ceased and shafts of uncertain sunlight risked a way through the dark cloud. Steam emanated from the horse's flanks and both it and its rider shivered with the wet.

What to do now?

Will knew that with prison clothing, he stood little chance of anonymity and he hankered for something a little more stylish. By nightfall they had moved on, keeping to covered ground or little used tracks, but always the discovery by federal patrols or prison guards was prevalent in his mind. A little way ahead, Will saw the yellow lights of oil lamps being turned on as the day faded. He rode in as far as he dared, then tied up the horse and made his way on foot. It was a small township with few buildings other than timber frame houses and he guessed it to be a farming community. Looking around, he saw the empty field which now lay fallow and he knew that his guess was accurate.

Skirting the houses, he saw the figure of a woman leaving one of the houses via the raised porch, to bring in washing that was only ventured out when the rain stopped and was still not dry. He observed the items hanging there, shirts, a blanket, socks and ladies' unmentionables. Waiting until she had gathered one basketful and taken it inside, he made his move, ignoring the ladies' particulars and helping himself to a shirt, socks and the blanket. At least it was a start.

He ripped a hole in the blanket and fashioned a poncho, felt the welcome covering of the socks and swapped the shirt for his prison grey jacket. He was far from dry and would be that way for some time, but Lord, he was free and riding again.

Later in the night he came across a barn, open and some way from the darkened farmhouse, so he led the horse inside, eased the girth and fell back into the hay. Early the next morning, he stole eggs and before first light was back on the trail, but this time with a morning sun that showed the way home.

By the second night, and a handful of more indiscriminate and welcome misappropriations, William Standing was dry and on his way. Keeping the setting sun to his left and a little behind he made good progress, well into the twilight hours, and felt that whatever pursuit might be behind him, he had made discovery of his whereabouts doubtful and difficult. Approaching another town, he waited until well after dark, hobbled the horse and without a coat to fend off the cool Autumn evening, found an outhouse on the outskirts to shelter him from the night. Outside, on the door, were three pegs, for the convenience of patrons who might wish to make themselves comfortable during their stay. Not the most positive of accommodation, he decided, but needs must and tomorrow he would resolve the overcoat issue.

Rising early, he abandoned his sleeping quarters and saddled up. In the first light he could see the silver threads that disappeared into the distance and told him that this was a rail stop. Perhaps it was time to reassess his plans. It was a long ride to Wyoming and many days ride, but a locomotive could move faster and not tire so often.

When more of the population were about, he found the rail stop, checked the schedule and saw the regular northern passenger service at noon, two days later. That would be a long, nervous wait. A small man appeared and opened the telegraph office, and Will followed him in, bidding the usual morning greeting.

"Ain't there any earlier trains north?" He asked the operator.

The man shook his head.

"Only one south, this afternoon at three," he explained. "There's a timber hauler waiting on the loop till it's past but it doesn't stop here and it won't carry people. You need somewhere to stop till the day after tomorrow, the hotel down the street is reasonable."

Standing thanked him. He worked out that if he could climb aboard the timber train, it might take him well on his way, and if it had to wait for the down service, it would not be until well after three before it passed through. It began to fall into place.

By early morning, he had ridden up the line and found a curve, where the train would have to slow down. It was about a mile from town, an easy walk. He returned to the livery stable and sold the horse, a deal that satisfied both parties. So now he had money and a ride if he could manage to get aboard, but he had no idea what the timber train might offer by way of comfort, so he considered the problem of warmer clothing.

Returning to the place where he spent the night he hovered in the area until the right person appeared to take advantage of the convenience. The man divested himself of his oilskin duster and black, flat brimmed hat, hung them on the pegs on the door and hurried inside. Will Standing gave the customer time to make himself comfortable, then took the coat and hat and began the walk out towards the bend.

The afternoon was warm and overcast and he settled in along the curve to await the sound of the southbound locomotive. Once that had passed, he knew the timber train would be free to leave the loop and make its way north. Often, when he thought the time near, he put an ear to the rail but was disappointed and pulled the stolen coat around him.

Dozing, he was suddenly awakened by a huffing of steam as it escaped the cylinders and the cranking of metal that worked the valves and pushed the connecting rods that turned the big wheels. He slid out of sight down a slope, away from the timber sleepers and pulled up his collar against the force of steam that was coming his way. For a long moment, he was engulfed in a white mist as the locomotive passed, slowing to pick up any passengers that waited at the halt.

An hour later, he was rewarded by arrival of the timber train, now free to make its way north. He picked the outside curve to make his move, where he would be hidden from the caboose and any railway personnel that might object to his free passage. As the locomotive went by, slowing into the curve, he rose up and leapt onto the passing wagon, a flat car with chained logs that gave purchase for his feet and spaces to crawl inside and allowed him to hide for the journey.

***

Cool morning mist covered the fields in irregular patterns as Autumn crept towards October. A single horse buck board moved steadily along the road, and its driver pulled his dark overcoat around him. Beside him on the seat was a Gladstone bag, almost new with shiny polished handles that met to form a single grip. The man's face was regular in features, clean shaven but with a neatly trimmed moustache which covered his upper lip. His hands were well manicured but strong and they held the leathers tightly.

It was a rented rig and the bay horse that pulled the vehicle stepped along with a regular gait, the noise of its hooves sharp against the quiet of the hour. A tug on the long rein brought the horse to a stop beside a large, dark green sign by the roadside and the driver satisfied himself that this was the way. He slapped the leathers and the horse continued down the road, where shortly a line of grey figures were already working to fill holes left by unseasonably heavy rain and weather.

Mounted guards balanced the stocks of repeating rifles on their knees and tipped their hats as the buck board passed. Soon, a side road led off to the big wooden gates of the penitentiary and the driver clicked his mouth and pulled the horse down towards the prison. A poorly uniformed guard walked towards the slowing horse, somewhat dishevelled and unready for visitors. He tipped his short-peaked cap at the well-dressed man who hauled back on the rein. A dark Derby hat returned the compliment.

"I am here to see the warden," the man said. "Mr Franklin, I assume it still is?"

The guard nodded once, and asked.

"Might I ask what your business is, Sir?"

The man on the buck board glared down at him.

"My business is with the warden, now if you would let me pass, I will proceed with the issue."

He took out a badge from his pocket and showed the guard, whose expression changed and so did his attitude. He walked quickly back to the gates and presently they swung open. Into the big courtyard rolled the buck board and

175

halted at the opposite side, near an open door that led to the formal office section of the building. The guard ran over and helped the man down and handed him his bag. He showed him through the door. Beyond, a single stairway went straight up and the guard led the way. At a large green door, he knocked and waited for response, then entered and held the door open.

The visitor was announced and he waked in, closed the door to exclude his guide and took off the Derby hat. The warden left the defence of his desk and walked around to shake hands, impressed at the gold Pinkerton badge that was presented to prove authority.

"Welcome, Sir. I am Warden Franklin. May I offer you tea, or coffee, or perhaps...?"

"Coffee would be fine, thank you."

Franklin opened the door ajar and called down. Over small talk, the coffee arrived and the two sat on opposing sides of the desk.

"So, what does the Pinkerton Agency require from us today?" asked Franklin, sipping from a hot cup.

The other opened his bag, and fished out papers, but kept them to himself.

"I have interest in one of your prisoners," he said, "an individual from the State of Wyoming under the name of William Standing?"

"Standing?" Franklin sneered. "A man of dubious character and considerable transgression, upon whom trust is a lost cause."

"Quite! May I see this man?"

"You cannot, Sir. For he is not here."

"But my information was quite precise..."

"Precise not enough, for he escaped these three weeks past, and has not been heard of since."

"Escaped?"

"With the theft of a fine horse, while good men toiled to bury the dead, God-damn his eyes!"

The visitor was obviously disappointed.

"And have you not had no sign as to his whereabouts?"

The warden raised his shoulders.

"Only the loss of minor items locally which might or might not signal a general direction, but nothing to tire horses upon, or waste the wages of men better employed on other matters."

"Then my journey has been wasted, do you by chance have a tin type of the man? I have only written evidence."

The warden smiled.

"We do. Every man we hold has his image made when he walks through the gates, and those here before that wonder was invented have been subsequently frozen for posterity."

More small talk filled the time until the tin type impression arrived and the Pinkerton man looked at a younger face than he expected.

"May I keep this?" He asked.

"Of course, he is no longer here, so we have no need of it. I expect never to see his face again."

The Pinkerton man stood and thanked his host.

"May I ask why you are after this man?" Franklin asked.

The Pinkerton man turned to face him, his teeth gritted and his face contorted. He held up the rolled picture in his fist.

"Justice, Mr Franklin," he growled. "Justice!"

***

They say a leopard never changes its spots nor a tiger its stripes, or all of the other stuff they make up to describe a person of less than moral fibre that advances the compass of their own. Another way to say it is that a horse thief always knows a good horse and if it can run, then moral fibre blows with the wind to the detriment of a careless owner.

When it looked like the iron rails turned more to the east, and he wanted west, Will Standing jumped off the wagon at the slowest bend that he felt a near fifty-year-old could survive. Even so, it was not a comfortable landing, and his aching bones told him that if he kept doing that, then something was bound to give. He guessed that breaking boulders and swinging a ten-pound hammer in the farrier's shop for near on twenty years had loosened up the sinews that age tended to tighten, but time drags you with it and there's not a whole lot you can do about it. It was the third train that he had ridden, taking him in a general northerly direction and he had skipped from one to another in the rail yards as the line made its way through more urban areas.

Lucky for him, the bend announced the proximity of civilisation that was both a good thing and a bad one. People meant people type things, which was just what he needed, but he had no idea how far or how fast the wanted posters had travelled, thanks to the invention of the telegraph. The good part was that the telegraph spoke words and not pictures, but any stranger was prone to be suspicious.

Food had been absent for several days along the way and his stomach almost kissed his backbone, so he chewed grass to fend off the ache, until a cabin on the outskirts of the township offered the heavy scent of apple pie, cooling on an open window frame. To prove his appreciation of the baker's skill, he crept up along the walls and helped himself to the larger one, gulped it down hot and returned the plate. He was not all bad.

He had money from the sale of the horse, but was a little short for what they were asking in this place, and he guessed he had reached Kansas, the way that the prices hiked. He bought himself a good meal at the local hotel and was astonished at the asking price, just shy of a dollar, and told himself, 'Lord how things are a-changing'. Leaving before the waiter could wince at the lack of a tip, Will walked over to the assay office and took on the role of a mining engineer, passing through and interested in the area. This gave him the means to check out local maps and discover where he was without suspicion. Kansas it was, and still a way to go.

By early afternoon, the bars were doing good business, but willing though he was to be tempted to go in, he made better of the diversions by weighing up the local transport against available time. The best opportunities were down by the hotel, where riders coming in for a late lunch at those inflated prices, tied their mounts off in a side alley, mounted and waiting and just asking to be stolen.

Checking the immediate side walk and finding them clear, all but a lady with a small boy, Will chose the bay and hauled himself up into the saddle. He untied the other, a half Appaloosa, and rode the two horses out by the outskirts and onto the open ground, hoping that the trick would have the law looking for two riders instead of one. It was an old ruse, but it might give him time.

A few miles from the township, whose name he had already forgotten, he unsaddled the Appaloosa, removed the bridle and released the animal to its own devices and galloped the bay into the afternoon.

Somewhere ahead were promises to keep, those for others, and those for himself.

***

The Pinkerton Detective Agency had become equally respected and hated since the Civil War. It had been a bodyguard for Lincoln and its motto of 'we never sleep', with the symbol of an eye on its stationary, a byword of forensic and judicial competence. Whether Mr Lincoln might subscribe totally to their description is debatable.

By those who fall into the category of felons, an agent of the Pinkertons was decidedly the last person they wished to meet, as their tenacity was legendary. The man who had returned the buck board to the livery stable was certainly one of this breed, and he would turn over every stone to find his target.

Reaching Atlanta, the city still wrapped in its traumas from the recent pains of the war, the man boarded the five thirty train that would return him to Washington. But he had not given up, and as the locomotive whistled and pulled out though a street in ruins, he looked intensely at the picture of the outlaw and escapee, William Standing, old and outdated. Determination was his byword. He had little doubt that one day he would catch up with him, no matter how long or how difficult, and what a day that would be.

***

Something told him that as a horse thief, luck had usually been with him, but perhaps it was his attention to detail and stealing the right one that gave him the edge. He would never take a grey or a paint, or one with a distinctive blaze or white socks, they would stand out too much and be recognised, and he had only taken horses out of necessity, never for money. Well hardly ever, and he had been young then, but still should have known better. Strange how once a habit starts, the road opens up for more of the same.

Riding free, Standing's mind wandered to that big black horse of years back. Never had he ridden such an animal, nor admired one so much, or owed so much to one. Looking back, he could see how Bellfield had become so obsessed with the horse and wanted it back, but for maybe the wrong reasons. Back in the pen, Thomas had told him that he had never known a new inmate put into the box immediately and for no infringement of the rules. His suspicions were that money had changed hands, and Will Standing had a fair idea whose money it was. They say that time heals most things, but with this thing, time would have to stand in line and take its turn. He was not a violent man, unless provoked, but

Bellfield was a wrong that needed putting right, and it was in his mind to do the putting.

Two days riding found him just short of the Wyoming line, not far, he guessed, from Fort Laramie, but it had been a while and he tended to doubt his own instincts. He had come across a Mormon immigrant train and used up most of what money he had left to trade for food. It had been a good trade and the salt bacon and biscuits would see him for a while.

Still moving north, he crested a rise and looking ahead saw a strange figure, sitting with two horses grazing. Will slowed to a walk and approached the man carefully, painfully aware that he was unarmed and a fugitive. It was an unusual sight to say the least and he halted when a few yards away. The man had seen him coming and waved a hand as he drew near.

Sitting upon a small stool, the man held brushes in one hand with a small folding easel before him. On his head was a slouch hat, pushed forward to shield his eyes from the sun. In the other hand was a palette with a riot of colours that Will had seen some way off, held in an awkward manner in the crook of his elbow. He was an artist, a young man around twenty and Will wondered what he was doing in the middle of nowhere.

"Good morning, Sir," said the artist.

Will looked around to check the area, but there was no one else around.

"Morning," Will answered. "A little exposed, ain't you?"

The artist stood and put down the palette and the brushes. He walked over to the mounted visitor and extended a hand.

"Russell," he announced. "Charles Russell."

Will took the hand and shook it.

"Will…" he said without thinking, then, "Ryder, Will Ryder."

"Do you live around here?" Russell asked. "You are the first I have seen for some days."

Will shook his head, and thought of something to say.

"Nope. Just ran some horses down to Fort Hays." He changed the subject, looking over at the easel. "Mind if I take a look?"

Russell beamed.

"Please. Please do. But it isn't finished by a long stick…"

The horse needed a breather, so Will dropped from the saddle and walked over to the easel. It showed a landscape, quite remarkable with, as far as he could make out, almost every blade of grass and cloud represented in detail. He looked closely over the whole canvas and shook his head.

"Think you missed a ladybug over there, about a half mile off." He grinned, spreading a hand across the painting. "You paint all this? You sell these?"

Russell was obviously happy at Standing's appreciation of the work.

"Oh, occasionally," he replied. "I work up north, just had a few days so I rode down, checked in at Fort Laramie and they told me the direction to go, where it was safe to be. Hoped to catch the last of the buffalo, but it looks like there's not a whole lot left. Maybe I should've headed north, they say they're still good in Canada."

Will shook his head.

"So I hear," he agreed. "Some time back, I seen herds so big it'd take all day for 'em to pass." He suddenly felt sad, but couldn't think why. "So, you just draw in the prairie and colour it empty?"

"Kind of," Russell said. "But look here…"

He reached under the easel and found a book of sketches. Flipping the pages he revealed drawings of Indians, afoot and with horses, in buffalo hunts and reclining on blankets with squaws, and a whole world of observations.

"I visit the camps where I can," Russell explained, "draw in what I see to make a composite, finish a whole painting in my own time." He indicated the easel. "Sometimes I make an oil sketch, like now. One day, I hope to have a real place to work, like the photographers do these days?"

"Well, I hope you do," Will said. "I sure would like to see some."

They spoke for some time, the artist explaining his work while Will filled in a little detail of what he recalled of the past and wilder times, without giving detail of his own of course, nor his current situation. Finally, Will mounted up once more.

"Keep your eyes peeled," he advised, "there was Indian trouble here some time back."

Russell shrugged.

"Ooh, it's pretty much safe around here, since the Custer fight in seventy-six, most hostiles are further north, up into Montana and Canada, or down in the south west. I hear they are having Apache trouble in Arizona and New Mexico, and over into Mexico. Most of the plains tribes are given reservations and I'm sure that will pacify them. Why, I hear that even Sitting Bull has found employment in Buffalo Bill's show and has toured both here and Canada."

"Bill Cody has a show? What kind of show?" Will asked.

"I haven't seen it but I hope to," Russell said. "Being going two, maybe three years now. Surely, you've seen the posters?"

"Er, no. Haven't been much by towns recently," Standing told him.

"Well, it's really something. Genuine Indians, bucking horses, even the real Deadwood coach, authentic historical reconstructions and the like. Lord, it sounds a wonder!"

"I guess so. So which direction is the fort?" He asked.

Russell indicated the east, so Will knew he must ride due west of north. He turned the horse's head, then halted. He crossed his palms on the saddle horn.

"So, you gonna picture in some buffalo on that sheet?" He asked.

"Maybe…"

"Sure would like to see it done," Will said, then waved and rode off to a walk, increasing to a canter when a hundred yards away.

Russell watched him go. He picked up the sketch book and began to draw frantically, then scribbled a few words to suggest a possible title:

'The man on the horse'

***

Dogwood was not as he remembered. Where Mr Bridey's store had been was now a hotel, wide and well made with painted window frames and even curtains at the windows. Seawell's livery was still there but the name was changed and the old barn had gone, replaced by a larger one with treated timber and professional signs. What had once been the bank that held memories of its own for him, was now a corner saloon and eating place, the 'Mountain Palace', with clients coming and going constantly. A larger and more impressive bank was now on the opposite side of the street, policed by an armed officer in a cradle chair by the door.

Will remembered the sleepy place that he last saw on that Saturday morning and found it now transformed. From somewhere behind the buildings came the constant lowing of cattle, and he had seen quite a few grazing free on the land as he approached the town.

As he rode down the centre of the busy street, avoiding wagons and carts and knots of riders, he looked for the Longhorn Saloon, but could see no sign of it.

He pulled over to the side and hailed an old man who sat on a rocker, smoking a pipe on the raised side walk.

"Whatever happened to Mr Bridey's place?" He asked.

The old man squinted up at him.

"Who?"

Will shook his head.

"Never mind," he said. "You recall a Marshal back some years, name of Deerbolt?"

The old man thought for a moment. He raised his pipe.

"Don't recall, but there's a woman that name, working laundry back of the Mountain Palace, don't know if it's any relation."

"Thanks."

Will rode slowly across the street, pulling his collar around his face, just in case. He allowed a cart to pass then dismounted and walked the horse through the fire break between the Mountain Palace and the next building. Some way off was a small cabin, and attached was a thick canvas tent stretched over wooden frames. Emanating from the open flaps of the tent was a cloud of steam and from the sounds, someone working inside.

He tied off the horse and stood in the opening, seeing an older lady, quite portly and with her hair tied in a bun on her head. She wore a faded blue dress and soiled white pinafore, tied at the back of her waist.

"Knock, knock," Will said.

The woman turned and wiped her forehead with the back of her hand, escaping the steam to see who was there. Will took off his hat.

"Ma'am, I'm looking for Marshal Deerbolt, I understand…"

The woman raised her cheekbones and took a step forward.

"Why, he's been dead these sixteen years, lost to the diphtheria, and he wasn't the Marshal for the two years afore that," she said, aware of the drop in the man's expression as she told him. "You a friend of his, from all those years back?"

"Not quite," Will answered. "I guess, you would be Edith, then Ma'am."

"I am that," the woman answered. "I am his widow."

Will shuffled, a little out of his depth, and certainly had not spoken to a woman for quite some time.

"Ma'am, do you recall a couple of kids, from way back, Tom and Alice, late of the Henderson family that lost everything in a Cheyenne raid?"

"Tom and Alice," Edith repeated, wiping her hands on a cloth, her eyes softening. "Yes, of course I remember. A nicer pair of children you could ever muster, we had them for over a year and would have kept them forever if I had my way, but it were not to be," she said. "You know of them?"

"I do, Ma'am," Will confirmed. "I'm trying to locate them. I expected your late husband to write me to tell me of their whereabouts, but I heard nothing all these years…"

Edith looked at him for a long moment.

"You are William Standing," she told him, not asking.

"I am, Ma'am, and I am looking for the children, though I guess they to be full grown by now."

"My husband wrote to you many times, but he received no reply, nor any confirmation of where you were."

Will turned his hat in his hand.

"I guess where I was saw no interest in passing mail to people, nor pressing encouragement to send out." He twisted a lip as he spoke.

"Then I am sorry, Mr Standing," she said. "As for the children, my husband spent some time in tracking their kin, and found them, somewhere east if I recall. That was why he wrote you, as he promised he would."

"Ma'am, do you still have detail of their kin, of where I can find them?"

She spread her hands.

"Mr Standing, you can see my condition. Since my husband died it has been quite a struggle and all of his papers have been gone a long time. I am sorry."

Will nodded slowly.

"I understand Ma'am. I'm sorry to have bothered you." He was about to leave, but turned back. "Might I ask, is Bellfield still around?"

Edith poked a finger in the air.

"You hear those cattle?" She said. "Bellfield beef."

William Standing replaced his hat.

"Ooh, Mr Standing," she called after him. "I do have something of yours. If you will come into the house, I'll get it for you."

He took off the hat again and followed her through the door into the single room. She reached up and pulled something from a dusty corner and handed it over. It was a Sharps long gun, and with it an old bag containing three cartridges, percussion caps and a folded telescope. Will took them and felt the weight.

"Old friend Ma'am." He grinned. "It's been a long time."

Edith wiped her hands on her apron.

"He said that maybe you'd come. Said if you did, I was to give you these. After all this time I doubted you would but he made me promise, so I did."

Will smiled down at her.

"Marshal Deerbolt was a damn fine man, Ma'am, and I thank you both for seeing to those kids," he spoke. "I wish I could pay you for…"

Edith raised her palms.

"Oh shucks, should be me paying you, it was the happiest time of my life. I never could have kids of my own, so I look on that time as a blessing."

William Standing thanked her again and shook her hand. He untied the horse and led it back into the street and looked both ways at the passing traffic. He put the loop on the Sharps over the saddle horn and mounted. One more promise to try to keep, this one for himself.

Chapter Sixteen
The Long Shot

By the next morning, William Standing had ridden the ten miles to the Bellfield place. He mused on how fortune had given him the means and the opportunity to fulfil the promise he had made to himself in all of those months in the box. How he would find the tools to commit to the idea was always something of a mystery, but he knew that one way or another he would. So, when Mrs Deerbolt handed him the Sharps, he was convinced that providence was urging him on to do the right thing.

It was still early, and he found a stand of silver birch, just right, on a rise, some three quarters of a mile from the house. And what a house it was. He had never seen the old one, but wondered how much it would cost to buy such a place as the mansion that Bellfield now owned.

Two stories, and painted in pale green and white, it stood like a monument with grass all around, where knots of quality cattle grazed. Closer to the side of the main building was a corral with several fine horses, two greys and a chestnut. Unfolding the telescope and cleaning the lenses, he rolled across the place, admiring at least the man's taste for good horse flesh and fine living. Today would be his last.

Will identified easily the timber veranda and the expensive furniture that was displayed there, to give a wide panorama of Bellfield's domain. He guessed that sooner or later his target would appear in the ornate doorway and proceed with his day.

All round the big house, workers were already visible doing chores that were their duties, from men seeing to the horses, to women tending the small garden off to the right, collecting no doubt the makings of their master's breakfast.

Putting aside the telescope, Will brought up the Sharps. He took a handful of grass and cleaned the rifle, blowing off the dust and pollen seeds that remained.

He levered back the hammer and found it surprisingly smooth, not rusted or stiff. With his fingers he let the natural oils rub into the weapon until he was sure that it was good.

A blue jay scolded him from above, hidden somewhere in the yellow Autumnal canopy. He slipped out one of the cartridges and pulled the lever under the trigger to its full lock, then slipped it into the breech until seated correctly. Then he placed a cap on the nipple and released the lever, allowing the block to trim the cartridge and leave enough black powder to ignite from the percussion cap and fire the gun. All he needed now was to calculate the distance and wait.

A clear, cold blue sky devoid of clouds allowed the sun admittance in the eastern sky. Will slipped his right arm from out of the coat to give more freedom when the time came. He put some thought to what would happen when he pulled the trigger and was certain that it would not be long before employees would figure it out and be up over the grass and after him. The horse was fast but it was no Midnight, and perhaps he might not be able to outrun one of those fine animals in the corral down there.

The speed of the bullet would outrun the report but it would only give him a second's grace and he could not stick around for a second shot. The first must do the job, and finish it.

The morning drew on and William Standing waited, growing impatient. Was Bellfield a late sleeper? Was he even home? How much longer could he wait for the man to show?

The sun climbed higher and Standing guessed it was around ten, or just before. The front double doors opened and a woman around thirty years old walked out and walked along the veranda. He put the telescope to his eye and saw her place a vase of flowers on a small table. Reclaiming the Sharps, he lay prone and supported the long barrel with his left hand, sighting the screw to a little over thirteen hundred yards. He looked again and gave the screw another quarter turn and waited.

Presently a shadow appeared just beyond the porch and Will put the Sharps into his shoulder and looked along the barrel, centring the sights upon whatever came through. He waited.

Something moved, but not clear enough to make out. He took the telescope again and located the doorway. He could see feet, raised from the ground, but they moved again. Someone pushed something through the doorway, onto the veranda and towards the small table, where it was turned to face his way. He raised the telescope again and adjusted the focus by sliding the brass sheath.

Bellfield sat in a wheelchair, a scarf around his neck and some kind of hat upon his head. He wore a red coat, a perfect target. A few seconds later, the woman returned and held a cup to his mouth, holding it there until the man had drunk. He seemed to hardly notice anything that the woman did for him, siting still and apparently aware of little. Soon, the woman would go, so Will waited.

When she went inside again, the Sharps was returned into position. He would take a final look through the telescope, then it would be all over. Will located Bellfield, who had not moved a muscle, his eyes looking straight ahead, his body wrapped in red and unmoving in the wheelchair.

Will raised the rifle and homed in on the red spot and what it represented. He pulled back the hammer to half cock, then all of the way. He was sighted and ready, just the pressure on the trigger, a hair breadth from revenge, a final act to resolve the wrongs that had been done to him.

Bellfield still sat motionless and Will saw the woman return. He held his position and could see the woman attending the man, possibly wiping his face or mouth, or wiping his brow, it was too far off to be sure.

She left again and disappeared through the double doors. Will felt beads of sweat on his temples. Now or never. He closed his left eye. He waited.

The moment left him, and he looked up slowly, moved his finger to the trigger and held the hammer with his thumb, letting it fall back on the cap without firing. He let out his breath, lay there for a while, then stood and walked back to where the horse grazed, holding the moment in thought, then mounted and rode off.

Some miles had been crossed. He pulled up the horse and looked down onto the ground, his thoughts distorted and damaged, promises broken and discarded. He took the Sharps from its loop on the saddle horn and pulled the hammer to full cock, pulled the trigger and the horse shied and danced at the explosion of the bullet that sped invisibly towards the open sky.

***

For a wanted man, some kind of employment might hide the past. He was too old to rob a bank and anyway they were not like they used to be, with armed guards and time safes, barred counterpanes and such. And to tell himself the truth, he had never taken enough to make it worth his while. Maybe he was too honest? His early misdemeanours had been amateur affairs and with the coming of the war, the army had knocked all of that out of him, or so it had seemed.

He was wanted, had no money, no place to go and was getting old. He knew nothing much just horses, so maybe he could find something along those lines. He was willing to give it a try, but he knew it was a long shot.

Saddle tramp is a harsh term, and one that he came to feel fitted him like a shrinking glove. He found that stealing food was harder than stealing horses and after a few days found his belly was making noises harsher than an unoiled barn door.

William Standing had decisions to make, and he knew it. Already he had despoiled his own promise to himself and let it go, but he made another to the children that he could not. In some strange way he could not resolve the mental issues that they were no longer kids but grown people, possibly with families and friends a world away from his. But a promise is a promise, and anyway, he guessed that this part of the world would be the first place where they would look for him.

Where the children had been despatched to their kin he had no idea, but logic told him that you have to start somewhere. East they had gone, and there he would begin the search, and if it took him another twenty years, what else did have to do with his time? He would head east, find some kind of employment and take it from there.

So, on an overcast morning, he sold the horse at the next township that had a railhead and found the ticket office. In his pocket was twenty dollars. He approached the counter and placed the money on the table.

"Where to?" asked the ticket clerk.

"East."

"Where east?"

"As far as that will take me," Will said, pushing the dollars further towards the man.

The clerk scratched his head and looked across at the dishevelled man on the other side of the counter.

"Well, St Louis, Missouri is the best I can do," he said. "And you won't get much change from twenty."

Will blinked.

"I was hoping for further." He screwed up his face in thought for a moment. "All right, it will have to do."

He took the ticket and went onto the wooden deck that was the platform and stood under the canopy, hands in the pockets of his tattered overcoat and looked up at the rain.

Back in the ticket office, the clerk opened a drawer and thumbed through a handful of papers, checking each and looking at the photographs, grainy and monochrome as they were. He found the one he was looking for and eyed it for some seconds, then fished for his spectacles in his vest pocket and looked closer. It showed someone younger, but it could be him. He knew a familiar face when he saw one, and this had only just arrived a couple of days back. Putting on the closed sign, he hurried over to the telegraph office.

***

The journey took three days. It was somewhat different from the last train he rode, and at least this time he had a seat, hard as it was on the intimate regions. Having sold the horse, he had spent a few dollars on food that would see him through the journey and although he could have seen it off in one, made it last until almost the last mile.

At every stop, the boredom of the ride became heavier, the carriage more crowded and the seat harder. Sleep was impossible due to the incessant conversations, the clack of the wheels on the steel rails and the constant impatience of small children.

Standing wondered what the children he searched for looked like now, how had they grown and changed from the faces he framed in his mind's eye. Would they know him, even remember him? He knew that it was a hard task he had set himself, but it was a task set many years ago and his conscience would not let it go away.

St' Louis, Missouri was a shock to William Standing's whole being. He had seen nothing like it and the Union Passenger terminal building was the largest building he had ever seen. He disembarked from the carriage and eased himself back into the upright stance that a human man should be graced with, even at fifty. Looking around, he found that the throng of moving people, milling and diverting along their own routes reminded him of the buffalo, when there used to be buffalo.

He walked on past the locomotive and looked up at a tower that held a clock of conventional design, and although the detail of the time piece was lost to him, he still found it impressive, wondering who had the skill and strength to climb the thing and wind it up.

Finding the way out, he could feel the cold wind of winter beginning to blow, and unaware of the name of the street where he now stood, he let instinct show the direction. He had no luggage, only the last of the clothes that he stood up in. 'Now what?' He thought.

***

Pinkerton's always moved immediately on information received, especially when a man was wanted and on the move. Three days was a tight fit from Washington on a frequently slow train, but with a photograph of the miscreant on hand it was worth the trouble. He had arrived at another passenger depot and had failed to find a carriage, so he ran as fast as he could until he found one free and urged the driver to hurry.

At Dearborn Street he stepped out and fumbled payment in his haste, dropping a five-dollar bill and chasing it for a few yards. The carriage driver made the conversion of change slow on seeing the man's need to hurry and was successful with his tip.

Rushing against the tide of de-training passengers, he looked to left and right, checking as many faces as he could as they passed him. On his hip was a forty-five calibre Schofield revolver in a polished holster that was part of his belt and worn high on the hip, where his suit jacket could easily be pushed aside to reach the weapon.

A railway guard stood by an iron rail, his hands clasped behind his back. The Pinkerton man showed his badge and a paper 'wanted' sheet.

"Have you seen this man?" He spoke urgently and quickly. "I believe he should be on this eastbound arrival. Perhaps a little older?"

The guard appeared to have little in the way of haste.

"Look, man. Look!"

The guard shook his head. Passengers still passed through and the Pinkerton looked dejected.

"What's he done?" The guard asked.

The Pinkerton man styled his moustache and pursed his lips in disappointment.

"Broke from the Georgia Penitentiary, looks like," he said.

***

It had been a mistake. What chance did he have in such a place as this? A saddle bum among suits and fine ladies that put his old rags to shame. He walked the streets, amazed at the high-quality merchandise that the shops offered, a ladder higher than that displayed in Mr Bridey's store some time ago.

He made sure that his dalliances were not overlong, lest one of the smart, uniformed policemen noticed him and thought to enquire as to his circumstances. They seemed to be at every corner, their thumbs in their belts and ever watchful, touching the peaks of their caps as pretty girls waked by in long dresses and high collars. The food had gone and his belly ached, and only a few cents rattled in his coat pocket, too few to purchase the smallest crumb from the bakery window that beckoned him forward to look in. He turned away and went to the next shop, a general store. He stopped and looked at the half sheet poster on the inside glass, colourful and bright against the tools and other sundry items behind.

'Buffalo Bill's Wild West'

Headed and personally introduced by

Col. W.F. Cody "Buffalo Bill"

The World's Greatest Educational Exhibition

Now touring the Provinces

Will Standing smiled and looked at the illustrations. He remembered Russell. Laughing to himself, he walked away, then stopped, a more serious expression on his face. He looked at the date and the location and asked directions from a dapper man exiting a restaurant. The man was perfectly civil, despite Will's looks and pointed the way, perhaps thinking that he was in the correct costume for such a spectacle.

"Are you with the show?" He asked.

Will tipped his hat at the presumption but let it go for the sake of his own self-respect.

"Sure," he spoke.

The show ground was not hard to find and before he got anywhere near, he came across knots of Indians and other obvious show people eyeing the emporiums, interested in what Chicago had to offer. Will found the strange sight of Cheyenne, Arapaho and Sioux, walking civilisation's streets as he was, something of a surprise, but he tried not to show it.

The back lot was open and civilians seemed welcome to walk around the horses, wagons, tepees and other western regalia that filled the site. He entered under the big canvas sign that stretched across the entrance, the bold red characters advising of 'BUFFALO BILL'S WILD WEST'.

Standing entered and walked around, wondering how all of this could have been gathered and brought east. He looked through at where the horses were stabled in long tented enclosures, and stayed a while at the temporary corral where the small herd of buffalo were kept. With all of the civilisation back on the streets, this felt like home.

A pair of riders walked his way, obvious by the sheepskin chaps that covered their legs and the high sugar loaf hats they wore, a little stylised and over coloured in their dress, but somewhat familiar. Will greeted them and asked for direction to someone who might be hiring. One pointed back through the smaller tents.

"See Major Burke, tumble kind of guy with a long blue coat, long hair and moustache."

Will followed the direction and found what looked like the man he needed, one foot up on a rail, his knee balancing a stiff handful of papers and scribbling on the top one.

"Major Burke?" Will asked.

The man turned to him, long hair flowing down his neck.

"I am, so?"

"Sir, I was wondering if you might be hiring folks? I've come a long way east and I need a job. I know horses and I can…"

Burke shook his head.

"We are close to finishing for the season," he said, "going into winter quarters. Come back then, if you are around."

It had been worth a try. Will tipped his hat and thanked him and turned to walk away. Burke watched him go, noting the general makeup of the man, despite his tattered clothing.

"Wait!" He called out after the departing man. "Maybe you'd better come see the boss, he's got more say so than I've got."

Standing thanked him and took him towards one of the larger tents, and entering was amazed to see rows of tables covered with clean white linen, polished cutlery and using them every facet of western costume. Bronco busters sat side by side with Indians of all tribal origins, drivers and workers of all divisions, casual and besuited alike. Food was being served by waiters who buzzed between the tables like busy bees and filled up half empty plates and cups. Along one side was a range wagon, where all of the food emanated from, steam and strong juices reminding Will of what he had missed for some time.

He followed Burke inside to where a figure sat with his back towards them, lost in conversation with his neighbour. Burke tapped him on the shoulder and he turned around. Will recognised him immediately, although he was a little older like he was, the same long hair, now greying, the same flamboyant dress style and the same demeanour. Burke looked at Will.

"This is Mr Cody, Buffalo Bill as we know him."

Will took off his hat as Cody eyed him, and his apparel.

"I told this man that we have no employment as we are into winter quarters before too long…"

Cody spread his hands.

"I am afraid that Major Burke is correct," he told Will. "We are disbanding shortly and we have little need of workers. If you had come some weeks past, we could perhaps have offered something."

"Thank you, then, Sir," Will said as he nodded to Burke and made for the exit.

"Perhaps you would care to join us for lunch," Cody's voice reached him across the chatter inside the tent. "There is plenty, and it would be the least we could do for someone who has offered service."

Will Standing spun around slowly and took off his hat again.

"I would like that, and most grateful for it, Mr Cody."

Cody smiled and waved a hand at a vacant seat across the table from him. Will would have preferred to be alone, but when providence offers lunch, how can the guest be less than courteous. He sat down and divested himself of his raggedy coat. What was underneath was little better. At Cody's direction, food came and Will dived in, finding silver service a little out of his reach, but he tried hard not to show his lack of formal manners.

Cody watched him eat, smiling. He waved a hand.

"I feel that I know you Mr…"

It took the devourer of beef a moment to think.

"Ryder, William Ryder," Will answered, "but I'm sure we never met before. Heard of you, though."

Cody shook his head.

"I never forget a face, I am certain our paths have crossed, but for the life of me I cannot recall. Old age, I guess."

Will swallowed.

"I think you must confuse me with another."

"Of course, you are probably correct, Mr Ryder," Cody agreed. "How is the beef?"

They spoke for some time, Will agreeing for a second helping, and it was a cordial conversation with Cody happy to explain the workings of the Wild West, how it had developed from a fourth of July celebration to become the reworking of history that it now was, although that was not exactly how he put it. Will kept his history to himself and when asked questions about his previous life that he felt inappropriate to his present situation, he side-lined the enquiries to a more mundane existence.

The diners had thinned out substantially, due to the proximity of the afternoon performance. Will stood and thanked Cody for feeding him and extended a hand across the table, which was returned with a firm grip. He pulled on his coat and placed his hat upon his chest with another grateful gesture.

"Thank you, Mr Cody," he said. "I hope your show goes well."

Buffalo Bill stood too and walked him to the entry to the tent. When about to take his leave, there was one more question from his host.

"Did you ever find those children that you were determined to catch up to, Mr Ryder?"

Standing turned to Cody and looked him in the eye, a little taken aback by the words. Buffalo Bill's face was without humour or contempt, just concern. Will nodded and put on his hat.

"I did, Sir. But I lost 'em again."

He started walking back to the entrance, to who knows where or what. Cody called again. Will looked back.

"Mr Ryder, we are shortly closing for the winter, but we have a contract with a local company for the housing of some of the horses, mules and other animals. We have our own staff who will oversee their welfare. It is not much of a position, and includes a considerable amount of unpleasant work, but if you are willing, I can pay you twenty dollars a month and found," he offered. "Are you interested?"

"I am, Mr Cody, and thank you."

"Then I will instruct Major Burke to add you to the payroll. You can begin immediately if you so wish, help out with as a general worker, and until we shut down, we will find you a bunk on the train."

Cody took him to Burke's tent and the arrangements were made. He was given better clothing, a place to get clean and invited to watch the afternoon performance and to look around the back lot to acclimatise himself with his surroundings, and promised that on the following day he would be assigned to a work crew until the winter break.

He felt that this was a new way to fulfil his promise to find the children. The show travelled far and wide and at every stop he would search, hoping that Henderson might still be their family name. There was no guarantee that it would be so, but the least he could do was to try. Also, the travel would keep his movements fluid and from anyone that still had an instinct to find him.

An hour before the show began, Will Standing was on nodding terms with other staff members and looked around from one tent to another until he came to the remuda area, where the horses were housed beneath canvas. Hands in pockets, he walked slowly along the line, admiring the quality of the animals, some being prepared for the opening revue in which Buffalo Bill would ride into the arena and address the paying audience.

Almost at the end of the line and moving towards the side exit, he noticed something that took him back to a different time. The high, blue black of a quality horse, was stabled between two roans. He stepped closer to take a look at the animal and slapped one roan on the hind quarters, moving it away so that he could have a better view. He was astonished.

Not only did the animal resemble Midnight, he was certain that it was the horse that he had known all of those lost years ago. He let his hand slide along its back, down its withers and chest. He knew it must be dragging twenty by now, but it still carried itself well and seemed strong and responsive, although he doubted that the animal remembered anything of their previous association.

"An old friend?" Cody asked, coming through the canvas.

Will sniffed away the emotion.

"Sure is," he agreed. "Thought he'd be long gone by this time."

Cody took the opposite side and rubbed the animal on the neck.

"We call him Charlie," he said. "He takes centre stage at the opening of the show. Quite the old fellow, I'm afraid, but he seems well and I've had him some years."

Will smiled.

"Summit Springs?" He asked. "You took him from a Cheyenne named Tall Bull, when he was in no condition to ride him no more?"

"Something like that," Cody agreed. "But I did not shoot that individual. I believe a man named Mr North did that service. I merely took responsibility for a horse that no one else seemed to be claiming."

Will Standing laughed.

"I like that explanation. I could've used it myself on occasion."

"Well, he'll be coming with me to the North Platte over winter, but you will reunite for the season of eighty-six, I hope."

"I hope so too," Will said.

That afternoon, William Standing watched the performance from a hole in the huge canvas backdrop that was hung on one short side of the rectangular arena. The beginning of the show began with a grand entrance of the various types of horsemen, and horse ladies, for women were by no means discounted from dangerous activities, including the riding of bucking horses. Buffalo Bill, himself, led the parade, mounted on Midnight, or 'Old Charlie' as he was now known. With the Stars and Stripes carried behind him, Cody advanced with the squadrons of riders who entered the arena, Indians of all tribes, wranglers, US cavalry companies and horse artillery.

Standing was mesmerised by the flow of horses and riders, Indians and bucking horses, the Deadwood Stagecoach repelling an attack by hostiles, a simulated buffalo hunt and so many wonders of his world that he had almost forgotten and had almost gone. At each segment, an orator announced the action through a large brass trumpet that expanded his voice, and curtains in the backdrop were pulled aside to let performers enter the long stage.

Half way through came an enactment of the Summit Springs battle, in which white women had been taken by Cheyenne, to be 'rescued' by Colonel Cody, Fifth Cavalry and attendant cowboys. It was too much for Will to see through that section and he pulled away, not wishing to recall the true horrors that such events symbolised.

The show travelled by special trains and performers had bunks on the passenger cars, with a little space below for personal items. Will had none, but soon found himself given used clothing by staff members and he realised that this was indeed a special family, working as one for the benefit of all. He still kept himself to himself but remained cordial.

A few days later, the season ended and as advised he found himself as part of a crew seeing to the welfare of the animals, housed in rented sheds. The personnel bunked above in the loft and apart from the occasional mouse that desired to share his bed, life was as good as it got for someone like him. Although some whined at the lodging, for him it was three squares a day and a bed better than an outhouse.

Cody left for his place at the North Platte as did others who had places to go, like Annie Oakley the shooter, and her husband, Butler. The train, the passenger cars and flat cars were returned to normal service and would be rescheduled for the next season and the wagons stored with the horses and the buffalo.

***

In the Washington office of the Pinkertons, the trail had gone cold and the file of William Standing was returned to the shelf. But one was not happy to let it go, and would not settle until it had all been resolved, and justice done.

Chapter Seventeen
Wondrous Wild

1886

Winter passed slowly, and William Standing grew into the routine of looking after the animals and seeing to their welfare. Much time was involved with a wide shovel, cleaning out the stalls and feeding them, and when this was done, there were sundry tasks such as repairing and cleaning tack and making new leathers where needed. There was also some work to do on some of the wagons that had been left there and all was overseen by a foreman that headed the small crew, which worked well together and got the job done.

As a distraction, early in 1886, Grover Cleveland came to town on a presidential campaign and Will and the others went into the street to see the short parade and cheer or not as the political persuasion prompted. He was to become president in March but. Will Standing had little interest in politics and no idea of which way he might vote, even if he understood the argument, and so returned to where the buffalo needed feeding.

In early April, Major Burke, who was the ramrod of the Wild West, returned to check on the livestock and the sturdiness of the wagons for another season. In all he appeared to be satisfied and even gave Will a curt nod of recognition. He then called him over and asked to be shown the repairs that had been made and the costs incurred. Burke explained to Will, who had yet to be involved in moving the show from one town to another on short 'stands', how these wagons were hauled up onto the flat railway cars on a daily basis by heavy horse and took a considerable workload.

By the end of the month, the whole area was a cacophony of moving animals and wagons, men and horses, buffalo and even elk. The Wild West rake of flat cars, sleeping carriages and wagons were hauled into a siding, awaiting the beginning of the loading routines. When time allowed, Will went down to the goods yard, to see for the first time the freshly painted orange livery on each piece of rolling stock and the shields of texts that boldly extolled the benefits of the Wild West in its role as an educational exhibition. He was impressed, and not only by the competence of the loading and the organisation, but by seeing famous people such as Annie Oakley and the legendary Buck Taylor, a six feet five giant who wore the title, 'King of the Cowboys'. Of course, none of the stars of the Wild West took much notice of a raggedy roustabout, but that mattered little, and he was paid twenty dollars a month.

By the first of May, Cody and his entourage appeared for a final confirmation that all was ready and on second of May, the show pulled out of St Louis on the special train that would carry it to the first performances at Dayton Ohio. By opening day on the fifth of May, the whole show ground was erected and ready. To Will, who had seen little of such a wonder before, it was like a moving town. His place was with the horses, and he worked diligently with long hours. He had helped with the disembarkation from the railway wagons and led them into their own stable tents, where they were allowed to be fed, watered and groomed ready for the afternoon show.

Almost the last animal to arrive was Midnight, now named 'Charlie', and led in by Cody, who patted the animal warmly on the flanks. Will walked across to receive the animal.

"William…" He searched for the surname.

"Ryder," Will added. "William Ryder, Mr Cody."

"Aah," Cody said, and then, "Call me Bill, they all do."

Will nodded, but found the request a little difficult.

"How well do you know horses, William?" Cody asked.

Standing turned to one of the heavy horses on the other side of the tent, a sorrel with a small blaze. He jerked a thumb at the animal.

"Enough to know he's got a loose shoe, left hind hoof, it already started a strain on the hock," he told his employer. "I'll take him over to the blacksmith tent and get him done before we leave."

Cody smiled.

"What do you think of the show, Will?" Buffalo Bill asked. "Do you find it… exciting?"

Will felt unsure of what to say.

"Well," he began, "reminds me of how things used to be, but ain't no more. Funny how things change so quick, sometimes for the better, but not all. What you got here is the last chance for people to see the old days as they were. I guess some of it is not as I recall, but it will have to do."

Cody took the words for what they were and left for his own tent, a marvel of life on the move, with writing bureau, comfortable cot and its own sign to announce the occupier. Will slept often with the horses, but sometimes on the train, where comfortable sleeping arrangements were available for most of the crew when the show was on the move.

Occasionally, he caught a glimpse of the Number One Advertising Car, the bright yellow railway wagon which went a week ahead of the show train to promote it in the next town. On board were all of the equipment and materials to cover the operation of bill posting and announcing the street parade that began the visit on arrival at a new venue. The posters were colourful and illustrated with dramatic scenes of every item in the programme and headed with a portrait of Buffalo Bill, with text to confirm what patrons would experience…

'Wondrous Wild'

Will Standing began to like the life, the routine, the working with horses, and three silver service meals every day, surrounded by the kind of people he felt comfortable with.

On the twenty fifth of May, the show had moved on to Wheeling, West Virginia, for a four-day stand. On the morning of the arrival, as the train pulled into the town before five in the morning, Will Standing was disembarking the heavy horses, the first to be needed to pull the wagons from the end flat car by means of a ramp. Others of the crew were similarly employed. Then, without warning, someone accidentally released the pressure of steam from the cylinders of the locomotive. One of the horses moving up the line and near the engine reared and bolted back the way that it had come, pulling clear of the roustabout that had held it. Galloping through the crowds that were disembarking, the horse thundered down the line, performers jumping to safety as it came.

Will Standing heard the drumming of hooves and turned to see the horse approaching. Without the thoughts that he had later concerning the matter, he calmly walked into the animal's path and threw up one hand and stood rock still. With the other hand he took off his hat and held it out straight.

"Whooooa!"

The horse slowed, recognising a familiar voice, and over several yards, came to a complete halt, its head jerking from one side to another, still confused and terrified by the discharge from the locomotive. Will grabbed the halter and spoke gently to calm the horse down.

The commotion was over and people returned to their duties, thankful that none had been injured. As Will led the panting horse away, he noticed Cody, sat on Midnight, some way down the line and watching him go.

Morning was the busiest time for the horse men. The animals had to be fed and watered and groomed, ready for the street parade at noon and the afternoon performance. Afternoons were generally free time, unless specific duties were given. Major Burke did not take part in the street parades and when things had become quiet, he found Will Standing finishing off in the remuda tent. He tipped his hat.

"Good day, Will," he said.

Will turned to respond. Burke continued.

"Pretty nice trick with that horse, this morning," he said. "Bill was impressed with the way you handled it. He said, we might have lost a horse, or worse a rider, and it might have cost the show dear in insurance."

He reached up and scratched his beard, not dissimilar to that of Cody's.

"Well, maybe if I'd given it some thought, I might have let the damn thing run itself out. Could have got myself trampled, and out of a job."

"But you didn't," the Major said. "Bill said to move you out, over to the bronc animals. Stock that wild need looking at by somebody who understands 'em. Means another five dollars a month if you're willing, and another dollar if you ride along with the street parade, in case one of 'em turns nasty."

The horses that were kept for the bronc riding section of the show were not ridden at any other time. Some were trained to buck, and others did so for no other reason but plain meanness. They were housed apart from the other livestock and handled carefully. Those that rode them in the performances were skilled horsemen and it was a dangerous profession.

"Sounds good to me," Will agreed, "when do I start?"

"You just did," Burke said.

Despite his going up in the world, Will Standing had not forgotten his primary reason for being with the Wild West. Finding the children and fulfilling his promise was always prominent in his mind. At every opportunity, he walked the streets, asked at local churches or other social centres and always asked the same question. Often, he wondered if names had been changed and if he might be on a wild goose chase, but he had to try. He bought paper and nailed small messages onto every prominent post he could find.

Giving his search considerable thought, he hit on the idea that everyone needed food, a blacksmith, general goods and the like, and so asked at every emporium that a family might need, 'do you know of the Hendersons?'

On several occasions there was a chink of light when someone recalled the name, but all came to nothing and his disappointment grew.

After a successful three day stand the show packed up and moved on to the capital, opening in Washington on the thirtieth of May. With the Wild West making camp at the city's Athletic Park, Will planned that after the street parade in which he had agreed to participate to oversee the livestock, he would spend the afternoon spreading his small notices and visiting the usual local shops. He felt that as this was the capital, maybe his chances to find Tom and Alice were perhaps a little better than normal.

The street parade was enormously welcomed by the Washington crowds, as it always was in any venue. All performers were assembled and advanced in procession through the city thoroughfares, a brilliant way to announce and advertise the coming exhibition. A cowboy band played the music of the day, rousing tunes from Sousa and other well-known composers. William Standing took a position as directed, around a third of the way along the parade, and leading the string of saddle-less horses. As he moved along, he scanned the crowds gathered along the sidewalks for anything that might give him hope in his search. He was to be disappointed.

***

Since the Civil War, the Pinkerton Detective Agency had kept a small office in Washington, performing services for the federal government and also private enquiry matters. Most of the limited number of personnel who worked out of the Washington office had their own individual tasks, mostly restricted along the east coast while the Central Office in Chicago dealt with major issues such as the James and Younger gang.

Returning from his unsuccessful journey to the Georgia Penitentiary, the agent who hunted William Standing fell back into other matters, but at least he now had a likeness of the man and as the agency always boasted, 'we never sleep.'

The weeks passed and one late sunny morning in June, he left his desk as he normally did to sit beneath the outside shades of Carmello's restaurant and take an early lunch. It was only a short distance to walk, but on that morning, his path across the street was blocked by crowds of people lining the side walk, hailing the parade that was just passing. At first, he thought it to be the Barnum and Bailey Circus returned, but was amused to find another great enterprise, the Wild West, led by the famous figure of Buffalo Bill riding a great black horse.

Children cheered and waved as Cody passed by, taking off his hat and returning the salute with a flourish. He was followed by a band of woolly-chapped riders, playing Custer's favourite song, 'Gary Owen'. The agent smiled as other squadrons of riders passed with their own individual qualities, Indians, Mexicans, United States Cavalry and the Deadwood Stagecoach, found, repaired and repainted by Cody from the wreck that it was found as.

Someone brushed by and the agent reacted in accordance with his training, and quickly dropped a hand down to the polished holster that held the Schofield revolver beneath his jacket. It was an automatic response that he soon realised was unfounded and he went back to enjoying the unusual free entertainment.

He moved along the line of excited people, three deep from the front where there were more children, completely absorbed in the spectacle. Ranks of horsemen filtered by in their own groups and he raised a hand to shield his eyes from the bright noon day sun. Several wranglers led the string of bucking horses that would thrill the public later in the afternoon, fire eyed animals that were billed as furious to the saddle and whoever tried to sit it.

Sharp eyes caught the half profile of one of the wranglers and the agent froze. He did not have the advantage of the poster likeness on his person and could not decide if his eyes were playing tricks in the hot, bright sun. He blinked away the moisture and tried to focus better, at the same time pressing forward through the crowd. The riders were passing so he forced his way through, until the father of a young boy decided that the man was disadvantaging the experience for his son. Without warning, he was shoved back with force enough to put him on the ground and struggling to regain his feet as more onlookers joined in to condemn his actions.

***

In his short time with the Wild West, William Standing had become friendly with one of the major performers in the show, John Nelson, who drove the original Deadwood Stagecoach in the exiting event, described in the programme as…

'An attack on the Deadwood Stagecoach by Indians,
and repulsed by Buffalo Bill and attendant Cowboys.'

It was overcast and a slight drizzle began. As Will was about to leave for the city streets to continue his quest for the children, Nelson ran over to him in a state of some distress. Will could see that something was wrong as the afternoon performance was not far from beginning, and Nelson ought to be checking the mules and the coach tack. He waved as he caught Will's eye.

"Gol-durn it!" Nelson gasped as he neared, almost out of breath. "Anderson come down with the damn measles, so I ain't got no shotgun, and the coach goes on in twenty minutes. I need a shotgun or them 'Injuns' ain't got nobody to shoot at 'em."

Will smiled at the explanation, and Nelson continued.

"I need somebody that can sit a wagon box without the damn fallin' off. Burke said he'd pay five dollars for anybody I could find that would do the afternoon show, until we find somebody permanent and Anderson gets over the measles. You interested?"

Will thought about it. He wanted to go about his search, but five dollars was five dollars, and there were other afternoons.

"Oh, I guess so," Standing agreed.

"Then come the damn on," Nelson growled across his substantial beard and drooping moustache, turning to hurry back across the back lot to where the coach was waiting for the afternoon performance.

In the arena, the US horse artillery was almost completing its routine. Some yards behind the curtains that allowed each item to enter and exit, stood the Deadwood Stagecoach, hitched to six mules. Nelson climbed up onto the driver's box and threw over a Winchester filled with blanks. A similar weapon was already up on the seat.

Will Standing caught the rifle and took his place beside John Nelson. This was the first time that he had actually taken part in a performance, and unlike the simplicity of the street parade, this was different. Will now felt that he was an actor without experience and he swallowed hard, wondering if he had done the right thing. He looked at Nelson, who was checking the longer reins to avoid any tangle.

"What the hell I do?" Will asked, nervously.

Nelson twisted his lip and shook his head.

"Pull down your hat and shoot at the varmints when I tell you and not until. And don't just pop at 'em all at once; you got two Winchesters so stretch out the shells until Cody kicks in to save us," Nelson told him. "And for Heaven's sake, don't fall the damn off, and if you do keep from under the mules!"

Will pulled down his hat, tight over his eyes. Applause emanated from the other side of the backdrop as the artillery completed its performance and a peal of thunder heralded a coming storm. Two huge curtains slid apart, actioned by manpower. The 'cowboy band' played off the horse-drawn guns, which passed by the coach on either side as the curtains closed behind them.

The orator in the arena announced the next item through a huge brass trumpet, supported on a wooden frame. Immediately the mules showed signs of excitement, taking their cue from what was happening around them, something they did on an almost daily routine. The drizzle became rain and another charge of thunder rocked the sky.

"Whoooa, Annie!" Nelson called across the team to an over anxious mule in the lead pair. He looked sideways at his 'shotgun'. "Ready?"

"Ready!" Standing answered, finding the words dry in his throat, despite the downpour.

He began to regret the show's promise of 'Two Performances Daily, Rain or Shine!'

The big curtains drew aside and Nelson needed little urging of the mules, the animals knowing perfectly well what was expected of them. The chains and leathers tightened and in a shudder, the original Deadwood Stagecoach lurched forward, splashing through the open backdrop and into the arena. The crowd roared and Standing winced at the sound, looking wide-eyed at so many people in one place and all looking at him.

John Nelson slipped into character and took off his hat with a free hand and waved it into the audience. He grunted at Will.

"Take off your hat, you damn fool," he shouted above the thunder of hooves, "shake it at the population that's paying your wages!"

Will did so and heard the people cheer. He smiled at the reaction and began to enjoy the experience as the coach careered along the long side of the arena and Nelson pulled it around into the first curve. Almost immediately, the speed of the coach meant another lean into the next curve and a long gallop towards the painted backdrop.

All of the crowd were covered by an oilskin canopy that protected from the weather. The audience in the bleachers stood as the coach passed them, waving their programmes and hats, cheering them on into another circuit of the field. Pulling around the end of the arena, for the second time, the orator drew the attention of the crowd to a sighting of 'wild Indians'. The curtains began to open slowly as the coach passed and headed down a long side once more, trailing a double line of mud and rain behind the rear wheels.

To a crash of distant lightening, and whoops and yells, twenty riders on painted ponies crashed into the open space in pursuit of the Deadwood coach. Nelson increased its speed with a shout across the mules and the animals rushed forward at the appropriate place. Will Standing turned in his seat, looking back through the tumbling rain at the screaming Cheyenne and Sioux, their bodies gleaming as water ran from their bodies and from the flanks of their horses. In that second, he was taken back to another time, another place, and for a moment his mind stopped working, until another flash of light lit up the sky.

"Shoot, you damn fool! Shoot!" Nelson shouted above the noise of thunder and splattering hooves.

Standing returned to the present and raised the rifle, remembering another time when a small hand had stopped him. Rain ran across his face in rivulets and he blinked away the wet. He fired, seeing the smoke from the barrel, but hearing little but hooves and the roaring crowds. He fired again as the pursuing riders, resplendent in painted faces and feathers spread out behind the coach and across the arena to cut them off at the turn. It all seemed so real and for a brief second, Will forgot the audience and the increasing rain. He fired once more and leant closer to Nelson.

"Pull around! Pull Around!"

Nelson looked back at him as if he were deranged.

"We gotta keep it down to give Cody his turn to get in!" He answered behind a frown.

"What?"

"Cody coming in to rescue us, like he always does, when we make the turn at the end," Nelson told him. "Just keep firing on them there Injuns!"

The coach was heaved around the end of the arena once more, Nelson letting out his right hand to ease the control of the mules on that side while pulling in his left towards him and driving the coach around in that direction. They were close to the side fence and as they passed by each section the crowds were bespattered by mud and rain, but they loved it. The drama of the weather, the sights and sounds of a world that was passing by enthralled their imaginations, children and adults alike. They had seen nothing like it, and many would never again, unless paying a visit to future venues.

The curtains drew aside again to another thunder clap. Astride Midnight, William Frederick Cody, Buffalo Bill, galloped into the muddy arena, followed by a group of bedraggled riders who drew their pistols and fired at the Indians who were attacking the coach to the thrill of the crowds. It was as if the poor June weather did not exist, either to the crowds or the performers, as time stood still for one more performance.

Will continued to fire consistently from his seat on the coach as the wild and colourful attackers drew close around them. The rain and the churned spray and mud made vision difficult and without thinking he rose and turned bodily around to rest his knee on the seat, trying to get a better view of the ground behind them. All that he could see beyond the back of the coach were the heads and uppers of both men and horses above the disturbance of mud and rain, jostling for position and enjoying the gallop.

"Set down, idiot!" Nelson shouted to his 'shotgun' when he saw Will rise.

The other was riding with the bouncing of the coach and playing his part well, the crowds applauding every shot, every whoop of a warrior and every time that Cody fired after them. Nelson pulled the coach into a turn again and Will felt his balance slip. He let go of the rifle with one hand, reached for something to steady him, but the momentary grip slid away and he felt himself falling, sliding and slipping on wet wood and metal, over the edge of the seat and towards the grinding wheels. Nelson flashed out a hand but Standing had gone over.

Will had a flashed vision of wheels and wet and his hand tightened on something, a handrail that was there to assist climbing up onto the seat. His legs were pushed away with the inertia of the curve and his feet found a temporary foothold on the board fencing that separated the audience from the performance. One after another his boots moved across the timber in quick succession while keeping his grip on the rail, running at an angle until he found the chance to heave himself out of the danger and pull himself onto the step that led up to the passenger door. The crowd went wild and he reached up and pulled his hat further down over his eyes, slipping his hands through the passenger door window and around into the side window and holding on through the wet and the rolling of the coach.

Nelson hauled back on the reins and looked over and down at the man who now held on to the side. As he became aware of the cheering crowds, Will Standing could not resist his moment of fame and with one hand took off his hat to show his appreciation, forgetting the rain streaming down his face and body. He knew that he had messed up his one and only chance and wondered as to the outcome.

Out into the arena, Cody continued with the general performance and chased off the Indians while the coach made one more circuit to the cowboy band's rendition of the 'Stars and Stripes'. And finally, to the appreciation of the crowds, the Deadwood Stagecoach made its way through the double curtains that parted to allow its departure through the wet and the rain, and out of sight behind the backdrop.

As the coach pulled up and Will stepped down onto wet ground and shook himself, John Nelson looked down at him and shook his head.

"God-damn, Will…"

Just then, Major Burke came through the rain, through knot of performers getting ready to follow next in the arena. He was covered in oilskins and grabbed Will by the arm.

"You all right?" He asked.

Will said he was and looked a sad sight, drenched from head to foot.

"Get yourself dry," he told Will. "Then get over to the Cody tent, he wants to see you right away."

Will Standing nodded without speaking further. He knew what was coming. Going over to one of the dressing marquees, he found a change in clothing, then found an oilskin horse blanket to keep him from the weather again.

Cody's tent was not far, next to the small conglomeration of tepees where the Sioux, Cheyenne and other tribes found shelter from the unseasonable June downpour. He stopped outside and called out.

"Will Ryder, Mr Cody."

The tent flaps opened to reveal the figure of Buffalo Bill, himself still wet with the previous adventure in the show, and pulling on a fresh shirt jacket.

"Come on in!" He said. "Some ride, huh?"

"I guess," Will said. "You want to see me, Mr Burke said to come over…"

"I did," Cody told him.

Will wondered what it might take to pull himself out of the mire. Maybe if he worked on the principal that he was only a last-minute stand-in, and did the best he could, surely that would be a reasonable excuse for making such a mess of his one and only performance.

"Mr Cody, I want to…"

Cody held up a finger.

"That was one hell of a performance, Will, and the crowd loved every minute of it," he said. "God-damn, that held the audience. Now if we can work along that line for every performance, and you can manage not to break you damn neck…"

"But?"

"Course," Cody continued, "if we get weather like today, we can tone it down a little, maybe just lean across, but if you can do that skip along the side fencing and Johnny Nelson can keep the coach steady around the curves it will be one daisy of a piece of action, so what do you say." He paused. "And maybe another twenty dollars a week to make it worth the effort?"

"But?"

"…And we can sort some kind of harness to make sure you stay in one piece," added Buffalo Bill, spreading his palms to describe his vision. "I can see it on the posters now…"

Chapter Eighteen
'We Never Sleep'

Will Standing wanted no part in the posters advertising the Wild West. He had always seen it as a means to an end, a way to continue his search, to fulfil the promise that he had made to others and, in some way, ease his own conscience. He was no angel, he knew that, but some things you have to keep to if you want to sleep nights.

It was still raining when he left Cody's tent, telling him that he would consider the matter. He knew that to deny his employer might mean the loss of his job, his income and the best chance to keep his word. Cody could be petulant and unpleasant when he did not get his way, but generous and confident when he did, and Will wanted no connection with the former. This was the man that paid and fed him, but now he was pushing fifty and leaping from a stagecoach twice a day was maybe asking a little too much, but he would give it a try.

Standing knew that he was still a wanted man, a fugitive and a horse thief and everything else in between that they could get away with throwing at him. To keep moving and his head down was his best way to keep his freedom, but he knew there were some who would not let it go, would pursue him to the end, whenever that might be.

After completing his premier performance in the show, Standing left the grounds to continue his commitment. He had made out several of the small handbills and although the spelling might not be the best, the sentiment was, although he had taken some time to ensure that the wording was somewhat ambivalent for his own protection. Asking at the usual places, he once more drew a blank, but at least felt that he was doing his best.

Protected from the rain by an oilskin duster, he looked down at the Washington streets and saw the smart black, glossy carriages, the horse-drawn cabs and men in top hats, with ladies in resplendent dresses sheltering beneath the awnings of expensive emporiums. He wondered how near he might be to the children, or how far he still had to go.

***

Another morning saw the rain gone, and the sun returned, although it was still quite muddy and puddles of water still reflected the fresh blue sky. As Pinkerton detectives did as a matter of course, he checked the mail but there was little of importance.

He still smarted from the rough treatment he had received the day before, when apologies went unheard. It would not deter him from his task. Finding the poster of the wanted man, William Standing, he folded it and put it into his pocket, put on the Derby hat and went out into the street, making his way towards the grounds where the Wild West was offering a second day of 'Enlightening Western Exhibition'.

Athletic Park was a short distance away and by ten in the morning, the sun was already warm. He wondered how such an organisation as the Wild West would respond to a Pinkerton investigation, there being many nefarious types aboard as far as he could make out from the street parade. He had no idea what to expect, but there was still the Schofield at his hip if needs be.

The grounds were already open and a thoroughfare for comings and goings of all kinds of people. Some had hardly ever been seen on the streets of the capital before, Indians with heavy robes wrapped around them, wranglers, workmen and others, moving in every direction.

A Pinkerton-headed handbill was pushed before one of the shirt-sleeved workmen and he was asked, "Have you seen this man? He would be older now, but I think it is a fair likeness."

The man looked briefly, shook his head and walked on. He asked another, then another, all with the same result. He was becoming frustrated and felt his temper fraying. He was certain he had seen the man in the street parade, so near and yet so far.

Soon, he had found Cody's tent and called, to no reply. Someone passed by and advised him to try the dining tent and pointed the way through a host of milling people, performers and the public who were encouraged onto the show ground as a form of positive publicity for the Wild West.

Finding the dining area, he went inside and looked around, quickly identifying the character of Buffalo Bill in his shirtsleeves. Cody was in conversation with another, but discontinued the discussion as he neared.

"Mr William Cody?"

"That is I, Sir. Can I be of assistance?"

The Derby hat was removed and he took a seat when it was offered. He produced his authority.

"I work for the Pinkerton Detective Agency, Mr Cody, and I am looking for this man."

The handbill was pressed forward for Cody to look at. The detective continued, "I believe he is working for you, Sir. His name is William Standing, as you can see, but I would imagine he has changed it to another by now."

Cody took the bill and put on a pair of small spectacles. He turned his head one way and then another.

"I don't believe I know this man," he confirmed, "although he may have been with the show prior to our present aggregation."

"The tin type is an old one, Mr Cody, and he would be older, but I still believe it to be a sound likeness."

Buffalo Bill looked at the bill again. He shook his head. "I do not recognise this individual. Perhaps you are looking in the wrong place, for he does not appear familiar." He showed the bill to his companion in conversation, who shook his head also. "Mr Nelson has been with the Wild West since the beginning," Cody explained. "If anyone might recall this Mr Standing then I would imagine he might."

Cody handed back the bill.

"I am sorry that we cannot help you, Sir, although I have the highest regard for the Pinkerton Agency and wish you every success in your efforts to apprehend this person."

"Then my search must continue," said the other, "although I am certain that I saw this man in your parade yesterday. With a string of wild ponies."

Buffalo Bill widened his eyes.

"You saw him?" Cody raised his voice. "With the horses?" He stood up. "Then let us go to the remuda tent and find this man!"

Buffalo Bill dragged his fringed jacket from the back of his chair and put it on as he led the Pinkerton man away towards the horse tent. They walked quickly across the grounds and found the large structure that stabled the livestock.

Walking inside, Cody called down the line, "Gentlemen, come here please, cease your labour and line up along the rail."

Seven men walked from the horses to press against a free wooden pole. Cody counted them. "Yes. All seven are here." He waved a hand to the detective. "Please, take a good look at each man. If the rascal is here, then we will assist you in your arrest."

The detective stepped forward and checked each one against the handbill, but it was obvious that none fitted the description or the tin type.

"Who is the man responsible for leading the animals in the parade?"

A wrangler stepped forward and gave a toothless grin.

"That is not him," confirmed the Pinkerton man.

Cody smiled; that smile that promised all would be well.

"Then perhaps you were mistaken, the sun was very bright yesterday."

"Perhaps."

The detective shook hands and thanked Cody for his indulgence. He thanked the wranglers for their patience and left the remuda tent for the open street, much downhearted and downbeat. Reaching the side walk beyond Athletic Park, he stopped once more to look at the tin type picture on the hand bill. It was certainly not one of the wranglers. How could he have been mistaken?

He continued his march back to the small office, wondering how he might try further to secure his man. Reaching into his pocket for the small case that held his cheroots, he found only one left inside and resolved to replenish it at the first opportunity. A block further on he found what he was looking for, a tobacconist beside a demolished building. And then he saw it.

It was like a bolt of lightning flashing across his vision, like some wild experiment of Leonardo that had come true, working in his favour. He reached forward and took it from the wall, a small white bill with poor writing and worse spelling, but nevertheless readable:

to anywone readin this note
I look for childran named Henderson
a boy tom and his sister alice
who was brung east around 18 years back
if you know of them, please find me at the show grownd athletic park
William Ryder

A tight smile crossed the lips of the Pinkerton agent. He laughed, almost aloud. How easily they had deceived him, how quick he had been to admit defeat, and then to find this.

***

Early that morning, William Standing had found Cody and agreed to the job of stagecoach shotgun and appearing with John Nelson in the performance. He was still nervous about the fall he had to make, 'twice daily, rain or shine', but the extra money meant more paper to turn into bills to post. Cody reassured him that the show's harness maker would fashion some kind of strapping that would make the feat easier on the bones, and so far, he could not fault his employers in the way that they had treated him.

He had crossed the path of Major Burke, the general manager, who had told Will that since he was now a performer, his days of shovelling for a living were now over and that another had been raised to the lofty position of horse manure overseer in his place with immediate effect. His place in the street parades on opening day was now up on the wagon box with Johnny Nelson. Standing pondered the fact that instead of him now chasing Cheyenne, they were chasing him, and both parties were getting paid for it. It was a sobering thought upon changing times.

It went without saying that at that specific time, the Pinkertons were already on his trail and he knew nothing about it. Had he been aware, then the whole damn thing would have been different and who knows what might have happened.

The day until noon was spent with Nelson, checking the chains and lines that connected the team to the coach, a daily chore that was necessary as the last thing anyone wanted was for the coach to wave bye-bye to the mules and go its own way into the crowds. Paying customers expected a little more.

Nothing was said about the visit of the detective to Will and probably everyone expected that the whole thing would simply go away. Doubtless there were many riders with the Wild West who kept a constant watch over their shoulders but the show was a family and it would take a lot to abandon one of their own.

Will Standing went down to the dining tent at noon and sat with his irascible partner for the silver service lunch that the Wild West offered. Over beef and gravy, they discussed the afternoon performance and how they would make it work with the least effort and fewest muscles pulled. It all seemed to fall into place, slip over the edge of the wagon box after firing a few rounds, struggle to get back up and make it look exciting for the delicate ladies watching. And if time allowed when they started to scream, give them a smile of resolve that was true to the all-American male, and perhaps encourage them to a second ticket later in the week.

Will told Nelson that he understood what was expected and that he would do his meanest to get the job done. At least the day was better than the one before, and sawdust had been purchased from a local sawmill and spread all over the arena to make a firmer grip for hooves. The Deadwood coach item was due to go on at three fifty, so after the meal, he walked back out onto the streets, as did other free members of the cast and found another virgin area to begin with the hand bills.

After an hour, Standing walked back to the show ground and found John Nelson with the coach. It almost appeared that the man and vehicle were joined at the hip, so careful was Nelson to check every moving part and possible problem and in the history of the Wild West, nothing had ever gone wrong with the original Deadwood Stagecoach, apart from the pitting from Indian arrows.

Nelson had collected the strapping that the shotgun rider was to wear and had made it to look like a regular pair of suspenders, but to support the man rather than his trousers, and disguised their purpose well. The strapping was connected to the metal hand rail by a loop which prevented its wearer from falling should he lose his grip. It was a clever contraption which could hardly be seen by anyone not on the coach.

Will tried it on and connected to the coach. It seemed to do the job and he was satisfied that he could prosecute the required manoeuvre while remaining safe from the spinning wheel below. And so, the afternoon performance came, and after the US artillery drill it was time for the 'Attack on the Deadwood Stagecoach' item.

Driver and shotgun were in place and as the curtains opened, in galloped six mules dragging the coach. Will waved his hat at the audience in perfect Thespian manner and they drove twice around the arena, now covered in sawdust. He was still waving when the backdrop opened once more to allow the knot of Cheyenne and Sioux onto the stage and begin their pursuit, whooping and yelling, their colourful shields held high and fringed with feathers and beads in the finest of decoration. Painted ponies kicked up the sawdust and what mud was left, giving the whole scene the feel of authenticity that the crowds loved.

"Git to shootin' ya damn sooner!" Came the order to repel borders in true Nelson fashion.

Will Standing complied and turning to kneel on the seat box, he kept up a steady fire upon those following. Twice around the arena in peril, and then Buffalo Bill entered with a string of rescue riders, the whole area enveloped in noise and gun smoke.

It was time for the fall on the next bend and Will prepared himself, testing the strapping out of sight of the audience. Nelson hauled the mules around the short bend and Will went over, grasping the rail with a gloved hand and making it look good. The crowd roared as he went over. Some stood, thinking it was not rehearsed and according to attendants on the bleachers, grown men fainted.

All in all, it had been a perfect performance, and Cody was ecstatic, shaking both Nelson and Will by the hand and wondering why no one had ever thought of such an existing finale to the presentation before. Extended drinks in Cody's tent tended to iron out the crinkles in Will Standing's muscle areas, but it was an extra five dollars and better than shovelling after the horses until lights out.

Every day, after the evening performance had finished, Will had made his way down to the remuda tent to visit old 'Charlie', as he was now known, and that night was no different. To William Standing he was still Midnight, and always would be. Whether the animal remembered him or not, hardly mattered, it was their mutual history that counted, and it served to remind him of promises made and some left unkept. The horse was still a fine animal, sleek and blue where the light caught his jet-black coat and the years had treated him kindly. He was still alert and strong and Will could feel the strength in his great chest muscle and sturdy legs.

Will put his fingers through the dark mane and remembered times gone, years back when they chased Cheyenne raiders across a lawless land. It seemed that with everything else that had happened around him, those days had faded into memory and only the proximity of man and horse could bring them back, partners who had shared the same dangers, the same hardships. Will smiled when Midnight grunted a cough.

"It were a wild ride, all them years back, weren't it?"

The ticket wagon was painted white with gold lettering, shadowed in red and black. About the size of a normal farm dray, it was built high enough for a man to stand upon the deck without bending and a roof to keep out the weather. At one short end was the entry door and at the other the ticket sales window.

The detective stood in line and waited his turn, pulling down his dark brown Derby hat as if not wanting to be unduly seen. A man with a greying moustache looked through the small opening at him.

"Four tickets, please, for tonight's performance."

The grey moustache animated.

"Where you wanna sit?"

"Oh," said the detective, "where will I be able to see the most?"

The ticket seller seemed to be irritated at the question. He thrust his head forward.

"All seats are good, Mister. Oilskin covered and dry against the rain. But I guess if you want to look left and right at the same time, then maybe one of the longer pavilions will suit you just fine."

The detective looked irritated.

"Four tickets, then. Longer pavilion side."

"Three dollars, twenty," the seller confirmed, "no beer, no hard liquor, no firearms on the bleachers."

He took the tickets and put them into his inside pocket and thought about how he might make his observations when the time came, and what he would do about it if he was proved correct, and he had found his man.

***

Everyone had been satisfied with the way that the stagecoach event had developed into something more exiting. Even Will Standing was reasonably happy with things, despite it being his bones at risk. Around the show ground he had become something of a celebrity, his quick rise through the ranks, his new role as performer and generally because they kind of liked his unassuming way. He was gentle with horses, kept to himself and was glad to help out when the need arose.

The evening performance was only the second time with the harness that would guarantee him safety during the slip from the coach, as the previous night they were awaiting its manufacture and they had gone through the act in the old way. As darkness was falling, the lamps were lit and a warm yellow light flooded the arena.

From all sides, the crowds closed in to take their places, drawn to Athletic Park by horse-drawn omnibus, carriage, cart and shoe leather. Even men on penny farthing bicycles made their way to the Wild West, propping their steeds against iron railings and inserting a padlock on the spokes, and trusting the rest to the uniformed police men who paraded outside the show as a bulwark against pickpockets. Seldom since the last inauguration had floods of humanity such as this been seen on the streets of the capital.

The man with the dark Derby hat pushed along with the flow of people entering the show ground. With him were two children, a boy and a girl, and a pretty woman in a long, light blue dress, augmented with a fashionable bonnet and parasol. The small party were ushered along until their tickets were checked and they were pointed along to the bleachers, rows of descending seats that dropped to the level of the arena. For an extra ten cents, a straw filled cushion could be purchased to ease the compression of wood on flesh and was usually found to be value for money. The detective took four and moved his family down one of the longer sides of the covered pavilion.

Around half way, he decided to halt and take their seats, but the stewards continually moved them along until they were not far from the short end of the area and could look back along the arena to the backdrop. It was not what he had hoped for, and his view was impaired somewhat by the distance. The children were excited and asked how much longer before the show began but were calmed to patience by their mother. At the request of someone on the seat behind, the detective removed his Derby hat and put it in his lap, becoming nervous as the time for the beginning of the programme drew near.

When the sky had turned a deep inky blue, the strains of the woolly-chapped cowboy band began to flow around the arena in the form of the 'Stars and Stripes'. Everyone in the audience hushed as the orator burst forth through the brass trumpet that extended his voice.

"Ladies and Gentlemen, Boys and Girls, Welcome to Buffalo Bill's Educational Exposition of the American Frontier!"

The backdrop illumination rose as the two large curtains in the centre of the backdrop opened wide to allow the entrance of Buffalo Bill on Old Charlie, the big black horse cantering along the right-hand fence of the covered stand. Following in squadrons abreast came the Mexicans, the Indians, the wranglers and all mounted groups that would be part of the coming event.

The audience stood as one person and applauded the incoming horsemen and women, carrying national flags and waving their broad brimmed hats. Fierce tribes carried their own regalia of shields, war bonnets and lances, all beaded and feathered to the highest quality and colour. The Mexicans emitting high-pitched yells and swinging lariats around their heads. This indeed was the opening of the mighty entertainment known as Buffalo Bill's Wild West.

Behind the backdrop, everything was being readied for the first event, sharpshooting from the saddle by Cody and others, chasing riders who threw glass balls into the air, to be shattered by expert marksmen and women. Other acts followed, the Virginia Reel on horseback, Indian tribal dances and other wonders to entertain and educate.

Will Standing felt nervous, more than he had done before, and put it down to the first serious performance in lamplight. The coach was ready, the mules were tense and nervous awaiting their cue to begin. Johnny Nelson did his last customary check on the traces and the chains and patted the lead animals, a superstitious act that he did on every show. Will climbed aboard and fastened the strapping that would keep him safe. He checked the Winchesters to make certain they were loaded with blanks and ready to go. More applause thundered over the top of the backdrop and across the back lot. Almost time. Nelson climbed up onto the box seat and took the traces in both hands, separating each leather into the correct grip.

"Whoooaa, Annie!" He called, noting the excitement of one of the lead animals. He looked sideways to his shotgun. "Ready?"

"You bet," Standing confirmed.

The curtains opened and out from the arena came a host of painted ponies and their riders, followed by squaws and pack animals, dogs and mules. They closed again as the orator bellowed through the brass.

"Ladies and gentlemen, Boys and Girls, the Wild West is proud to bring you the attack on the original Deadwood Stagecoach by Indians, and rescue by Buffalo Bill and his attendant western riders!"

The huge curtains fell away and Nelson slapped the traces but the mules knew their moment and lurched forward to the canter, then the gallop, and burst into the yellow glare of the arena to the thunderous applause of the American public. Twice around the perimeter the coach drove, still with applause and cheers, with Will Standing waving his hat in response.

Out on the bleachers, eyes with a different interest than the rest of the audience had scanned each item on the programme as it played out, and this event was no different. It was not a perfect light to see by, but most observers were interested only in the spectacle as a whole and not individual faces within it.

Having completed the second circuit, the coach drew by the backdrop and as it passed the curtains parted once more to allow in the attacking Cheyenne and Sioux warriors. Will turned to take his position on the wagon box and shoot over the top of the coach, cheered on by excited onlookers. He leant in as Nelson took the short bend, his back to the audience. On the far turn, his face was covered by the stock of the Winchester, held up tight to his chin. Distant eyes blinked and tried to make out the features in the yellow illumination.

Will levered a round into the block and fired another blank at the make-believe attackers and continued for another circuit, until Buffalo Bill and his men once more entered to save the day. Now was his time.

Travelling the long edge of the fencing, the coach approached the coming curve. The nearest warriors let off a volley at the gallop and Will saw it as a good moment to act. He dropped the rifle into the well of the box seat and rolled over the edge, gripping the handrail as he had planned. His body jerked as Nelson prepared for the curve and he fell sideways, still held safely by his harness but with his back to the coach and his legs flailing against the fencing. However, he fell over the side of the coach he was safe and it took but a moment to right himself and complete the thrilling deed. But it gave someone at the right place and time to get a good view of the man's face, like the flash of a photographer's tin type exposure in his mind's eye.

He leant forward.

"That is him," he said, barely audibly. "That is William Standing!"

The detective's heart pumped with excited blood and beat against his chest like a jack hammer. He pulled out the 'wanted' bill and stared into the paper, shuffling it into the best light. He turned to his wife, who had detached herself from the drama in the arena.

"I am sure that is him. I am certain."

His wife's face tightened. She was fully aware of her husband's obsession with finding the man and seeing justice done at last. He crumpled the paper in his fist and set his lips beneath the heavy moustache.

Out on the sawdust, the coach had finally been saved by the efforts of the hero of the show and his attendant riders. The final shots to see off the Indians were being made and the original Deadwood Stagecoach was heading for the opening backdrop and safety. As a last flourish, Buffalo Bill paused at the last moment and reared Old Charlie in a final salute, the silver trimmings on his saddle flashing in the limelight.

Chapter Nineteen
Justice and the Man Who Stole Midnight

Cody rode slowly up to the coach as it came to a halt behind the arena backdrop. He sloped his large brimmed, white sombrero.

"That was a damn good showing, Gentlemen." He grinned. "Damn good. I shall expect you for a small appreciation in my tent after show time, if you are so inclined?"

Nelson grunted an 'all right' in his usual manner. Will Standing thanked his employer and agreed that he would certainly be willing to comply with the request, knowing that it might be slightly more than that, if Cody's reputation was to be believed. He unclipped the harness and climbed down. It would be another hour before the show was over, and so he decided to go down to the stable tent where Midnight had been walked down to be unsaddled.

Reaching the ground, Standing stretched away the minor aches from his exertions and felt the satisfaction of doing something right for a change. It was about time, and there was only one important thing left for him to do to feel complete, providing he could avoid his more recent misdemeanours catching up with him, of course.

The applause could still be heard over in the main part of the grounds and he felt glad to be a part of it. He walked slowly between the tepees and the blacksmith tent, the short avenue to the dining area where coffee was available for performers and crew alike twenty-four hours a day, and the concession wagon where sundries might be purchased at low cost.

Up ahead in the low light he could see the remuda tent and headed for the entry, flipping aside the flaps. Down at the far end he could see one of the wranglers easing Midnight into his temporary stall and start to take off the saddle. When he reached the place, Will slapped the animal on the flanks as he always did and helped with taking off the rest of the harness. The crewman walked off and busied himself elsewhere.

"Looks like the boss liked the show tonight," Standing said to the horse, which turned and pushed its nose into his abdomen. "Remind you of anything?"

He continued to rub the animal down after the excesses of the arena, easing his hand down the forelegs and checking for any strains. Rising, something caught his eye. Halfway along the centre line stood a man in a tailored suit, complete with dark brown Derby hat, the face tight and stern with a moustache. Will could see the tip of a polished holster protruding from the bottom edge of the jacket and knew that it would be useless to remind the man that personal firearms were prohibited on the show ground.

William Standing stepped away from the line of horses. At his hip was the Colt that he used in the show. He tried to think fast. Perhaps bluff might work.

"Are you indeed the man, William Standing?" The detective asked.

Will knew it had to come sometime, but was surprised that time had caught up so soon.

"My name is William Ryder, Sir. I have no knowledge of anyone of that name."

As they spoke, the crew among the horses made themselves scarce, leaving the two alone. The detective slowly reached into his inside pocket and drew out the 'wanted' bill.

"I have your likeness here," he said. "I have little doubt that you are my man."

Standing knew that it must be an old picture, but dare not admit to it for fear of incriminating himself. The world was closing in.

"I know of no picture, Mister. You are mistaken."

"Then I must trust to my instinct and take you for William Standing."

Will shook his head. "I might tell you where you may shove your instinct, Mister, if you do not stand down and walk away."

His own instinct slipped in and his right hand moved closer to the pistol at his hip. His eyes glazed and his mind weighed up the odds, an empty revolver against a loaded one, dead or another ten in the Georgia Pen? It seemed there was not much of an advantage either way. It was all over. His hand still moved involuntarily towards his hip. The detective threw up a hand, the palm presented towards the other.

"That is not my intention," he said. "There is no need for that!"

Behind the suit, the flaps of the tent opened and a pretty woman in a light blue dress appeared with two children. It was all over. Standing laughed hollowly.

"The gun's empty anyway, just blanks from the show business," he told the other. "I knew you'd be coming."

"You did?"

"Sure, just a question of time before it all caught up with me and bit me in the slats. The law always likes the last bite."

The detective looked confused. He pushed back the brown Derby.

"Uncle Will, do you not know me?"

William Standing frowned and looked hard at the face in the poor light. A knot of furrows dug deep above his eyes. His mouth opened but words were difficult.

"Tommy?"

"I am."

They both took a step forward, hardly believing what was happening, how they had at last found each other after so much time gone by. Hands reached out and became an embrace.

"I, I just…"

"I've been looking for you," Will laughed and cut in, "well, since I broke out from jail."

"I know," Tom said. "I found the note, the one you nailed to a wall. I searched for you too, but the story is long and I have to tell it."

Will looked across at the woman in the tent opening. "Alice?"

Tom shook his head. "We lost Alice these six years gone. She died from the consumption but it may be seen as a blessing, for she had little insight of the present since we were taken. She spoke little and uttered only the song that Mother used to sing on occasion." He turned to smile at the woman and children who were approaching. "This is my wife, Elizabeth, and our children, William and Molly."

Will let go his grip on Tom and took the hand that Elizabeth held out.

"Thomas has told me so much about you, Mr Standing." She smiled warmly. "I am so glad he has found you. It has been his life's work."

"Then I am glad that we worked it through," said Will. "But saddened that Alice cannot be here to see us all."

The side flaps burst open and in came a knot of men, led by Cody, who moved towards them.

"There must be some sensible explanation to all of this," he blurted, "I have known this man for many years and…"

Standing held up a hand.

"It's all right, Bill. You remember those children I was chasing the first time we met up?"

"Of course."

"Then this is my boy, Tommy, and his wife and kids, and we have at last closed the gap." Will grinned. "He is a mite older than I recollect and he's grown lip hair, but I know him now and I am glad of it."

His uncle led Tommy to where the black horse stood quietly in his stall.

"Remember him?" Will asked.

"Surely not the Bellfield horse?" Tommy asked.

"As was, but not no more. Now he's the Cody horse," Will told him. "Had my sights on Bellfield not long back. You once put a hand on the hammer once, but I guess somebody else did that day. Had him cold, but I walked away."

Standing slapped the animal on the flanks. He looked at Tommy.

"Ain't this something? All together again."

The party in Cody's tent that evening was somewhat different to that which had been planned. It went on for longer and drew in more participants than was expected. That Tommy was now a Pinkerton man and respected for it, was something of a surprise and a shock for William Standing, the notorious miscreant and jail breaker, but he was assured that tomorrow all would be explained and at least for the moment he might sleep soundly. He wondered what that might mean.

They walked to the show entrance just after midnight. Tommy held his daughter, asleep in his arms, while his son held Will's hand and walked along with them. Cody had his personal carriage brought to the gates and arranged to take the Hendersons home. It was agreed that they would meet again at Ebbit's, a large and established hotel not too far away, at noon on the next day.

As Will waved them away, he wondered what else this world had in store for him, but a promise was kept, on both parts, and for now he would go along and see what would come next and bite him in the indescribables.

***

Morning came with an ache in the head which made him late for breakfast in the dining tent. Most had come and gone but the range wagon still had bacon, eggs and beef for any late comers. He washed them down with strong, hot coffee and felt the better for it.

He borrowed a good jacket and shaved to make himself presentable for the meeting. Around eleven twenty he left and followed directions to Ebbit's Hotel and found Tom and his wife waiting in the restaurant. It was a warm reunion, as it should have been, but Will felt out of place and ill at ease in such salubrious surroundings. He removed his hat and took the seat offered him.

"You hungry?" asked Tommy. "Anything you want…"

Will put up a hand.

"I just ate, you know, a little late after last night."

Tom grinned. "It was a little, wasn't it?" He agreed, remembering Cody's stories.

"Just coffee, that'll do fine," Will added.

He noticed a pile of folders on the edge of the table and wondered if they might be his downfall. The coffee came and the small talk evolved into something more serious. It was for Tommy to tell the story that Will was totally ignorant of.

"You remember, Uncle Will, when Marshal Deerbolt came to see to us after they took you off somewhere?"

"Sure," Will agreed. "They took me off to Fort Laramie and a twenty stretch in the Georgia Pen."

"As I now know," continued Tom. "Because of the Indian emergency the trial was held at the fort, or so they said. From what I later found out, Bellfield encouraged the judge to resist a hearing any place else. There were as I understand it, financial issues, and also both were in the same Confederate commissary unit during the war."

Standing laughed, but it was not a humorous one.

"That figures."

"That's not all," Tom went on. "Because of the place and the time, the court papers went missing. The following year Wyoming became a state and for a long time, nobody was interested in pursuing any non-standard appeals. I know, I tried." He looked earnestly at his uncle. "There's no way on this good, green Earth that you should've done anywhere near twenty years on those charges."

"If it came to what they gave me and what Bellfield wanted to do to me, maybe I got the good end of the deal," Standing argued.

Tom went on further, "Marshal Deerbolt found our dad's brother out here by letter, and before long they agreed to take us in and raise us. The Deerbolts were good people."

"I know, I owe them," Will said.

"Well, Uncle Bob was a state lawyer and when I was of an age to set to and find you, he helped me work it through. I wrote Marshal Deerbolt to see where they put you but I got no reply."

"He died of the diphtheria, long time back," Standing explained. "When I broke from the Georgia Penitentiary I worked my way back to Dogwood, see if you kids were still there but he was long gone. So was you. All his papers got trashed; such a long time passed that nobody saw no value to 'em." He smiled. "I guess his widow missed you two."

"She was a nice lady," Tom agreed.

"She still is. A little edging to the portly and taking in washing, but she's still going strong."

"So, we had no idea where they sent you," Tom confirmed.

"And Thomas wrote to this Bellfield man to ask for help, but he also failed to reply," Margaret added in her strong southern accent.

"Why would he?" asked Will.

The coffees came. Will downed his in one go and was poured another.

"I wrote to every penitentiary and jail I could find," Tom said, "but either none knew of you or failed to answer."

Standing nodded.

"The wardens were never none too eager to worry about mail from home."

"I refused to believe you were dead," Tom hit the table with his hand, "not after all that..." He calmed a little. "So, when I left school, with help from my Uncle Bob, I found employment with the Pinkerton Detective Agency and that gave me a better way to investigate what had happened to you." Tom paused. "I requested prisoner lists for every jail that had failed to answer my letters, under powers from the Justice Department and friends of my Uncle Bob of course, and eventually found your name."

"He was very persistent," Margaret said.

Tom laughed aloud.

"I was, but when I got to the Georgia Penitentiary, you had flown the coop, as it were. Something about a burial?"

"I did," Will answered. "It was."

"Then I missed you at St Louis, at the railroad terminal. We sent out bills to the main junctions to see if we could track you down."

"Huh!"

"The important thing is, Uncle Will, that we applied to the Justice Department for an appeal in your absence, and told them the whole story. The courts agreed that you should have served no more than ten years, and you served eighteen. Mr Grover Cleveland is a friend of my Uncle Bob and has been the president since March."

"He has?"

"Yes, and it has done us no harm," Tom said. "Uncle Will, you are a free man, and should have been for a long time. It is up to you if you wish to pursue Bellfield in the courts. My Uncle Bob recommends it. You have much to gain, he is a rich man. Judge Flanders died of the bottle some way back, so he is beyond the courts of this world."

William Standing thought about it, remembering the state of the man the last time he saw him.

"Oh, I guess not." Will jerked a thumb over to Midnight. "We still got his horse."

"Uncle Will," Tom was serious, "you are no spring chicken and you cannot keep jumping from stagecoaches forever. A settlement with Bellfield would benefit your later years, and no doubt about it. It is something to consider."

Will shrugged off the thought.

"I already considered it, Tommy."

Tom sat back in his chair, not really understanding. Will smiled.

"I do thank you so much for what you have done for me, and for what I knew nothing of all these years. And you must thank your Uncle Bob, he sounds a decent man. I am grateful for what he did in my absence and would like to meet him some time."

Tom reached over and took Will's hand.

"And he wants to meet you." He moved his chair forward a little way. "Listen, we rent a small house for work's sake, but we also have a place away from the city where we raise horses, my Uncle Bob and I. It is small at the moment but things are going well and we have good stock. There is good green grass and tall timber, you would feel right at home. On a good day, you can see the sea and the sky beyond, and tall ships coming in from the east with square sails."

Will smiled.

"We can use someone who knows horses," Tom went on, "Its a permanent job and found, and we want you to do it."

"Ain't never seen the ocean, nor a ship for that matter, unless you count keelboats or the ferries," Standing said. "But it's a world away from mine. It ain't that I'm not grateful for the words, but I ain't just fixed for the east, settled in one place, I just ain't."

"You should think about it, Mr Standing," Margaret offered, "Thomas would be so pleased to know you are around."

"It's Will," he answered, smiling again, "or William, or just 'hey you'. My family name's been a little vacant these last few months."

"Please, Will. Do think about it," she pleaded.

"I already thought on it, Margaret," he answered.

"Uncle Will, I know you have a family here with the Wild West, but age is the friend of no one, and you can't fight Indians for the rest of your days. There is a future for you, with us. Take it."

Tom knew it was decided and pressed no more.

"By the way," he grinned, "the horse you borrowed from the Georgia Penitentiary. The warden tried to press a charge for it, but he decided to forego the matter if other more serious issues of the past were forgotten."

"I owe you much," Will said.

"I owe you more," Tom answered.

They shook hands and hugged and left it there, with Tom confirming that there would always be a place with the Hendersons. He wrote down the way to find them and asked if Will needed money, which he declined. William Standing watched the carriage until it disappeared from sight, and then went back in time for the afternoon performance.

That night, Standing walked across to the commissary station, known as the 'pie wagon'. He purchased an envelope, a stamp and some better paper than the kind he used for the hand bills. Finding a quiet place, he wrote in his own personal style, the envelope addressed to 'The Widow Deerbolt, Deerbolt's Laundry, Dogwood, Wyoming'.

Deer Mrs Deerbolt,

I write to tell you that I fownd the childran. They are growd now and much as tall as myself. But sad that Alice went under from the consumption some years back. Tommy is growed tall and works for the Pinkartun Agency and is well looked on. He has wife and 2 kids. They was well cared for by there uncle bob and there ant. They live arownd washington and are good peeple. I have good employmant and enclose fifty dollars by way of thanks for what you done. Your man was as good a law man as I ever known.

Sinserely yourn,
william standing

Will slipped in the notes and sealed the envelope, added the stamp and mailed the letter.

***

The Wild West moved on to long stands in Philadelphia and then Staten Island and eventually Madison Square Gardens, New York. The days were becoming cooler and shorter and Will Standing had fallen into the routines of the show business, twice daily, rain or shine.

Money jingled in his pockets but often it jingled in the wrong direction when he saw the street urchins and beggars in the big cities. He wondered how a body could stand it in that condition when within a horse distance were tall trees and open land as far as the eye could see. Granted, there were few buffalo any more, but times were what they were and as you find them.

The stagecoach routine was always popular and thrilled the audiences. It was a hard way to make a living at dragging fifty, but the food was always plentiful and on time and he had Sundays off. Still, he regularly made a point of visiting Midnight, finding his time with the horse helped to punctuate his day and ward off an overcast sky. He could feel that they were growing old together and wondered where the Wild West would take them.

On a cold afternoon in October, Will was greasing the wheels of the coach when John Nelson sidled up to him.

"Billy wants to see ya," he told him. "Over in the 'eats tent'."

Will looked for somewhere to wipe off the grease and found an old copy of the programme to clean most of it from his hands. The residue he wiped on the seat of his pants.

Entering the dining tent, he found waiters clearing the old tablecloths and fitting new ones. Cody was sat in his usual position, a seat that no one else dared to take by the entry flaps. He was smoking an expensive cigar.

"You wanted to see me, Bill?" Will asked.

"Ah! Mr Standing, would you care for a smoke?"

Will shook his head.

"Don't do smokes. Always seemed like setting your innards alight for no good reason."

"Ah!"

"So, what's it about?" Standing asked.

Cody leant forward and rested his elbows on the table after the waiter had replenished the cover. He pursed his lips.

"I feel that the routine is unfair," he said.

"Huh?"

"Well, think about it," he explained. "If one is on one long side of the arena, and the action happens on the other side of the arena, then there might be some weight to a complaint. In fact, there have been a couple, minor ones admittedly, but when the posters show drama on that side of the coach, well, you can see the dilemma, can you not?"

"No."

"Well, let's say you do the fall as you presently do, and then repeat it on the opposite side of the circuit, just before I lead the rescuers in to save you? Problem solved?"

William Standing stood for a moment, hardly believing his ears.

"You know what it takes to throw yourself off that thing twice a day?" He said. "Now you want it done double?"

Cody puffed the cigar.

"Well, it's entirely up to you. If you find that you cannot manage the strain of such a routine, we will find you work back in the remuda. I realise that age is something that catches us all in time."

Without answering, Will stormed from the dining tent and stomped back to the coach. He found Nelson still there.

"You hear what he wants me to do from now on?"

"I heard." Nelson grimaced. "That's Billy Cody for ya, always lookin' for somethin' better to grab the payin' customers."

It was a short time until the afternoon show. Cody's words hung heavy around his shoulders. Will Standing kicked a stone along and wished it were something else.

The band began with the 'Stars and Stripes'. He saw Midnight, saddled and waiting for his rider as the applause began its appreciation of the music. Leant against the stagecoach, Standing watched as the opening revue began, the squadrons of horsemen streaming through the gap between the curtains and into the arena following the regal figure of Buffalo Bill, his long hair flowing and mounted on the big black stallion.

William Standing should have known human frailty better, he had the experience and yet had failed to use it. He could no longer put it down to youth or lack of education.

The show rolled on through until it was time to prepare the attack on the coach. Nelson was already going through his regular checks and superstitions. Crescendos of applause came and went with each event. Cody had dismounted and tied off Midnight to a rail behind the backdrop, near to a peep hole where it was possible to look onto the arena without being seen to monitor the performance. He walked a little distance away and began speaking with Major Burke.

"Better git on up," Nelson told Will, seeing that it was almost their entry time.

Standing did so, but did not secure the strapping harness. He had other ideas. The music began for the stagecoach act and the mules pricked up their ears in response. They shuffled in their traces and twenty-four hooves danced on the spot. Nelson hauled back on the reins a little more to hold them back until the curtains opened and line up the coach. Over the other side, the orator sang out his introduction and slowly the curtains began to be pulled back. Standing was ready for the moment.

When John Nelson slapped the reins and urged on the mules and in between the heavy widening canvas, Will slipped over the side without restriction before the coach had picked up speed, and landed on his feet. On at the gallop went the original Deadwood Stagecoach, with the driver looking back over his shoulder, his eyes wide with surprise.

Standing sped across the space between himself and the black horse, untied him, threw a foot into the stirrup and heaved himself over the saddle. Pulling around the animal's head he pressed him forward after the coach and into the arena as if in pursuit. Nelson looked around at Will Standing, coming up on the inside and riding Cody's favourite horse. Taking the first curve, Will eased the animal around and took off his hat to a shrill yell of psychological and actual freedom, the first he had felt for many a year. He knew what he was doing and would do it well no matter what the consequences.

The whole cast somehow became aware that something extraordinary was happening. Many stood frozen, wondering how it would pan out. Ushers among the bleachers, aware of a difference in the routine, watched in disbelief. Only the audience were totally unaware of the undercurrent of drama that was unfolding.

When only one circuit had been traversed by the coach, Cody ordered in the Indians, who entered rapidly. Standing cut the corner and gained ground, finding himself ahead of the mules. He took out his revolver and twisted in the saddle, firing back at those that yelled after them. He leant far back and extended a leg to balance himself as he fired but Midnight felt the shift in weight and compensated as he ran flat out. It seemed like they had done something like this before, a long time ago.

Cody had found a new mount and also before the rehearsed time, led more riders into the performance, on the heels of the Cheyenne and Sioux. Will's revolver emptied and he put it back into the holster at his hip and concentrated on the ride. Screams and yells and gunfire filled the area between the covered stands and smoke began to hide one group from another. Will kept close to the coach and discarded the curses that Johnny Nelson cast at him.

Out of the smoke and confusion, Buffalo Bill signalled the orator and the curtain crew and the gap in the backdrop began to open to allow all to exit for the next act. Cody was furious at the demolishing of routine and the trashing of the performance but the crowds had loved it. Waves of clapping hands echoed around the show ground and gave approval to the spectacle and the horsemanship.

Will Standing saw the ebb of the presentation through the gun smoke, the contraction of horses and riders as they left the arena and the dark red colour of the Deadwood Stagecoach as it pulled away towards the opening in the backdrop. He too turned away to make his departure, but then turned back. He slowly cantered towards the centre of the rectangle, through the fading mist from the guns and pulled back on the rein. Midnight reared and kicked the air as he had been taught by Cody, but this time for another. Will Standing pulled off his hat and saluted the audience, who responded with a standing ovation as the big black horse touched ground again, curving his strong neck over pawing the sawdust.

Will patted the horse on the neck and pulled away towards the painted backdrop and to whatever awaited him.

As the curtains closed behind them, horse and rider came to a halt. Cody and a group of wranglers stood in a line to deter any further progress. From his employer's face, Will knew he was in trouble, but then why had he taken such an extreme dissent? It had all seemed quite natural, almost automatic to make such a show of defiance, but right then he felt almost petulant, like a schoolboy deprived of candy. But in his heart, he was glad to have done it.

"Well, Mister?" Cody growled, his hands on his hips. "And do we have explanation of your action?"

William Standing felt his anger return. Not a fierce anger, but one of right against wrong, and no going back or giving in to compromise. Words would be wasted on such a situation and he knew it.

"Mister Cody," Will said, with a half-smile on his face, "You can stick your stagecoach up your ass and send the mules on after it."

Bill Cody saw humour in the state of affairs that others probably could not. His frown turned into a smile of sorts.

"Are we saying that this may be an end to our association, Sir?"

Will grinned back.

"You're damn right!"

The wranglers began to slowly creep forward, towards the man on the big black horse, but they were not fast enough. He pulled to his left and used his heels to encourage a gallop and Midnight responded in what he did best. Up ahead lay the gate to the show ground, always closed during performances. Will dropped low and drew up his feet, urging the horse through the milling performers readying themselves for their acts. Cody's mouth dropped as he watched them go.

Reaching the closed gate, will pulled back on the rein and Midnight knew exactly what was expected of him. Almost in slow motion, the animal took the four-bar gate and sailed over. In mid-air, Will removed his hat and presented it to those behind him.

"Damn you to hell, Billy Cody," he called back.

The black horse touched the ground and galloped away down the street, through the lines of black glossy carriages, cabs and pedestrians. Behind on the back lot, those who had seen the incident stood watching them go. Cody grinned and turned to the others around him. He took off his wide sombrero and waved it after the escapees, his head back, his voice deep and loud.

"Now that, gentlemen, is how to steal a horse!"

***

By dark, they had left the capital behind. An abandoned barn served as shelter for the night and taking off the saddle, Will rubbed Midnight down with a handful of clean hay that he found in a corner. Then, he let the horse loose to graze in the moonlight while he thought about what to do next. Watching the animal, he leant against the pen door frame and thought about how strange things had worked out. Lord, how he always seemed to make a mess of things.

He searched his pockets and found a few dollars and change, not much but at least it was something. And he had a horse, the best damn horse this side of the Missouri. Sure, it was getting on a mite, but then so was he.

In truth, Will Standing's options were few. He thought back to his conversation with Tommy and remembered the offer he had made. Would that be so bad? Food and found and a world away from trouble if he kept his nose clean, providing he could get away with his latest misdemeanour. He wondered if they were once more after him, and why he had let himself fall into bad ways again. Like always, he would take things as they came, and deal with the consequences if he had to.

Tommy's words jangled like an old, rusty wind pump and would not go away. Midnight loped over and stuck his head into Will's shoulder.

"Well, what now?" he asked. "Seems like we just can't escape ourselves, can we?" He rubbed Midnight's head. "Lord, I must be the world's worst horse thief, stealing the same animal twice. Whatever I'm doing wrong, I keep doing it."

Will laughed at himself.

"'Course, I'm also the worst bank robber, never took no more than I needed, nor shot nobody, nor even cursed at 'em." He looked up at the moon, disappearing behind cloud. "But I guess I paid my dues one way or t'other."

The horse grunted.

"I know, you been through the ringer too, and ended up more or less where you started. Maybe you would've been better with Bellfield, run once a month and regular feed."

William Standing looked to the south, where he guessed Washington would be. The horse nuzzled him again.

"We're gettin' old, you an' me." He smiled. "But we ain't dead yet, and we still got some bark on us. Tomorrow, we'll head south, see if we can find Tommy and all of those mares just waitin' for a stud like you. It's a long ways, but maybe we can find a train, take us part of the way. How about that?"

It was maybe shooting high, but hell, it was something to do.

***

After two days or more and the occasional pilferage from a washing line or a corn crib, they rode into a small railhead. Will Standing dismounted and rubbed his discomfort. He tied Midnight to a post while he walked across to the rail office.

Opening the door, he entered and crossed to the counter, looking around. A tubby individual with a rotund red face looked across at him and smiled. He wore a white shirt and dark waistcoat, with the buttons open.

"Can I help you, Sir?"

Will took a deep breath and smiled back.

"Got a horse and myself, looking for transport to Washington, or nearby," he said. "Need to know how much."

The official looked down onto the counter and with his index finger moved down his printed pages. He expressed a price and noted Will's concern, then made another suggestion, "There's a service train an hour from now, if you don't mind riding the boxcar. Goes all the way, but you'll still need to pay the baggage prices."

Will asked how much again and checked his finances. He was eight dollars and twenty cents short. "Can I get partway?" He asked.

The officer shook his head. "Tickets got legs, Mister. They run all the way."

Will thought for a moment. "When does it come through?" He asked once more.

"Fifty minutes from now; at ten-five, it pulls out."

Standing tipped his hat and walked out. He looked over at Midnight and knew that he could not expect the animal to go all of the way to Washington. He looked back through the window to the clock inside the office, then went back inside. He spread what money he had on the counter.

"Will you keep this for me, and the ticket? I'll be back before the train leaves. I need to go to the bank."

"Sure," the officer said, pointing over to Midnight. "That the horse?"

"Uh-huh."

The sun poked through the low cloud and cheered up the day. Standing walked slowly along the short street and stepped up onto the board walk. Looking through the window of the small bank, he checked the time by the big clock. Just after nine-thirty. He walked on, keeping moving to pass the time, self-conscious of the thumps that his heels made on the wooden boards.

He felt for the pistol beneath the folds of the stolen overcoat and felt reassured, despite the fact that it was his performance pistol and carried nothing but blanks. This was not the first bank that he was about to rob, but he hoped that it would be his last.

He touched his hat to fine ladies that passed by and offered smiles to any menfolk that he encountered and tried to look casual. Time passed slowly, as it did when the conscience told you it was wrong.

Nine fifty-five. Will Standing entered the green double doors and saw only one woman at the counter. Against his manners, he found that waiting for her to complete her business was inadvisable as the train was already pulling into the halt. He recovered the Colt from beneath the coat and held it at arm's length.

The teller behind the screen stepped back wide-eyed and put up his hands as the woman turned around. Will tipped his hat. "Excuse me, Ma'am," he said. "This is a hold-up, and I'm a little short on time."

She gasped and stepped away, throwing up her hands. Standing waved away the gesture with his free hand. "No need for that, Ma'am."

He turned back to the startled teller and levelled the Colt.

"Now," Will Standing said, "eight dollars and twenty cents. And if I don't hit you over the head, will you promise to give me ten minutes before you raise the alarm?"